THE
ANATOMY
OF
MAGIC

THE
ANATOMY
OF
MAGIC

J.C. CERVANTES

PARK
ROW
BOOKS

PARK
ROW
BOOKS™

Recycling programs for this product may not exist in your area

ISBN-13: 978-0-7783-1082-2

The Anatomy of Magic

Park Row Books
22 Adelaide St. West, 41st Floor
Toronto, Ontario M5H 4E3, Canada
ParkRowBooks.com

Printed in U.S.A.

For that kid in California who
never stopped believing in magic.

"You can't go back and change the beginning, but you can start where you are and change the ending."

Unknown

1

I'm still breathing.

My heart is still beating. Both scientific indicators that, yes, I am technically alive.

And yet...

I speed down the remote highway with the window half down, an unlit cigarette in my mouth.

I've been driving for two days.

Closer to three if you count the time that I spent in traffic trying to get to LAX before I passed the exit. I couldn't do it, couldn't shove through the crowds. I couldn't face all those strangers going about their lives with some kind of purpose they believed mattered.

I suppose we're all guilty of it. Believing whatever version of reality suits us.

Still, a flight home would have been so much easier than sleeping at rest stops and ignoring my basic hygiene. It would have been faster at the very least. But I wanted to drive, to feel the open road beneath me, to be the decider on this journey.

To just once, be someone else, someone who wasn't a serial perfectionist believing in the glossy illusion of control. Sometimes I imagine a normal life with normal expectations. Maybe I could be that person who has a house with a lawn and a walkway lined with pumpkins every fall.

What would that feel like? I wonder as I adjust my sunglasses and hike my left leg up to rest on the seat. Probably boring as hell.

As I drive along the deserted highway, the Sonoran Desert is its usual beautiful. Forever skies, columnar cacti, and a horizon I'll never catch. The view, for just a moment, takes my mind off the reason that I'm here in the first place.

Because I ran.

Because I couldn't stare at my colorless apartment walls another second. Because I wanted to crawl out of my own skin. Because I'm a failure and a coward.

Ultimately, running away fell woefully short of my expectations. The memory followed me anyway.

I can still feel the cold of the operating room, can still hear the clanking of metal, and the voices. God, there were so many voices. And then came the horrific silence. The kind that stays with you forever. It's the kind you can never outrun.

I turn down the podcast that's automatically rolled over from my original playlist: *Terror in the Deep South*. I would never subscribe to a show like that. Who knows? Maybe it's a ridiculous sign from the universe. Regardless, I prefer happier topics like health or fitness or some other version of living your best life. Ironic for a doctor who's going ninety-five with a cigarette pressed between her lips.

Although I'm pretty impressed that I haven't lit the thing yet, a habit I broke in med school six years ago. I don't even know why I bought the pack—a desperate attempt to reach into the past maybe? My therapist cousin, Dahlia, would tell me that there's an avoidance message in there somewhere as well but I'm too exhausted (and uninterested) to attempt an analysis.

Two hours and three non-murder podcasts later, I pull off the highway into La Ventana, a spellbinding town tucked into the rolling highlands of Mexico. The sweeping hills are dotted with colorful haciendas for as far as the eye can see, with miles and miles of gold and green between. It's like a painting that never fades, never changes.

The closer I get to our family farm, the more the knot in my stomach tightens. Mom only knows what I texted her: **Coming home early. Don't ask or I'll turn around. I'll talk when I'm ready.**

I half expected her to balk. Instead, she surprised me with, **We can definitely use more help with the wedding.**

Wedding? Whose wedding? Between a gaggle of family friends and neighbors, it could be anyone's but I was too spent to even ask.

Easing up on the pedal, I feel that same painful heat winding through my heart, spreading like fire across my chest. I've been in denial, pretending that it was heartburn, or stress. I know better.

Just like I know when the symptoms began.

Now I glance at myself in the rearview mirror—tangled dark hair I haven't bothered brushing in over a thousand miles, sunken eyes, and a worn face. My mom might accept the mystery of my early arrival, but she'll never accept a ghost for a daughter.

Still, how can I tell her what happened when I haven't even processed it myself?

I pull over near a street stand selling tacos to try and freshen my woeful appearance. Where did I put my makeup bag? Shit. Did I even pack one? I rushed out of the house so impulsively the memory of it sends my pulse skyrocketing.

I take a deep breath and then another, remembering the five senses technique Dahlia taught me.

"Okay, sight," I say aloud, looking for five things to name them.

"Boy with a stick of corn," I say as my eyes dart about the scene. "Agua fresca. Orange handbag. Bus with way too many people. Scrappy dog in a hurry."

Next, I search for four scents. Carne asada, poblano, and cilantro fill the air, making my stomach grumble. I realize all I've eaten on this journey is half a bag of Doritos.

Just then my phone buzzes and I never get to the fourth scent.

It's my oldest sister, Harlow. **Is it normal to weigh a thousand pounds two months before giving birth?**

Seeing her name, along with the tiny photo of her face that accompanies it, forces me out of nomad mode and back into the expected identity of Lily Estrada, youngest sister of three, fixer of all things, weaver of memory magic.

Biting down on the end of the cigarette, I text back, **Definitely.**

We're all excited for Harlow's baby to arrive, but when our mom heard the news that she was finally going to be a grandmother she nearly exploded with confetti-like joy.

At least we won't all be subject to the torment of a gender reveal party. Harlow's having a girl just like every Estrada before her. It began generations ago when my great-grandmother Margarita accepted the Aztec goddess Mayahuel's blessing that every female descendant would be blessed with her own brand of magic. We were given the ability to grow mystical flowers on our land, to create enchantments, and be committed to forever protecting love, passion, and beauty. But there was a catch, a price that each of us would have to discover and bear on our own.

A price I thought I'd paid ten years ago.

I'm a miserable stuffed potato, Lil.

You're growing a human, I manage to type back. Of course you're miserable.

While we know Harlow's baby's a girl, we won't know her name until the birth when Mayahuel whispers into my sister's ear. Like each of us, the child will be named for a flower. The only one without this designation is Harlow herself, who up until four years ago believed that the meaning of her name, heap of stones, was a cruel fate meant only to remind her of her lack of power. That was until she discovered that she's the most powerful of us all, an encantadora who multiplies our magic.

She's not human, I swear! I'm growing a new breed of the kraken.

I fumble through my purse to find the boot lighter I bought at a convenience store on the Tijuana border. More dots flash across my screen, and Harlow clearly isn't done with her rant.

It's a lie you know. There is NO GLOW, Lil! You're an OB. You should have warned me!

Lighter in hand, I lean my head against the headrest, close my eyes, and take a deep breath, grateful for a moment of privacy that's rare in my family. If this were seven months ago, Harlow and every woman in my family would have already known something was very wrong with me.

We've always had a deep psychic connection, opening channels to our emotions and signaling to the others when something significant was happening. But ever since Harlow got pregnant, those channels have all but closed. Mom said it's typical. *After all,* she told us, *Harlow is growing a new generation of magic. That takes tremendous effort and there are only so many mystical resources to go around.*

I'll have to thank the little kraken when I meet her.

My phone buzzes again.

Are you trying to get out of this? Harlow asks.

Out of what?

That you didn't warn me.

About the kraken?

About all of it!

To try and take her mind off it, I respond, How's the new book coming?

She sends an angry-faced emoji.

That bad? I start to rub out the Dorito stain smeared across the front of my white sweatshirt.

Worse than that.

Before I can reply that she has dreadfully underestimated the value of *worse,* I get another text. This time it's from Seth, a radiologist I went out with a few times. Up for a drink?

Seth's intolerably handsome, has a disarming smile, and can talk about nearly any subject as if he's part AI, but there's no *it* factor, no spark. Just like nearly all the men before him.

I realize he must not have heard the news yet, which makes me wonder how the hell I'm supposed to respond. I go for the least complicated version. Out of town for a bit.

As soon as I hit send, I realize the text went to Harlow by mistake.

In an instant, her confusion flashes across the screen. Huh? Wait, where are you?

There's no sense trying to lie. She's going to find out soon enough that I'm home two weeks earlier than planned. We're all scheduled to be at la Casa de las Flores y Luz later this month for the annual Celebration of Flowers, a sacred tradition when each Estrada woman asks for the goddess's blessing as we press our hands into the soil to enchant the new crops.

Favor? I'm too exhausted to explain anything.

Shoot.

I'm home early and please don't ask why. I'm still figuring things out. Can you just accept that I'll tell you later?

As I wait for her response, I tug my dark hair into a pony-tail, pinch my cheeks, and swipe some mint balm across my chapped lips.

Okay, Harlow texts back. I can feel the tension in those four little letters. Are you all right?

No. I'm not.

I've never been a wisher, never wanted to hand over my power like that, but right now, in this fragile moment I wish that I could use my memory magic on myself.

All it would take is the exact right blend of blooms made into a breathable concoction. One inhale, maybe two, and all the pain would be gone.

I've seen the effects of my magic, the relief in people's faces the moment the memory they no longer want to carry evaporates. Even then, I've never liked being the thief who carves away someone's history. I prefer the giving of a memory—

when someone relives a beautiful moment, every sound, scent, touch. As if they've traveled back in time to experience it once more.

I slump farther, realizing that in the end, it doesn't matter; the women in my family aren't allowed to use magic for our own benefit, at least not for anything significant or life-altering.

I send Harlow a thumbs-up, turn off my phone, and toss it onto the passenger seat, knowing that eventually I'm going to have to face this, that I'm going to have to talk about it. The inescapable reality presses against my chest with a heaviness that's making it hard to breathe.

I consider going back to Dahlia's senses exercise, but a mass of storm clouds is sweeping across the sky, so I pull back onto the road and drive toward home. With each mile, my anxiety expands. The darkness closes in.

I flick open the lighter and press the cigarette to the tiny flame, inhaling deeply, drawing in the poison, reminding myself that I'm still breathing.

I'm still breathing.

2

The moment I'm halfway up the long stone driveway, a different world comes into soft focus.

It's a trick of the eye really, as if the house doesn't want anyone to see its grandeur and rugged beauty until just the right moment.

From a certain distance, our home looks unassuming with its thick adobe structure and red tile roof half hidden behind sweeping palms and high walls.

In my mind's eye, I step through the romantic archway into a colonnaded courtyard with a verdant garden and trickling waterways. The house holds myriad secrets and hidden corners that even I haven't discovered yet. There are winding staircases that lead to dead ends, walls inexplicably erected over the years, and unexpected doors tucked here and there that have either been sealed shut or open to mysterious alcoves no one uses.

Beneath the canopy of trees, I stop the car, roll down the window, and sit idle, basking in the one thing I can always count on whenever I'm home: a sense of calm that washes over me.

I take a deep breath and then another, filling and emptying my lungs with the oxygen-rich air. The anxiety slowly retreats like a cowering animal, but I know it isn't gone for long.

The January air is crisp, clean...

I search for the scents of my childhood: honeysuckle, lavender, rose. There's nothing. I inhale slower and more deeply this time, waiting for the floral aromas to reach me.

Alarm bells begin ringing in my head.

There are no traces of jasmine or peonies or orange blossoms wafting across the farm. Why can't I smell the flower fields?

Was it the cigarette? Did it mess with my senses? No, that's ridiculous. I had no trouble smelling the tacos from the street stand.

I jump out of the car and take another breath, searching for any flowery scent at all. All I smell is tobacco and distant rain.

Tobacco. Shit.

The last thing I need right now is a lecture from my mom. "Mija, you are a doctor." I can see her finger waving at me. I try to anticipate a way out of it and come up with a half-baked lie about a smoky restaurant. But she'll never buy it. Magic aside, you can't keep anything from that woman. Definitely not worth it to be a smoker *and* a liar.

I pop open the trunk, tug a clean sweatshirt out of my luggage, and do a quick change. A part of me wants to sneak right inside, take a soothing shower, and fall into a forgetful sleep, but the other part of me is determined to investigate why the hell the farm doesn't smell like the farm.

I mean, seriously. The flowers, this house, this land, our magic—these are my constants in an otherwise unpredictable world. Things have been shaken enough these past few days, I can't bear to imagine what I would do without them. Hell, my own magic *depends* on scent—it's how I choose which flowers to use for a memory spell. An unspoken language between me and the blooms.

Slipping through the shadows, I go in search of some flowers, cutting across the expansive driveway and down a dark flight of uneven stone steps that leads to a cascading jungle of wild plants and trees. Even now, at the ripe old age of nearly thirty, I cower the way I did as a little girl when the trees looked like monstrous figures waiting for just the right moment to pounce.

When I reach the first landing, I glance around, wishing the moon was just a bit brighter. I'm certain there are flowers here somewhere.

Quickly, I power on my phone and turn on the flashlight. By the crumbling stone arch are a group of potted white geraniums, symbolic meaning constancy, folly, and deceit. The trio of words seems at odds until I rearrange them to mean "foolish devotion leads to deception."

Leaning down, I press my nose to a bloom, and breathe. There aren't the usual notes of citrus with hints of rose. As a matter of fact, there's nothing. How is that possible?

Trying not to panic, I run through a mental list of medical possibilities, coming up short. Sure, there are lots of reasons someone might lose their sense of smell or taste, but I've never heard of someone losing the ability to specifically smell flowers.

I drop onto a wooden bench, tug my knees into my chest, and wrap my arms around myself, tighter and tighter as my body tenses and the familiar heat blazes in my heart again.

How can this be happening?

I tell myself to get a grip. To focus on the facts.

The peculiar symptom began soon after I met my patient's son. I can still see his thinning hair, the lines around his deep-set blue eyes, his crisp pilot's uniform.

A pair of wings pinned to his chest.

I answered his questions, assuring him that this was a routine surgery. He was edgy, chatty—I felt for him as he tried to convince me that he had nerves of steel, and it was only when his feet were on the ground that he was out of sorts.

Each word he spoke about flying was another step into my past.

And then he uttered those five words: *the sky is my home.*

Instantly, the memory I'd locked away came rushing to the surface, stirring my magic. Forcing me to remember a different time, a different me, and...a desperate spell I had cast so long ago that I'd all but forgotten.

Until now.

Here in the dark of the garden, I take deep even breaths, searching for the calm rational part of me.

There's no evidence that old spells can cause physical symptoms. And even if they could, why now?

Lightning cuts across the sky in a series of bold flashes, as if the goddess herself is trying to send me a message: *even magic cannot fix this.*

"Lily?" My mother's voice comes from the shadows, startling me out of my reverie. I look up and see her slim frame at the top of the steps, backlit by some distant garden lights.

"What are you doing down here?" she asks.

Her voice is a soft, comforting sound that instantly turns me into a child. But I was never the needy daughter like Harlow or our other sister, Camilla, preferring to either ignore whatever was bothering me (still do) or bury my emotions so deep even a mole rat couldn't find them.

Before I can say a word, she closes the distance, lithe and graceful, pulling me to my feet and into a solid hug, one that says, *I'm sorry for whatever you're going through.*

A part of me is terrified that she's going to break our agreement and immediately start asking questions, but to her credit, she says nothing, only holds me closer, "I'm glad you're home."

All I want to do is sink into her embrace, but years of training in the science of fortitude, resilience, and, above all, a detached persona keep me from falling. In my line of work, I don't have the luxury of breaking down, or giving in to my emotions, and the practice of it has left me a ghost of who I once was. I went into medicine to heal, to make a difference in the health outcomes of women, and over the years, I was introduced to a broken system, one that values profit over patient care.

I squeeze my eyes closed, fighting the tears. Remembering to breathe.

When we break apart, my mom's gaze is intense, yet soft and sympathetic. She's wearing jeans and a long white button-down shirt. As always, she looks effortlessly elegant. "Why don't I draw you a bath?" she asks. "Geranium and lavender."

It sounds like absolute bliss but I'm too tired for even that. "I think I'll just take a shower tonight." I realize I'm avoiding my mom's gaze, afraid of what I'll see there—pity, disappointment? Or maybe I'm terrified of what she'll see in me.

With a sudden scowl, she inches closer, sniffing. "Have you been smoking?"

My mouth goes dry. I roll my eyes and force my perfected all-is-well smile; it's small, moderate, leans more to the left. The smile of a woman who would never lie to you. "Of course not."

Her penetrating eyes circle my face, landing on my hair.

"Yes, I know I need a haircut," I say, not bothering to tell her it's been six months, a record for even me. Then, quickly changing the subject, I ask, "Is there something wrong with the flowers?"

"What do you mean *wrong*?"

There's a moment when I vacillate, trying to decide if the truth is worth telling, or if it will only lead to questions that I'm not ready to answer. My curiosity wins out.

"I... I can't smell them."

In a flash, Jasmine Estrada's gaze hardens, and her entire persona shifts from tender mother to stoic soldier. "Are you sick? Do you have a cold?"

"No, and even if I was getting sick, that doesn't explain that I can still smell everything else, like food or the rain coming." I'm struggling to remain calm. Surely there's an explanation and surely my mom has it. "I have to be able to smell the blooms," I tell her as if this is somehow news, "to cast memory spells but how can I—"

"Lily."

I freeze. Waiting. Sinking into the night, into fear, into the *thereness* of my mom that somehow soothes me.

"It's going to be okay."

Which part? I want to ask her. The flowers? The agonizing pain that's been following me mile after mile, no matter how fast I drove? The worry that my future looks so far away that I don't think I can ever catch up?

She studies me for another moment with deep brown eyes, ones I didn't inherit. My light honey eyes belong to my dad, who stopped being a husband to my mother decades ago when he realized that the magic was too much for him to live with.

"You look frail," Mom says. "Have you been eating?"

Yes. Half a bag of Doritos to be exact.

"Can we not do this?" I instantly regret saying anything.

"Don't you ever rest?" she goes on, gaining momentum. "You know how important your well-being is, especially to your magic, and I'm sure if you can get some sleep—"

"We've been over this," I tell her, trying not to groan.

"And you know rest isn't a thing for chief residents." What I wouldn't give for another cigarette.

Another life.

"Lily," Mom begins, and I brace myself for the lecture, but she stops herself. Shaking her head, she sighs. "Well, rest *should* be a thing. I read an article that it takes six straight hours for your body to get rid of negative emotions and heal itself."

My mom devours information, reading articles, books, anything she can get her hands on. Her curiosity is actually impressive, and most of the time, I love the tidbits she shares, but right now, the last thing I want to talk about is negative emotions and healing.

"Sounds like a research nightmare," I tell her, already mentally probing all the scientific problems of whatever piece she read.

She frowns. "Not everything can be measured by science."

Magic. She's got me there.

She hooks her arm in mine and escorts me back toward the house.

My mom and I are so good at this dance, saying the right words but never answering the real questions. Evading the truth for the sake of peace. Like me, my mom has bent and stretched and broken, but the difference is she put herself back together.

As we walk in silence, I'm hyperaware that she suspects something about why I can't smell the flowers. I saw it in her expression, in the quickness of her breath. But I don't press for more, worried it might be an invitation for her to interrogate me again. Or maybe I just don't want to know any truths tonight.

Reality is so overrated, and all I want to do is sleep, even if the nightmares will come like they have for the last seven nights.

★ ★ ★

In my bedroom, a fire burns in the stone hearth. The roomy space is filled with antiques, left over from the many lives that have slept here before me. After my great-grandmother made her deal with Mayahuel, the goddess told her to build the house in this exact spot, and for the last hundred and fifty years, new rooms, corners, and walls have been added like paint on a canvas that isn't quite finished.

On my nightstand, a single white gardenia rises from a narrow vase.

"So, you're the emotional support, huh?" I ask, dropping my luggage next to the bed.

The gardenia is known for healing and peace. A symbol, a gesture from my mom that I appreciate. But Jasmine has also been known to cast her dream magic by placing just the right flower beneath a pillow: holly for prophetic dreaming, or maybe a white poppy for deep sleep. I quickly look under my pillow, but there's no petal. No magic to be found.

After a punishingly hot shower, I wrap an oversize towel around myself, open the balcony doors, and step outside. A cool wind twists through the trees and cuts across my damp skin, causing goose bumps down my arms.

For a single, hopeful breath, I imagine that the shower cleared my sinuses, but still the flowers' aromas evade me.

Even magic cannot fix this.

I light another cigarette and watch as the flame burns away the paper.

Bursts of lightning illuminate the black sky, a stunning light show escorted in by deep rounds of thunder.

With every flash, I stare across the endless rolling hills of flowers, each marked for a magical purpose, each a symbol of hope for health, peace, connection, love.

Fields and fields of wants and wishes.

Cold rises out of the ground and, with it, the memory of that operating room.

Vivaldi pipes through speakers. Surgical techs buzz about. Weekend plans, a recent concert, the patient in Room 205. Tidbits of conversation that float right past me.

I look through the scope, into her abdomen. Ligate vessels.

Her son's voice echoes across my mind.

The sky is my home.

Searing heat takes hold, expanding across my chest—the forgotten spell winds its way around my heart like a thorny vine. My hand trembles. I lose focus—a fraction of a second.

I slam the door on my memory. The rain comes without warning, and for a moment, I let the cold drops fall onto my bare shoulders.

The spell did this.

Another moment and I defiantly lift my face to the dark sky and take a long drag of the cigarette, feeling the rush of nicotine.

I did this.

Another moment and I open my mouth to scream, but I don't, because in the end, I'm a coward, too afraid to give up control, too afraid to begin something I can't stop.

And when the cold and the rain and my so-called defiance become too much to bear, I put out the cigarette, go inside, and bury myself under the fluffy down comforter.

Shiver. Shiver. Breath.

Shiver. Shiver. Breath.

Until I fall asleep.

And for the first time in many nights, the nightmares don't find me.

3

I was wrong.

My mother spelled me. Evidenced by two facts: first, I slept for an obscene sixteen hours straight, something I haven't done since college, and second, I found a sprig of purple thyme *inside* my pillowcase, a bloom known for the power of healing and deep sleep.

Well, it did its job in one regard.

Nevertheless, the ache is still inside of me, and I'm worried it will never go away.

I roll out of bed in my old UCLA T-shirt, pad across the cool stone floors and into the bathroom. Leaning against the vanity, I peer into the mirror. Even bleary eyed I can see that my cheeks are sunken, my eyes look hollow, everything about me is pale and tired and bruised.

I guess I do look frail. But I'm not...am I?

Frail indicates fragile, and fragile doesn't graduate at the top of her class, or match at her first-choice residency, or get elected chief resident.

My heart ignites again.

Rubbing my chest in slow circles, I take a deep breath and squeeze my eyes closed. I wish I didn't remember the moment when things went from the dream of healing others to becoming the "best."

Time and heartbreak eroded bits and pieces of that dream (and me) on my way to the top. But now I reach back to that little girl, the one who loved intricate puzzles and fine instruments, like the tweezers I would spend hours using to extract seeds from a packet, planting each into the earth like some kind of promise. I remember the thrill of receiving my first microscope. It was like magic—the way it revealed a different view, a more nuanced image of what the naked eye couldn't ever possibly see.

I knew then that science and magic weren't too far apart.

"I'm not fragile," I whisper to my reflection.

My jaw clenches as if grimacing at the lie.

I *was* fragile...once. Or at least my heart was. Regardless, that was a long time ago.

With a grunt, I tie my dark hair into a high bun, splash warm water on my face, and brush my teeth.

I don't bother changing out of my tee before making my way downstairs where I find my mom in the west garden beneath a red umbrella, having lunch with Tía Rosa.

Even in early January, the garden is bursting with delphiniums, hydrangeas, and too many roses to count.

"Only you could make that ratty old shirt look like a fashion statement," my aunt says as she rises out of her chair and gives me a strong abrazo.

"I know nothing of fashion," I say, taking a seat. "Scrubs are basically pajamas." The table is laid out with delicious food. A silver bowl brimming with figs, a basket of fresh pan, and a tray of chilaquiles. My mom is already serving me before I can even set the cloth napkin on my lap.

"You spelled me," I say to her matter-of-factly, giving her a quick glare as I pour some watermelon agua fresca into my glass.

"You're welcome," Mom says. "Now eat."

Tía Rosa smiles conspiratorially, pretending to be busy cutting her tiny bit of bread with a knife and fork. She's changed her hair since I saw her last and is now sporting a blond pixie that suits her spunk.

I jab my knife in Rosa's direction accusatorily. "And you assisted her."

My aunt rolls her eyes. "I do not possess dream magic."

"Oh, okay," I say flippantly, "but the flowers talk to you, so I'm betting you helped her select the right ones." It's a gift Rosa and my older cousin, Lantana, share. They are the only ones the flowers speak directly to, using a language only they understand. It comes in handy when one of us isn't sure about a spell, or if we're choosing between several options.

"The flowers are very happy you're here," Rosa says. "Although they missed you for Christmas."

"If only hospitals closed for the holidays," I say teasingly, but there is a seriousness beneath the words, a hint to my family, who has never quite understood the rigors of my life, the sacrifices, and challenges. It's what I love about medicine, identifying patterns, diagnosing problems, weighing risk and benefit, all to reach a solution. It never pauses, a drive I used to crave, but it can have its drawbacks.

Mom huffs. "Are you really going to complain about a good night's sleep, Lily?"

"Absolutely not." But there's a part of me that would like to think I have the natural ability to sleep on my own. Eventually I'm going to have to go back to my life and I can't take my mom's magic with me.

Rosa claps her hands jovially and leans forward. "I almost forgot! Lily, do you remember Antonia?"

"Mom's friend, the photographer?" I say slathering some butter onto a bit of cuernito. My stomach grumbles. Hunger. That's a good thing.

"The *famous* photographer," Mom says. "Her work has been shown in galleries all over the world."

"That isn't the point," Rosa says. "The point is that her son is getting married."

That's the good news? I was totally expecting something better, based on Rosa's dramatic outburst. And then it dawns on me—the wedding Mom mentioned before I came home.

"You mean Charlie?" I ask, scrunching my face. "The scrawny kid who used to hang out at her studio acting like a morose old man?"

"Yes!" Mom says.

"Isn't he only, like, twenty-three?" I ask, savoring my buttery croissant.

Mom shakes her head. "Twenty-four."

"Great," I say. "Congrats to Charlie and…"

"Amanda," Rosa puts in. "But that's not the best part."

"They're getting married in two days, here, at the farm," Mom interjects with a smile that makes me nervous. "You can help us get everything ready."

"Me?" I bark out a laugh. "I don't know anything about weddings or decorations or—" I look down at my plain tee "—fashion. So, I'm pretty sure I'm the last person who can help." Plus, the idea of attending some Insta-worthy wedding sounds like torture to me.

"It's going to be small," Mom says as if this is somehow a perk.

Rosa's nodding vigorously. "Only one hundred people."

"Is that all?" I tease.

"You'll know many of them," Mom goes on. "Of course you don't have to go, but Antonia hasn't seen you in so long and she's always asking about you and your sisters and cousins. And I was hoping…." She pauses. Her gaze flits to Rosa's.

I'm almost afraid to ask. "What?"

"I was hoping you could help with a memory-magic bouquet," she says, "as a gift to the couple, so they can relive the moment they met."

And there it is. The true reason I'm invited to the wedding.

I take a huge bite of my croissant to avoid having to answer, and as I chew very slowly, my aunt and mom stare at me expectantly. Hopefully.

"Well, that's going to be a problem," I say around a mouthful, "since I can't smell the flowers, which means I can't select the right ones for the happy couple."

"I can help with that," Rosa says, tilting so close I can smell her musky perfume.

"Oh yeah?" I turn to her. "How?"

My aunt pats my hand gently. "Mira, I know we aren't allowed to ask questions about why you're home early, but obviously you've been through…*something*." She pauses, an invitation to define the *something*. When I don't indulge her, she goes on, "and if you don't want to talk about it, that's fine. Although, there is a reason the flowers' scents aren't reaching you."

Oh. Good. Finally someone with definitive answers. Maybe now I can put my lingering theory to rest, and that it's not because of an old spell I cast on a summer night forever ago. "I'm all ears."

"It's because something else is taking up space in your heart, and you have to heal that."

A part of me thinks, *This is your chance. Tell them. Tell them the truth*, but I can't seem to get the words out. "Except that all of us have had terrible experiences and no one else has ever had this issue."

"We think it might have to do with the fact that your magic requires inhalation," Mom adds.

Huh, maybe she's got a point.

Each form of my family's unique magic comes down to the delivery. Dahlia uses tinctures and brews because the power of her healing magic must be ingested. Whereas Mom can use her dream magic with a simple spell and a petal under a pillow. Cam's magic is definitely the most complicated. If she wants to conjure a ghost, she has to not only enchant the right flowers but also bury them at the exact right time, sometimes carving a name into the stems of the blooms.

"Think about it," Rosa puts in. "You, more than any of us, draw in the very essence of the flower, its magic. You become one with it. Heart, body, and soul."

Does she really have to make it sound so dramatic?

Mom sets her napkin on the table. "We went to your garden this morning."

Each of us has our own, and the jardín never lies—it's a mirror to our souls, and whatever grows there will not only carry a message but will also reflect our emotions if they're powerful enough. I've been actively avoiding the idea of even going there, afraid to see my hellish life represented in a little plot of dirt.

"There's just a single bloom," Rosa offers. "A purple anemone."

My mind immediately conjures an image of the poppy-shaped flower that grows in an array of jewellike shades, and while I can't recall its meaning or power, I remember it's also known as the "Wind Flower."

"Estrangement," Mom says, filling in the gaps of my memory.

A loaded word that can mean so many things from antagonism to alienation. To the depth of what I'm truly feeling: *isolation*. From others, from my profession, from myself.

Rosa folds her arms over her chest and looks at me with purpose. "I'm going to speak honestly. The flower also means withered hopes and suffering."

"Rosa!" Mom chides.

"It won't do any good to color the truth and baby her," my aunt argues. Then, to me, she says, "Its power is to heal and protect and although the bloom wouldn't speak to me, I still think the answer to your nose problems has to do with your heart."

"Sounds pretty abstract," I say, twisting my napkin, afraid but growing more certain that she's right.

"Magic is never a straight path," Mom says.

I feel suddenly trapped by symbolic meanings and hidden messages. "Well, I really doubt I'm going to get very far with my nose or heart before the wedding so you should definitely have a backup plan."

"Hearts are such complicated fragile little things," Rosa says with a smirk.

"We are here to *encourage* her," Mom insists.

Ignoring her sister, Rosa says to me, "I can select the memory flowers. You can still cast a spell without the ability to smell their aromas."

"Really?" I ask, encouraged. "You...you can do that?"

"It won't be as powerful as if you selected the flowers yourself," my aunt tells me, "but it will have to do."

I nod, and suddenly I'm filled with longing to fully reconnect to my magic, to figure out what else the Wind Flower has to tell me. It's never as cut-and-dried as one might think. Flower messages are like labyrinths that you can only discover one step, one wrong or right turn at a time.

"I'll do it," I finally say. As much as I'm hesitant, giving a beautiful memory is one of the best gifts possible, and I don't want to ruin it for Charlie.

With a sly grin, Mom extends her open palm to Rosa. "Pay up."

Rosa rolls her eyes then pats her denim jumpsuit's pockets. "No dinero, hermana."

"You guys bet on me?" I ask, feigning offense.

"I knew you'd say yes to the bouquet," Mom explains. "Rosa was sure you'd turn your nose up at the whole affair."

"Only because you don't like weddings," Rosa argues.

"It's not the weddings I don't like, it's the whole tying yourself to one soul for the rest of your existence." As if love could ever last that long without some kind of spell. It's almost incredulous to me that I once believed it could.

Mom stands and begins to stack a few dishes. "This one is going to have horses."

I groan. "Oh, God. Please tell me there isn't going to be a horse-drawn carriage."

"Of course not," Rosa chimes. "The horses are going to wear flower wreaths and stand in the field like the magnificent steeds that they are."

"Like decorations?" I grimace. Poor things.

"No, like guests," Mom puts in. "Apparently, Amanda loves them. She grew up on a horse farm in Montana and when she was in a car accident a few years back she suffered from PTSD."

"What does that have to do with horses?" I ask.

"She went to a horse ranch just north of here and they helped—"

"Or maybe the handsome trainer had something to do with it," Rosa cuts in.

"She was engaged," Mom argues.

"I wasn't implying anything," Rosa adds, feigning shock.

"How do you know he's handsome?" I ask. "Have you been to the ranch?"

"Oh no," Rosa says, looking a bit flustered. "I've only heard stories. Evidently, he keeps to himself quite a bit."

"So a recluse," I tease.

"Something like that," my aunt says, and for a split second, she shares a glance with my mom.

"What are you guys not telling me?" I ask, hating that I'm not in on whatever their eyes are talking about.

Mom looks back at me, ignoring my inquiry. "The ranch is for healing. Perhaps..." I begin to see her wheels spinning, when thankfully, my phone buzzes, interrupting what I know is going to be prescriptive advice that I'm not about to follow. Thankfully, it's my sister Camilla on FaceTime.

I answer it with, "Mom and Rosa are telling me about Charlie's wedding."

Harlow's on the call too. She's right. She does sort of look like a stuffed potato.

I love my sisters' random just-to-chat calls, especially now when I need normal so badly.

"Little Charlie?" Camilla says. She's wearing a red silk scarf on her head. Wisps of jet-black hair peek out. Her perfect skin and naturally long lashes make her look like a starlet from old Hollywood.

"He's all of twenty-four now." I laugh. It feels good and I realize how much I needed this—my family, shared memories, sunshine.

"Oh, right," Harlow says, adjusting a pillow behind her back. "He's marrying the nurse. The one with the horse obsession, right?"

I laugh, enjoying our banter. "Exactly. So now we're going to have horses at the wedding. At our house. As guests."

My sisters bubble with laughter.

"Not funny," Mom sings.

"It sort of is," Harlow asserts, still laughing.

"Hold on," Cam tells us. Then, to someone off camera, she says something about towels in Room 213. She and her husband, Amir, own a small inn on the California coast, a slice of heaven, really. "So, Lil, are you going to the wedding?" she asks.

"Looks like it."

"You hate weddings!" Harlow says while Cam nods her agreement.

"Maybe I'm just more of a realist than the rest of you."

"You can be both a romantic and a realist," Mom argues.

Except I've never been one for the gray areas of life.

With a dramatic sigh, Harlow switches topics to the Celebration of Flowers in two weeks. "I can't believe you're all going to be together without me. I really think I could come. I'll barely be eight months along and—"

A chorus of "no way," "not a chance," and "forget it" explodes from the rest of us.

And while Harlow argues, our family banters, love erupts, and the flowers are in bloom, I don't feel so lost.

Later, when the sun has nearly set, I decide I need to get it over with and visit my garden and the message waiting there.

I walk a narrow path at the north end of the farm. From here, I can see the peaks and valleys of our land, the rolling sea of vibrant colors that has always felt more fairy tale than real.

I took the long way just so I could meander through the vibrant purple tunnel of jacaranda trees. When I was little, my grandmother Azalea told me that the garden was a special place where time stood still, and if you visited under the light of a full moon, you could reverse time. Or more specifically, you could change a moment in time.

If only, I think as I marvel at the thriving buds even in winter. Here, there are no seasons by which we plant or cultivate. Here, magic is always in bloom.

My garden is a minute's walk on the other side of the passageway. The twenty-by-twenty patch of land is bordered by river rocks I placed there as a child, along with a handmade Keep Out sign that is so weathered it now reads just as "p Out."

I pass the old tire swing that hangs from a nearby tree and squat next to the single anemone poking through the soil.

"I hear you've got something to tell me." I lean closer to the silky petals, remembering that this is an odorless flower, and one without nectar to attract bees. I'm not sure if it's the flower's way of standing in solidarity with me or if there's some mysterious message that I'm too daft to get.

That potential mystery is why I brought along the "Libro de las Flores." Hand-written by many ancestors, it outlines everything we know about each flower, including symbolic meanings, connections, potency, and magical uses.

I tug free the cigarette and boot lighter tucked into my jeans pocket and make my way to the tire swing, where I perch with the book.

A cool breeze drifts by. Clouds amass in the darkening distance as I light the cigarette and inhale deeply. It's a near-immediate effect, calming my nerves. I'll stop tomorrow, I promise myself.

Flipping through the pages, I land on "Anemone, Flora de Ventana."

The Wind Flower is a complicated flower, and one with many meanings. Abandonment, fading youth, suffering, refusal of love. This flower denotes estrangement. It possesses powers of healing and protection. Wear in an amulet around your neck to cast away darkness, nightmares, and unwanted thoughts.

I take a drag of my cigarette, feeling disappointed that this entry isn't telling me anything concrete. Well, except for the fading-youth part, which I'm going to choose to ignore.

Through a plume of smoke, I reread the passage, landing specifically on "refusal of love."

With an annoyed groan, I rotate the swing, once, twice, staring up at the twisted branches of the old oak tree as the last bits of daylight fade.

When the rope is nice and tight, I release my hold. I spin so fast that everything is a blur, even my mind, which is churning at the same speed.

I come to a stop.

And when I do, the world *looks* and *sounds* different. Everything is quiet. Still. Colorless.

In that single moment, I see myself from above.

A black-and-white photograph, a still frame, forever locked in the space-time continuum. The small voice inside of me whispers, *There is no path forward, no path back.*

How can there be?

Nothing can fix this—not magic, or my family or this enchanted land. Not even the goddess herself can make any of this go away.

I know I need to tell my family the truth about why I'm not at work, about why I ran away from my life, but the words feel too heavy, too big for my body.

How would I even begin?

I'm on leave because one of my cases is under investigation by the hospital.

True, but only partially.

I'm on leave because... My brain stalls. Tears form.

The memory floods every cell in my body, and once again, I'm back there.

The cold room shrinks all around me. My heart thuds in my ears.

The magic twists around my heart, distracting me. A second, maybe two. Not enough to interrupt a routine hysterectomy. But then...

Blood. So much blood. From where? Must seal the vessels. Must...

The music is fading. Her blood pressure's dropping.

Wiping my face with my sleeve, a tremor works its way through me. I've never lost a patient. Not like this.

I light another cigarette, each inhale calming me, each exhale forcing the truth up and up.

I'm home because I killed someone.

And now I allow the unthinkable to take form: what if the forgotten spell really does have something to do with all of this?

4

As the words climb out of my consciousness, I feel a burning sensation blazing through my body.

Grief. Regret. Rage.

They've all moved in. Unwanted visitors that have made themselves at home, and for the first time in my life, I don't know what to do. I don't have a next step, or anything close to a solution.

I'm certain I tried to stop the excessive blood. I tried to seal the vessels. I followed all the right protocols. I converted to open, cut the long incision in seconds. Searched desperately for the location of the bleeding.

I wasn't fast enough.

Those two seconds of distraction could have mattered.

And no matter how many times I go over every detail in mind, I can't reconcile the horrific truth that my patient, Sarah, is gone forever.

As darkness descends, a yellow moon rises, and I pluck the anemone from my little garden and make my way back through the time tunnel. Halfway through, I consider my grandmother's words about standing under the light of the full moon. It's foolish, really. I know I can't reverse time. I can't change the moment that brought me here.

I stop and take it all in anyway.

The moonlight weaves its light through the branches, a gossamer-like effect that is both tranquil and magical. It makes me think of another relative, of my great-grandmother and the deal she made with the goddess.

Instantly, I draw up the memory of Margarita walking that dirt road, alone and afraid with no future in sight. I was born with this memory, one that's never faded. One that's created a connection to her, and her pain.

I've never felt closer to her than I do now.

I see her in her worn skirt and tattered scarf. She was young, married to a faithless, abusive man. I can feel the ache in her body. The heaviness in her heart. I open the memory like a book, to the pages that matter the most.

My memory magic surges, warming me from the inside out. The air shimmers with it, as the vision appears before me in a silvery haze.

The goddess Mayahuel stands with the glazed sun at her back. Her skin luminous. Her black tresses shine with hints of indigo.

She speaks softly when she tells Margarita, "I will give you and all of your descendants the magic to grow enchanted flowers."

My great-grandmother's stomach grumbles with hunger, not for food, but for purpose and meaning. For power in a world where power is never given, especially to women. She's smaller than the goddess, her shoulders hunched forward, her hands worn. Even then, even amidst her hunger and suffering she asks, "What do you expect in return?"

"You must always protect love, passion, and beauty."

My great-grandmother studies the goddess. I feel her admiration, the desperate hope to escape from a life she never asked for.

"But there will be a cost," Mayahuel says, inching closer.

"What kind of cost?"

"That is for each soul, each of your descendants, to discover."

Margarita lifts her chin. Her dark eyes flicker with a rebellion that courses through each of us. Then, in a voice bigger and grander than her stature, she says, "I agree."

I stand at the edges of the memory, wanting to scream at her, to tell her to get a more detailed definition of *cost* because the devil is always in the details.

That night, when I fall asleep holding the Wind Flower, I dream I'm on a sailboat alone, drifting across a placid sea.

My grandmother's voice echoes across the water. *Go back to the beginning.*

What beginning? I ask. There is no answer.

5

The next day the hacienda is a flurry of wedding-prep activity. People are running in and out of the house, asking questions, looking busy and hyperstressed.

This. This is why I hate weddings. They are a parade, a performance, an extravaganza of perfectly poised details that will look great in photos for social media posts, but they'll never be fully occupied moments.

As I descend the stairs, I see a young, nervous-looking guy in black pants and a white shirt, who looks entirely lost. "Bathroom is down the hall to your right," I tell him.

"Actually," he says, "I was looking for a Jasmine Estrada?"

He pulls out a clipboard from behind his back, stares at it, then flashes it in my direction. "Need her to sign for the tables."

"Follow me."

A minute later, we find my mom in the kitchen, up to her elbows in pink roses. She's so deep in flower-design mode, she doesn't notice us come in. Catalina, a thirtysomething employee from our flower shop carries in a basketful of greenery. "This is the last one," she says with a huff, setting it down on the counter.

"Oh, hey, Lily," Catalina says when she sees me.

"Need help?" I ask.

She shakes her head. "That was the last load... I hope."

Catalina's been working for us for two years and knows nothing of the magic, but she is one hell of a floral designer. Actually, none of our employees at our flower shop in town know about the enchanted blooms. Only Fernando, our farm manager, does and that's because he was born into it. His grandmother handed the job down to his mother and she handed it down to him.

We operate our magical-flower arrangements entirely off a whisper network. And those who come to us are required to fill out an application and sign an NDA. It's a bit ironic that something so magical and nuanced is also so incredibly businesslike. Once my aunt and mom approve specific applications, we hold our annual Celebration of the Flowers. It's the most important time of year for us, entirely centered on that year's hopefuls' requests.

Most of the requests are things like rekindling a lost love, or healing a broken heart, or reliving a memory, or talking to a deceased loved one. We then hold our ritual to prepare the blooms accordingly.

I've seen thousands of applications in my life, and I have to say that the majority are centered on matters of the heart. Although once, I did see an outlandish and impossible request for superpowers and another wanting the ability to time travel.

My mom looks up from her roses and spots me, offering a half-hearted smile, then glances at table guy. "Finally," she exhales. "Are you with the furniture delivery? Did you bring the antique pine? The long tables, not the round oak ones? And the comfy chairs, right?"

She's still asking questions as she leads him outside to inspect the furniture and make sure that, yes, he's indeed brought the antique pine and not some other inferior wood.

I pour myself a coffee and plop down on a barstool. "Very pink," I say, wishing I could smell the sweet fragrance that I'm sure has consumed the kitchen.

Catalina brushes a bleached-blond bang from her eyes. "More like a baby shower if you ask me."

We both laugh as Rosa sweeps into the kitchen. "Why aren't you dressed?" she asks me with a scowl. I know that voice. It's her we-have-work-to-do-and-why-are-you-just-sitting-there voice.

I glance down at my sweat suit, another relic from my old bedroom. It's pilling badly. "I am dressed?"

"Ay, Lily! Go put on something more suitable."

Right. The selection of the flowers for Charlie and Amanda's memory bouquet. Does that require a dress code I'm not aware of?

Catalina offers me a sympathetic expression as I head upstairs to put on something more suitable for walking through the garden, which ends up being a pair of jeans, one of Harlow's designer cardigans that's already making me itchy, and a pair of work boots.

Twenty minutes later, Rosa and I are bumping along the ditch in a utility terrain vehicle.

"Maybe you could slow down?" I tell her over the roar of the engine.

She smirks as she makes a sharp right, forcing me to grab hold of the handle above me before I fly out of the vehicle.

"Azalea came to me in a dream," I say.

"And?"

"She told me to go back to the beginning."

Rosa nods, frowning deeply like she's mulling something over. "What do you think it means?"

I shrug. "Seems pretty vague if you ask me."

"These kinds of messages are never on the nose, Lily. You know that. There is…" She pauses, considers.

I know that look.

"Please don't tell me something about the value of the journey."

She huffs. "Fine. I won't." Then, with a knowing smile, she adds, "But it's true."

I fight the need to groan. "*Beginning* could refer to a million-and-one things."

"A specific point in time or space, a feeling, any kind of start," Rosa muses. "It's the something you need to figure out."

Azalea wouldn't have referred to an inconsequential something. So I immediately rule out obvious beginnings, like my career, or the something that led me home. But I rule that out, too, because that was a definitive end.

My aunt and I descend a steep hill before Rosa slams on the brakes near a wooden fence. Beyond are fields and fields of gladiolas, primroses, impatiens, magnolias, and too many others to count.

The colors are glorious, rich, and vibrant.

I turn to my aunt. "Can I ask you something?"

"Anything."

"What does the past have to do with the present? I mean, why would I need to go back to heal something from years ago that's not even related to what's going on now?"

Rosa scans the fields, taking her time, pondering my question. It's one of the things I love about her. She's thoughtful, measured, and entirely focused.

"The heart is a strange vessel," she says, and for a second, I think she used the wrong word, until she adds, "Whatever we fill it with is mirrored in our lives. So, I imagine that this so-called beginning was a moment when your heart was at risk."

Like now? When I'm questioning my love for medicine? What if it's not enough? What if *I'm* not enough?

Rosa adds, "But since Azalea specified *beginning*, it could mean the first time your heart was at risk. And that memory is still present, a shadow of the past that is affecting how you heal today."

First time.

Heat ignites inside my chest, reminding me of the spell.

A simple enchantment to place a veil over my heart, to keep my family's prying eyes out of my business for once. How could that possibly be so significant? What am I missing?

"The wedding is tomorrow," Rosa says, getting down from the vehicle. "Magic takes time and we have already wasted too much. Ándele."

I don't argue. There's no winning against my aunt when she is on a mission.

I hop out of the UTV and stand next to her as she surveys the fields, which go on farther than the eye can see.

"Did the happy couple tell you the memory?" I ask.

This is the starting place for any memory spell. I don't need every specific detail, just a brief description.

"Of course," Rosa says, taking a crumpled piece of paper from her pocket and handing it to me.

I unfold the note and read it aloud, "'We were at the beach. The sun was setting, and the sky was orange and pink and it was the perfect temperature.'" I feel a groan climbing up my throat, but I resist because it'll just tick off my aunt. "'A sexy song was playing somewhere in the distance.'" I glance up at her. "Seriously?"

"Just keep reading."

"It's so sappy!"

"Lily, it's romantica."

I look back to the note. "'We were happy,'" I read, "'wrapped up in each other and a perfect moment of total bliss.'"

I'm fighting the urge to roll my eyes. Then, as I read the last line written in another hand, Charlie's hand I'm guessing by the straight blocky letters, my body tenses. *The song was "Thinking Out Loud" by Ed Sheeran.*

I nearly laugh at the universe's sense of humor. Every note and word of that song is a ghost of the past that I've expertly avoided until now.

"Are you okay?" Rosa asks.

I swallow the pain and nod as my aunt begins to high-step through the fields, floating her hand over the flowers, whispering to them as she passes. Waiting for them to tell her which ones to choose.

I follow behind her quietly. The fields buzz with so much magic, I can feel the hum beneath my feet. When we get to the west end of the pasture a few minutes later, she's picked three flowers: a yellow coreopsis, which signifies love at first sight, a lavender forget-me-not, for true love and remembering, and a pink camellia.

"Remind me what the camellia is for?" I ask.

"Pink signifies longing and desire," she says almost reverently.

I take the little bouquet from her, knowing that the couple will never see it. For my memory magic to work it must be inhaled and that means I need to blend the flowers into a breathable concoction, sometimes powder, other times liquid. I'll know by absolute instinct once I begin the alchemical process.

Rosa drops me off at a small supply shack on the way back to the house.

"You know what to do?" she asks.

"I've done this hundreds of times."

"Call me if you need anything."

She peels out, kicking up an enormous dust cloud as I make my way into the shed.

Inside, there are dirt floors, shelves of dozens of amber tincture bottles, rows and rows of various floral oils, and a mishmash of baskets, pots, and vases.

Not exactly the kind of place one would imagine magic is created.

After I grab a tincture bottle and some vanilla oil made from the vanilla orchid, known for its purity and mental clarity, I sit at the distressed, lopsided table. Using a molcajete bowl and a pestle, I begin to crush the petals, grinding them into dust.

Bits of sunlight break through the roof's crevices as my magic expands, vibrating through my fingertips. It feels good...natural to be here.

And for the briefest of moments, I feel content, as if the memory of my patient's death can't touch me here. But I know better. Memories go with you no matter how far you travel. Or how much time passes.

I take a grounding breath and scoop a tiny handful of the powder into the tincture bottle. Magic swirls all around me, a simmering, comforting presence, as I place three drops of the vanilla oil inside and spin the spell.

Inside the container, there's a glimmer of pink, then a soft blue glow. Any moment now, I will get a hint of the memory. Sometimes it's a brief image; other times it's a sound or a scent. Today, I hear the ocean, waves crashing onto the shore as if they're right outside this shed.

I feel the familiar hum of magic twisting around my heart. *The strange vessel.*

That's when I know the memory spell is complete.

Just as I close the bottle, I hear that Sheeran song, a few simple notes that echo across time and space. A warm mounting sensation begins in my belly, rises to my chest. The light shifts, the edges of the room fade.

Suddenly, I'm no longer in the shed.

I'm at the top of the waterfalls, dangling my feet over the edge.

I know this memory vividly.

Eleven years.

That's how long it's been.

I don't want to be here, don't want to see…to feel. To remember what I've tried so hard to forget.

Cool water sprays my toes and ankles. It's nearly night. The air is warm, gentle. That's when I hear that same song. I know what comes next.

Just like the first time, I stand and look over my shoulder. He's there, running toward me, singing the chorus of that melody, so out of tune I laugh. He races past me, a blur of motion as he cannonballs over the falls into the lake below.

I'm smiling, staring down into the waters as the sun slides into the horizon, casting a warm glow across the cascadas. He's going to emerge now and when he does his face will catch the light and that's the moment I'll know. That's the moment my heart will no longer be my own.

I inch closer to the edge waiting for him to come up for air.

Any moment…

The memory slows. My body aches all over. I wait. And wait.

The water stirs.

Then, just as he surfaces, before I see the light on his face, I'm mercifully jerked back to the shed.

My heart is thrashing against my ribs.

Everything is out of focus, distorted like I'm peering

through a magnifying lens. I cling to the table, trying to orient myself, to catch my breath.

What the hell just happened?

Dizzy, I squeeze my eyes closed.

A face comes swimming into focus, one I've kissed a hundred times, one I've loved more than any other. One I thought I'd cast out with magic.

It's him. It's Sam.

6

I run back to the house at full speed.

My grandmother's words are in each footstep.

Go back.

Go back.

Go back.

The sky is my home.

A single sentence that conjured Sam. The boy I grew up with, who I spent every summer with. The boy who dreamed of being a pilot and spoke these exact words to me so many times. The first and only man I've ever loved. I hadn't heard those words for ten years, not until my patient's son repeated them to me.

I race over the pebbled paths, through the shaded orchards, remembering the truth I buried deep and that shame kept hidden.

The pain and confusion of Sam's abandonment were unbearable, and the anger that bloomed afterward fueled my desire to reduce him to a distant memory, one that didn't ignite so much emotion. Which is why I intensified the original veiling spell I had used. So instead of simply hiding our relationship from my family's prying eyes, I ended up shielding myself from it too.

Never knowing that the magic I used to protect my heart would end up wounding it all these years later.

I rush across a small courtyard that leads to a side door of the house where I won't bump into anyone.

As much as I want to ask my mom or aunt about what just happened, I can't. I'd have to explain Sam, and I'm not ready to do that. I've never told anyone about us.

At first, it was because I wanted to hold a space for just the two of us and I was so young and didn't really know how to explain that I'd fallen in love with the nephew of our closest family friend, Roberto. I didn't want to face the teasing and the questions, and the longer the secret was kept, the harder it was to reveal the truth. Which meant that I had to hide my emotions before my family sensed them, so I shielded my heart with a masking spell. One that would afford me an ounce of privacy. At least where Sam was concerned.

I never planned for it to get so out of control. It was just a fun, secretive fling at first, and then came that moment at the falls when I realized that he'd stolen my heart when I wasn't looking.

We made love for the first time that night.

We stared up at the stars, dreaming, laughing, making plans for the future carelessly, the way only the young can do. And as he held me, he told me things I wish I could strike from my memory, things like, *I'll always love you* and *Your magic will never be too much for me.*

I believed him. I let him into my world, secrets of magic and all.

After that I knew I had to tell my family about us.

Except that everything blew up before I got the chance. In

the weeks that followed, Sam changed into someone I didn't recognize. He became cold and distant, a storm of chaos that confused me, and when I asked him about it, he told me that he didn't love me anymore, that he needed to move on.

I felt like the earth was disintegrating beneath my feet, like there was no oxygen left in the entire world. I went against my nature and begged him to reconsider, to tell me why. What about his promise to always love me?

He wouldn't even look at me when he said, "I was wrong. I'm sorry."

As I watched him walk away, I shattered into a million pieces. He all but became a ghost that night, and for years after, I sometimes thought maybe I had imagined it all, had imagined him.

It took weeks to find the strength to get out of bed, to control my obsessive desire to call him, to try and make him change his mind.

But time has a funny way of forcing you to see reality. He was never coming back. He'd lied. He'd never loved me, or at least not in the forever kind of way he'd promised, and I'd been foolish enough to believe him.

Anger became my oxygen.

I rebuilt my life. I threw myself into academics, and then medical school. My family has always teased me about my brief affairs; they think that I just haven't found the *right* one. But after Sam, I became an island that no man would ever reach again.

I learned that power comes in having the upper hand, in being the one in the relationship who cares the least.

And somehow those words, *the sky is my home*, disrupted the spell I thought was protecting my heart, creating a balm that made the memories of Sam bearable.

I hurry up the back staircase and into my room where I

pace restlessly. I light a cigarette, taking long drags as I go over every detail, try to answer the *why* of having to relive that goddamn memory.

I quickly realize that I can't figure this out on my own. I need to talk to someone, but who? One of my sisters? One of my cousins?

I choose the one person who won't pity me, who won't judge me, who is the Fort Knox of secret keeping.

After I finish my cigarette, I call my oldest cousin, Lantana. A kick-ass lawyer, Lana's absolutely the most objective person in the family and would die a slow death before she even considered giving a secret away.

She answers on the second ring. "You caught me between appointments. I've got seven minutes. What's up?"

"I need more than seven minutes," I say, rubbing my forehead.

"Oh, so it's a big problem."

"Bigger than that."

"Hold on." There's a sudden radio silence and then she comes back with, "Okay, shoot."

"What happened to the seven minutes?"

"I moved my schedule around."

"Lana."

"Look, if *you* of all people call with a problem, which to my recollection has never happened, then it must be serious."

"That's not true," I argue.

"Of course it is! You're always the one fixing things. Always finding solutions to everyone else's issues."

That's because it's so much easier than focusing on my own.

"And I can't think of a single time," she goes on, "that you've ever reached out for help. At least not for anything serious."

Lana's right. In not asking for help, I created an image of

strength, an iron fortitude, and a world where vulnerability didn't exist. Now all I want is a shoulder to lean on, someone to scoop me up and tell me it's all going to be okay. "Lana. Please focus."

"Fine," she says breezily. "Did you call anyone before me? Am I your backup?"

I manage a small smile. "Nope. You're the only one I called because you're the best secret keeper on the planet." It's her favorite quality about herself.

"So, it's a secreto," she practically purrs. "Okay, tell me."

I hesitate, scared I won't be able to get the words out without falling apart. "Something really awful happened last week at the hospital, and I can't discuss it yet, but it's why I'm home early."

In typical intuitive Lana fashion, she lowers her voice and says, "But that's not why you're calling."

"Well, it's kind of related."

"You know you can tell me anything."

I nod. I feel the memory bubbling up, forming into words I so badly want to spill. *A patient died in emergency surgery. As part of hospital protocol, the case is under investigation and if I'm found negligent, I'm going to need a good lawyer. I'm never going to get over the guilt. I'm never going to heal.*

"I'm just not ready...but I will." Eventually. I'm not sure what I'm so afraid of. Reliving the horror? Being judged? Living with a truth that will follow me for the rest of my life?

For now, I stick to the magic.

That feels more manageable, simpler, something I might be able to fix. I tell my cousin how I can't smell the flowers. I tell her about the dream I had of our grandmother echoing the anemone's message, and then my speech slows. "I walked into one of my own memories," I tell her quietly. "When I was creating a memory concoction for someone else. That's never happened before, Lana."

She's quiet for so long I feel a wave of anxiety rising. I hear her tapping a pen on the desk. "Hmm."

"That's it?"

"Tell me about the memory you walked into."

Why is this so hard? Why do I feel like I'm betraying some part of myself by sharing my first and only love? As if the Lily I am today is the only version I can ever show anyone?

"Lil?"

My eyes burn with tears. "I… The memory was from ten years ago. It was the same night…" I take a shaky breath and drop onto the edge of the bed, forcing the words up and out. "Okay, look, I was in love once. A long time ago and I never told anyone and—"

"Holy shit!" she shouts. "*You* were in love? You don't even believe in it!"

Where Lana is objective, she's also dramatic. Maybe I should have called my sister Cami. No, she's way too romantic and unrealistic to give me advice.

"Who in the hell got to you?" she asks.

"You don't know him," I lie. Any marginal clue that she might, and I'll be met with a storm of inquiries that I'm not ready to face.

"Whoa. Is this…is this why you can't commit to men?"

"No." Maybe. Who knows how deep the spell has affected my heart?

"Wait. How come none of us sensed it?"

"I, uh…" I press my lips together, then say, "Promise me you won't ever tell a soul."

"Cross my heart and hope to die," she says eagerly.

"I *spelled* my heart."

"YOU WHAT!" Her voice rises for the second time. "How? Why?"

"It was just a little masking spell to keep you guys out, to give myself some privacy."

"Seriously? You were that bent on keeping this guy a secret?"

With a wince, I add, "It's even worse than that."

She goes quiet.

"I sort of..." I hesitate. "I intensified the spell."

"Intensified it how?"

"I... I don't know."

"How can you not know!"

I squeeze my eyes closed, inhaling, exhaling. "I was so hurt, Lana. I wasn't thinking clearly."

"I get it," she says gently. "But can you recall what your intention was? Did you try to erase him from your memory or..."

"It wasn't a memory erasure. I... I just wanted to shield my heart from him forever. So that if, you know, a memory sprung up, it wouldn't be so awful."

"Lil," she says gently. "You used magic for your benefit?"

"It was a tiny spell!" I argue, even though I know she's right. If there's anyone in the family who thinks she can bend or break the rules of magic, it's me.

"Look," I add, "I was confused and practically a kid and I don't need a lecture. I need to know your best assessment..." I feel a headache coming on as I lie back on a pillow. "How—" the fuck "—did I step into one of my own memories?"

At my clear distress, Lana goes into lawyer mode, asking questions like what time of day I came home, and about my dreams, and every detail of when I blended the memory for Charlie and Amanda. I don't even fully get the answers out before she's rapid-firing another question.

Then, she sighs. I can hear her heels clicking on a hard surface. I can see her pacing in her Dallas high-rise office. I wait.

"Lil?" she says softly. The kind of voice I use when I give a patient bad news. My heart drops.

"What's wrong?"

"Not sure if I'd qualify it as wrong as much as I'd qualify it as a message from the magic."

"Which is?" My heart is crashing against my ribs violently, stealing my ability to take a breath.

"Did you ever *unspell* your heart?"

"I mean, to be honest I forgot about it until…"

"Until what?"

I tell her about the pilot's words. "I felt this weird spark in my chest, and ever since then, it comes and goes."

"That's the spell talking to you."

"How do you know?"

"I've been doing magic longer than you," she reminds me. "But I think that those words, this trauma at the hospital, maybe it stirred things up or somehow messed with the old magic in some way. I think the first step is making sure this spell isn't hovering anymore."

"So I should undo it?"

Silence.

"Hello?"

"Oh, sorry—I was nodding."

"And then what?"

"And then figure out why your own magic forced you to relive a memory of this man."

Traitor.

"I'd rather not."

My skin is prickling with anxiety. I'm being punished. That's what this is. Punished for bending the rules.

Lana says, "Maybe this is about clearing out the cobwebs of your heart. Your unspelled one, I mean."

I thought I *had* cleared out the cobwebs.

What's the point anyway? Even if I undo the spell, even if I figure out what the magic is trying to tell me, my patient isn't coming back. I can't undo the trauma of that night when she took her last breath on *my* watch.

"One more thing…" Lana trails off ominously.

"What?"

"Undoing a spell that old is precarious."

"Precarious how?"

"The heart you've been walking around with isn't natural. It's magicked. And has been for what did you say? Ten years? That's a hell of a long time, Lil. Once you pull back that veil, you might see things differently. You might *feel* things differently."

"Is there any way to avoid that?" I ask, already knowing the answer.

Lana chuckles. "They're only emotions, Lil. They won't kill you."

Except emotions only get in the way of logic and restraint, two characteristics that have served me well.

A dreadful thought occurs to me. Will I have to relive the feelings I had for Sam? The agony of letting him go? That will be like throwing gasoline on the flames and the idea of it terrifies me. What if I'm not strong enough to shut that door again without magic?

"Listen," she says, "when I get there next week, I can talk to the flowers. Maybe they can shed more light."

I bury my head under the pillow, thinking how nice it would be if I could block out the entire world. "Okay."

"Hey, Lil?"

"Yeah?"

"You're the toughest of us all," she says gently. "I know you're going to get through this."

Except that I don't feel tough. I feel like some unknown entity has ransacked my identity and I'm never going to find the way back to the truest version of myself.

After we hang up, I stare at the now-wilting anemone. "You could have been clearer," I tell the violet bloom as I grab the "Book of Flowers" from the nightstand and flip through the pages until I reach the right entry.

The Wind Flower is a complicated flower, and one with many meanings. Abandonment, fading youth, suffering, refusal of love. This flower denotes estrangement. It possesses powers of healing and protection. Wear in an amulet around your neck to cast away darkness, nightmares, and unwanted thoughts.

I find a pen and pad of paper in the drawer and copy the words. Using a method of deduction and intuition I learned in medical school, I begin scratching out words until the entry looks like this.

~~The Wind Flower is a~~ **complicated** ~~flower, and one with many meanings.~~ **Abandonment, fading youth, suffering, refusal of love.** ~~This flower denotes~~ **estrangement.** ~~It possesses powers of~~ **healing and protection.** ~~Wear in an amulet around your neck to~~ **cast away darkness, nightmares, and unwanted thoughts.**

Frowning, I study the words.

"A complicated moment of abandonment, fading youth, suffering, and refusal of love," I say aloud. "Okay, so maybe that leads to estrangement, which requires healing and protection but only if I can cast away darkness, the nightmares…"

I look to the bottom of the page where I notice a near-faded entry that I can't make out. In a fit of energy, I rush toward the window and hold the book up to the sunlight so I can read the small, slanted words I hadn't seen before.

I left my heart in the dark...

The *K* dangles off the edge of the page.

I turn it quickly to find a continuation: *...And there it rusted, a decomposed box of memories lost in the cold. Until spring came. Until it emerged from a cocoon of dreams.*

The words come to a sudden halt as if the writer got distracted or had nothing else to say. Beneath the message, though, is a black-and-white drawing, an elegant sketch of a water lily. A flower that signifies both birth and death.

Instantly, I remember a family folktale about the water lily needing hibernation in order to bloom, but once the winter was over and the spring came, the lily emerged from a cocoon of dreams that had been spun by a goddess of sleep.

I reread the entry, feeling a kinship with the writer, understanding what it is to leave your heart out in the cold dark.

A decomposed box of memories. Until spring. Until it emerged from a cocoon of dreams.

A cocoon...

Like the veil I folded over my heart.

It might sound ridiculous, maybe even unhinged, but there's something oddly comforting about allowing Sam's memory back into my orbit, or at least the goodness of him.

When we were twelve, he asked me why in the world I wanted to be a doctor. "Doesn't that mean you'll have to look inside of people with all their guts and blood?" he asked.

"So?"

"So, that's creepy."

I laughed. "Not any creepier than flying thousands of feet in the air. I mean what if the engine died, or the wings fell off or lightning struck?"

"I'm not scared of pain."

"Yeah, well you'd be a goner for sure."

Sam narrowed his dark gaze, considering my logic, and just when I thought he was going to acquiesce, he smiled and said, "Still better than touching blood and guts."

Lifting my gaze, I stare out across the rolling hills of golds and pinks and greens as the sun floats closer and closer to the horizon.

How can there be so much color in the world when all I feel is gray?

I don't close my eyes against the glare, afraid the afterimages of that night in the hospital will come.

I've decided.

Tonight, I'll undo the spell. I'll pull back the veil. I'll prove to myself that I'm not a coward.

Lana said it might be precarious, but that's not what I'm fixated on. It's the pain that is likely to follow.

I take a long drag of my cigarette, hold my breath until my lungs begin to ache. Slowly, steadily, a plume of smoke escapes my nose as the thought unfolds.

I want it to hurt.

Because in the end, I deserve nothing less.

7

After everyone is asleep, I slip out of the hacienda and into the darkness.

The moon is hovering low tonight, as if it's dangling from an invisible string.

Using the ambient light to lead the way, I head to the small pond beyond the barn, and I find what I came here for: a pink lotus.

The bloom is known for evolution, and resurrection, among other things, but I'm most interested in its powers to open a lock.

With the lotus in hand, I begin my hike up to the water-falls, the place where I intensified the masking spell. Ironic that the place where I gave away my heart is the same location where I plan to unspell it.

With each step, I remember that night in Technicolor—the climb up the mountain, the scent of rain floating in from the east, the wild fennel in my pocket used for the spell that I consumed slowly.

The hike should only take fifteen minutes, but tonight, it's as if an enormous expanse of hours has replaced the length of minutes. My legs ache by the time I walk up a few steep trails where I lose the moonlight due to the tree cover.

Night creatures hum, silvery leaves rustle. My own voice keeps me company.

You can do this. No matter how much it hurts, you can do this.

I don't want to get ahead of myself, but my mind is already racing ahead before I can stop it. Once I break the spell, I can begin to heal. Once I begin to heal, I can go back to my life. My very carefully curated life.

When I reach the clearing that leads to the falls, my heart sinks. I haven't been back here since that night. I pass the shaded grove where Sam and I laid out the blanket. It was red with little gray stars.

The memory of Sam's voice finds me.

I'll always love you.

"Except when you stopped," I whisper, thinking that lies are always the most powerful when served on a platter of trust.

The sound of the waterfall rushes up to meet me as I inch toward the edge, making promises to myself that I know I can't keep.

I won't think about him again.

I won't imagine a future that doesn't exist.

I won't feel the warmth of his arms around me no matter how cold I feel.

I won't wake with his name on my lips.

Cold water sprays my ankles and bare arms as I sit at the edge of the cliff. From here, I can see the shocking white falls crashing into the dark waters twenty feet below. My gaze follows the ripples that drift toward the black woods beyond.

With a shuddering breath, I fold the flower into my palm. I feel the throb of my own pulse as my magic surges, thawing the fear in my chest and stomach, waiting for my permission to enter.

A chill emanates from the water below.

I want to be brave and stoic, but for this to work, I have to picture my heart, really see it, and well... I'd rather not.

Closing my eyes, I imagine my heart—the anatomical version, thinking that if I stick to science, this won't be so bad. But then the textbook-looking image shifts and I see only a small door, half eaten by rust and time.

Right.

I open it slowly, begrudgingly. I swear I hear the thing grind on its hinges as the pale misty magic rushes in.

Quickly, I place the flower on my tongue. Bitterness spreads through my mouth.

I don't chew. I don't swallow.

The lotus's essence spreads through me as I lie back and wait.

The memory comes like an old movie, aged and slightly out of focus, but I can still make out the important parts. He's here. Of course he is.

I see Sam clearly.

The way the sunlight glinted in his eyes, the way his mouth curved into an unforgettable smile. I hear the echo of his voice.

Jump and I'll catch you. I promise.

A tear slips down my cheek.

Then, in the quiet of my mind, I say the only three words that matter in the moment.

Unlock the spell.

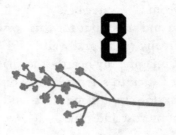

8

In an instant, the world vanishes into cobwebs and darkness. A hazy figure comes into focus.

The figure comes closer. A little girl, I realize, about seven years old. She walks with a skip in her step. Closer and closer until…

I see that she's me.

Blackish hair falls around her face in a tangled mess. Smears of dirt stain her cheeks. She stares at me in mute fascination, then, with defiance burning in her eyes, she says, "You used to be fun."

I'm stunned at this kid's audacity. "Excuse me?"

"Now I'm stuck here because of you."

"But you *are* me."

She shakes her head briskly. "I'm the better version of you."

Anger swells, but what am I going to do? Duke it out with some kid version of myself?

Sam's boyish voice echoes across the terrain. "Chapulin!"

A nickname he gave me because he said I was as restless as a grasshopper. I feel the stab of that name deeper than bone.

Everything is fine. This is only a dream.

My mind conjures up the memory of seven-year-old Sam, the shy, awkward boy I met at a Dia De Muertos parade. His face was painted like a skeleton. Shockingly white with uneven black circles around his eyes. He wore a bright red cape, a bit tattered and smeared with makeup.

"Are you a superhero skeleton?" I asked him, thinking that's exactly what he looked like.

He merely shook his head and muttered, "I need it to fly."

"Skeletons don't fly."

He swept his cape behind him and whispered like it was a secret, "Ghosts do."

Now young me points a long skinny finger at my chest. "You have thorns in your heart," she says.

As if on cue, my heart begins to twist painfully.

I lift my shirt and glance down to find agave spines growing out of my chest. There isn't any blood. Just a burning agony that could drive me to my knees if I wasn't so damn stubborn. "This is only a dream," I remind myself.

"Is it?" she asks, tilting her head to the side. "Thorns cause scars you know."

Scars. The body's natural way of healing and replacing lost or damaged skin. Yes, I'm scarred; my heart is damaged.

She steps closer and stands on her tippy toes, her dark, endless eyes circling my face. "Time to open wide."

A dark cold grips me.

I feel something taking shape inside of my mouth. I feel the silky slip of a petal curling, twisting, reaching past my lips. And with it, a scream that's climbing up my throat, but I won't let it out. I won't give it the power to come into this world. I won't let it win.

My mouth flies open, and the lotus flower tumbles out and onto the ground.

Young me picks it up, twirls it between her fingers and says gently, "It wasn't your fault."

The air turns thick and hot.

An aching sadness digs its claws into me, ripping me open from the inside out. And suddenly, I feel the weight of that moment, of my patient's last breath. The final beat of her heart. I can still smell the blood. I can still feel the icy fingers of death curling around my hands.

My legs give out and I collapse onto the earth, pressing the tears back into my eyes with numb fingers.

I take an unsteady breath. Two.

"You don't believe me," the girl says.

And I don't. This is a dream, slanted and cut into too many parts to make any sense.

The girl sighs as if she's been trying to convince me for eons and not mere seconds. "Well then…"

Her voice trails off and the thorns in my chest vanish into a swirl of mist.

"Good luck," she tells me before she turns and skips toward the sound of Sam's voice, back into the misty darkness, humming a tune. That stupid Sheeran song.

I run after her, toward Sam. I feel a sudden urgency to *see* him, to see the boy who was everything I couldn't be, reckless and free, a boy who grew into pure fortitude on two legs. A boy who's haunted my dreams, who I've tried so hard to forget, even if it meant leaving pieces of myself in his wake.

Up ahead, there's a long pale ribbon of light.

I run toward it, faster, harder, gulping in the hot night air.

Their laughter echoes softly through the trees. And all I want is to be closer to them, to the unnamable something that they share.

With a jolt, I wake in my bed.

It takes a moment for the world to come into focus, as if I

have sand in my eyes. My body throbs with a dull ache as I roll over onto a damp pillowcase.

Tears.

I know because they're still drying on my cheeks.

The memory of last night drifts into my consciousness and with it a million questions.

How did I get here? I don't remember walking home. As a matter of fact, all I *do* remember is seven-year-old me skipping back to Sam as if the two of us had created a world that time and reality couldn't touch.

A vicious, cruel dream, I tell myself, rubbing my temples in slow circles.

"And I am fun," I groan.

Then, remembering unlocking the spell, I sit up and snatch the anemone from my nightstand, breathing in its petals.

There's no scent. No lingering sweetness.

Shit.

I stare up at the rough-hewn timbers on the ceiling, wondering if maybe I did the ritual wrong.

No, I'm sure it was right, I think as I reach for a cigarette. My hands tremble, fumbling with the boot lighter as I spark up, aching for answers.

Whoever said that healing was good for the soul was way off track. It hurts like hell.

As I inhale, dark, ashy flavors sweep past my tongue and into my skull, giving me an instant headache and I nearly gag. In a fit of disgust, I throw the cigarette onto the floor.

What the fu...?

Whirls of smoke suddenly start to rise from the ground.

I leap out of bed, grab the cigarette just as it's about to burn a hole in the vintage rug, and, with a grunt, put it out on the terrace before I race into the bathroom and brush my teeth to get rid of the horrid aftertaste.

I frown at my reflection in the mirror, as if *she* has all the answers. Chewing my bottom lip, I tell myself firmly and repeatedly that there is a logical explanation, that the spell must have done something to my taste buds instead of restoring my ability to smell the flowers.

I'm no stranger to nighttime oddities and nightmares, but this one... It felt so real. Like a long-forgotten memory that resurfaces when you catch a whiff of a familiar scent, or you hear a dreadful song.

I try to shake the girl's voice from my now-cramping brain: *it wasn't your fault.*

It.

My patient? Sam? The spell?

I'd love to know which *it* she was referring to because I swear there are so many, I've lost count. And what does some little kid from the dream world know of culpability? Nothing.

For so long, I didn't have room for wanting, for needing. I focused on my career, on making a difference, or at least that's what I've told myself.

And then I remember Sam's voice, the innocence and affection, the voice that grew and deepened and held me with a ridiculous promise of forever. In an instant, I'm that nineteen-year-old girl, shattered and curled into a ball on the floor desperately searching for answers.

I spit into the sink and shake off the memories. I'm no fucking wallflower. I can't change the past. I can't bring my patient back and I can't make Sam love me. I can't make him pay for his lies, and believe me, I've fantasized about it.

I shoot Lana a text.

It didn't work!

Almost immediately, my phone buzzes with her reply.

How do you know?

Can't smell the flowers.

And now my taste buds hate cigarettes, which is probably a benefit, but still. I can't help but feel that the magic is toying with me, making a game of it all to see how much I can take before I break.

Lana texts, Undoing spells can take time.

How much time!

Well, you did spell your heart for ten years, so who knows?

The girl's voice rings through me: *You have thorns in your heart. Thorns cause scars.*

Thorns.

Just like Mayahuel, who was locked up by her wretched grandmother because the old woman was jealous of her beauty, but it wasn't enough to keep away the god Echuetl who whisked Mayahuel to safety. Unfortunately, the couple was bad at hiding. Eventually the only way the goddess could free herself entirely of the hag was to become an agave, a thorny spiny bush that in the end became her weapon.

I hear footsteps followed by my mom's voice. "Lily!" The door swings open. "It's nearly four!" she says with a disapproving scowl. She's wearing an emerald-beaded dress that falls to the floor, a perfect complement to her dark, striking features. "The wedding is in an hour, and you're not dressed."

Did she say four? Was I really out that long?

"What am I supposed to wear?" I ask, thinking the pilling sweats I have in my closet aren't going to cut it. Hope surges in my chest. Maybe this is my out. Maybe I won't have to watch Charlie and Amanda exchange vows promising forever.

Mom sighs with more exasperation than the moment calls for. "Nice try. Lucky for you, Harlow ordered a gown and shipped it here when I told her about the wedding."

Of course she did. My sister, the shopaholic.

"Did you say *gown*?" Ever since I adopted the social life of a vampire, due to countless night shifts, and essentially lived in scrubs, I stopped thinking of style the same way that others do. Not that I don't own any dresses or non-scrubs clothing, but I left all of that back at my apartment, instead stuffing my luggage with comfortable, oversize grunge wear that I could get lost in.

"I hung it in her closet," she says. "Be ready in forty minutes."

After a three-minute shower, I wrap myself in a towel and hurry into Harlow's room down the hall, pretending the dream isn't lingering at the edge of my memory. God, I just want to take a hammer to it and smash the images to bits. The more I think about it, the angrier I get.

Good luck.

Why do those two words suddenly feel spiteful?

I find the gown, still wrapped in plastic, hanging in the closet. The dress is gray, strapless. It's understated and simple, even spectral. Harlow knows me well. This is the perfect dress to disappear in.

I blow-dry my hair straight-ish, letting it fall to my shoulders, and after a two-minute makeup routine that consists of tinted moisturizer, bronze eyeliner, some mascara, and a dab of pink lip gloss, I slip on some strappy heels Lana left behind, and head downstairs where my mom and Rosa are waiting.

"Que linda!" Rosa sings.

Mom nods her agreement. "I haven't seen you this put together in…"

"A decade?" I hand over the amber vial that contains Charlie and Amanda's memory potion.

Rosa eyes me appreciatively. "They will be so happy."

As we leave the hacienda, I close the front door, and for a split second, I think I hear a slow exhale behind me. But when I look back, all I see is a long, slanted shadow guarding the entrance.

9

Rosa and Mom are chatting it up as we walk past the valets parking cars in the driveway and the wedding crew directing and escorting guests down the path that has been scattered with pink peony petals.

We don't get much farther when I realize, "I forgot my phone. And I promised Harlow and Cam I'd take photos."

Mom sighs. "There will be a photographer to handle all that."

"They want the unedited version of the wedding," I say. "Go on without me. I'll meet you there."

"Please don't be late," Mom says, looking at her watch. "You've only got another twenty minutes."

I rush back to the house as best as I can in these damn heels, wobbling up the stone stairs and into my room where I find my phone on the bathroom counter. As I head back out, I realize that these leather straps are already digging into my skin and there is no way I will last the night with them on my feet.

After I slip the shoes off, I find a pair of flat sandals in Lana's room, not exactly elegant, but the dress is long and hopefully no one will notice my mismatched fashion choices, or my desperately in-need-of-a-pedicure toes. On the plus side, I'll be able to run, cutting short the ten-minute walk to hopefully five.

With each step, I try to puzzle out last night. I start with the most obvious: *when did I fall asleep?* The last thing I remember before the dream is placing the pink lotus bloom on my tongue. If I'd been counting back from ten, I wouldn't have even reached nine.

The thought of dream-induced me sleepwalking home sends a chill up my spine. Never in my life have I walked in my sleep, so why was last night different?

To avoid guests and dreadful small talk, I take the back route past the hydrangeas and orange blossoms. I dash past the lemon trees and through the herb garden, which leads me to a small orchard of pomegranate trees, northeast of the ceremony.

Standing at the edge of the orchard, I take it all in: the altar decorated with an arc made of white roses, the silk pink runner lining the aisle, the dozens of chairs, each adorned with a sprig of pink heather for good fortune.

A hippie-looking harpist with red hair to her waist floats her long fingers across the strings. The minister is shaking hands with some guests. Mom and Rosa are seated near the front, heads bent in whispered conversation.

I can't help but think that this is a lot of pomp for two people to make a forever promise. Why not just run off into the forest or get lost at sea?

While everyone waits for the bride, I begin to head over and take my seat when I see two horses. The white steeds stand in the field beyond the altar about thirty yards away.

Purple and yellow wildflowers sprout all around them, making them look more fairy tale than real.

They're wearing French lilac wreaths around their necks,

a bloom that signifies first love. An unexpected smile fans across my mouth.

I can't help but marvel at their muscular forms, and how elegantly they hold themselves. Maybe Amanda had the right idea by bringing them to the wedding.

The subtle sound of movement catches my attention. The guests have gotten to their feet. A new song begins, soft, and slow, and bright.

I spin to see Amanda making her way toward the aisle, clutching a tiny bouquet of daisies with one hand while looping her free hand into the safe crux of her father's arm.

Her blond hair is woven with baby's breath. Her tiara's stones shimmer in the waning light. I'm about to make some snide internal comment when I catch myself and look at her with fresh eyes. I must admit, she sort of reminds me of a summer queen returning to take her throne.

I lean against the tree as my gaze trails to the altar where Charlie stands, closing and opening his fists. He's tall, made up of broken angles that seem to soften when he smiles. He's not at all the grumpy kid I remember.

And my God, he stares at Amanda like he's falling in love with her for the first time, like he'll never get enough of her.

An odd pressure begins to mount in my chest. Then comes the tug.

A magnetic, gravitational pull that forces my eye to the wildflower field beyond the altar, where a man emerges from the back side of the hill.

He walks with purpose through the knee-high flowers toward the horses.

My throat tightens.

I know that stride. I know those shoulders. The curve of those arms.

Bitterness grows inside of me.

And somewhere between the haze of *I do*s and magical flowers, I want to run, to never look back, but his head is already turning toward me.

His face is older, lined as if he's lived a decade longer than I have.

And just when I think he might lift a hand to wave, just when I think he might acknowledge my presence with even a tiny grin, he scowls, his body stiffens, and Samuel James turns and walks away.

10

Something ignites inside of me. I tell myself I'm just tired from my night of magical happenings. I tell myself that the bile rising in my throat is because my heart is no longer magicked.

I'm a lone flower caught in a windstorm.

Lana said I would feel things. This must have been what she meant, and still—the idea of it does nothing to console me.

Would it really have been so hard for him to smile or wave or acknowledge my presence in any way? Am I really so awful that he can't stand the sight of me?

Nausea rolls through me as I realize the bitter truth: my heart still beats to his tune, and I hate myself for it.

I spin toward the trees, running deeper and deeper under cover before I stop, bend over, and vomit all over the earth and Lantana's sandals.

Tilting against a tree, I wipe my mouth and pull myself together. Why is he here? He walked toward the horses like they belonged to him.

I recall Rosa's words: *the handsome trainer. The ranch north of here.*

But how? Why?

No matter how many times I ask the same questions, my brain doesn't compute. What does Sam know of ranches and horses? Nothing. All he ever wanted to do was fly planes. To get his feet off the ground and his head into the clouds.

Each question that rises is just another dagger to my heart, reminding me that I know nothing of Samuel James or how he's spent the last ten years.

Could he ever know that for me those same years have been nothing more than a series of tally marks, the passing of days under the false light of all my ambition?

The last bits of sun stream through the tree branches. Dappled shadows dance at my feet, reminding me of summer, of those warm and wondrous days on the farm when I was a kid. When life was simple. When Sam was my best friend.

It's a strange thing to have someone in your life for so long that they carve neural pathways in your brain. They cement themselves in your memory and then one day, they're just... gone.

And in the space of their absence, you can't help but wonder who they've become without you. Clearly, some big details have changed, but it's the little, seemingly insignificant things that peck away at you, like, does he still hate sushi? Does he still love rainstorms?

Over the years, my family's mentioned him in passing, saying they heard he'd moved away, asking what I knew. I acted as if it was the least-interesting topic in the world, and that quieted the inquiries. Plus, I wasn't at all surprised that he'd left town, figuring he'd gone off to school, to fulfill his life in the sky.

Still, every time I've come home since we broke up, I've

avoided certain places and refrained from asking his uncle Roberto about him. Oddly, Roberto never mentioned him. Maybe he knew about the breakup and didn't want to make me feel worse.

Even with the enhanced spell, I've lived with the fear that Sam might be visiting at the same time and that I might run into him in town, and the magic would fail me and I'd melt into the ground, because what do you say to the person who crushed your heart inexplicably?

Jesus, the guy could be married with seven kids for all I know, and here I am, retching over something he probably never even thinks about.

In that moment, I realize that I have a choice.

I can rejoin the guests for the reception and risk seeing Sam or I can hightail it home and bury myself under the covers and pretend him away.

I consider the loveliness of lingering in the dark of my bedroom, but then he'll win. He'll know I'm a pathetic coward avoiding him, and I refuse to give him the upper hand.

With my head held high and my shoulders thrust back, I go back toward the white tent, heart hammering like I'm on a death walk. Each step a mantra: *I can do this. I can do this.*

When I arrive, the party is in full swing. The tent is filled with cherry blossom trees reaching toward a weblike constellation of baby's breath that droops from twisted branches where candles are balanced delicately.

"Where have you been?" Rosa says, startling me from behind.

"I… I felt sick," I tell her.

Her eyes take me in like she's trying to decide if I'm telling the truth. "Are you okay?"

"Better now."

The quasicourage I felt a moment ago has all but dissipated. God, I just want this night to be over so I can forget I ever saw him. So he can crawl back into whatever hole he's been in for the last ten years.

Or maybe I should concoct a spell that mimics food poisoning to the tenth degree.

The idea of it, fragile and villainous as it is, buoys me somehow.

Or maybe it's the unlocking of the spell, but either way—

This is my home, my territory, and damn if I'll let him run me off. Never mind the fact that he's clearly over it. I mean who has the audacity to show up at the person's home whose heart you obliterated? And not even wave!

Weaving through the crowd, I am heading over to the bar for a glass of much-needed wine when I run into Charlie. He's taller and less toothy, as if his face finally caught up to his body.

"Lily?" He wraps me in a hug.

"Congrats," I tell the beaming groom. He's so far from the kid I used to know, and I can't help but think how funny time is. How it can whittle away the strongest stone and shape the most distant hearts.

"Thanks," he says, still smiling. "What's it been? Fifteen years?"

I chuckle. "Last time I saw you, you were maybe nine or ten and training for that taco-eating contest."

He barks out a laugh. "You've got a good memory. But if I recall, I came in last place and was sick for three days."

"At least you still got a medal."

"For participation," he says. "I think I've still got that thing."

Just then, another guest comes up to Charlie, jabbering on about something, and as their conversation gets going, I turn to leave. He grabs my arm gently, leans in, and says, "Hey, thanks."

No other explanation is required. I know he's talking about the memory spell, and I feel a sense of joy and pride that I was able to do something so special for them.

Lost in my thoughts, I nearly slam into my mother. Her silence screams disappointment, but her maternal instincts must kick into gear because her face softens into one of sympathy. "Rosa said you were sick."

"I'm fine now. Probably just need to eat."

"Try the sopa. It's…" She doesn't get the rest of the words out because Amanda's at the microphone, thanking everyone for being here and pointing our attention to a tent wall, which is now sweeping back like a theater curtain to reveal the two steeds draped in the French lilacs.

And between them is Sam, holding their reins loosely, like a man with no fear that they could buck or run away or otherwise tear through the elegant party.

Sixteen people stand between us. I counted just to keep my mind and anxiety from spiraling out of control. I should go. But I don't. My legs are stone pillars.

He's dressed in a plain black T-shirt and jeans. His hair is darker than I remember, as if it hasn't seen the sun in many summers. It hangs to his chin in a heap of careless black. And his brown eyes, those are brighter than I recall, flashing with an emotion I can't read.

I used to be able to though.

Sam could never hide his feelings from me, no matter how practiced his smile or how fixed his expression. His eyes always told the truth.

The night he walked away, when he told me he didn't love me anymore, I searched his eyes for the inevitable lie, knowing *they* would never betray me, but all I saw was anger and resentment and I knew then that it was over forever.

Amanda is going on about how much she loves horses, about how *Sam's ranch* saved her.

The words land like grenades.

"As you all know, I had PTSD from a car accident," Amanda

explains to the crowd, "and these lovelies, they saved me." She raises her glass, her gaze floating over my shoulder. "And so did Charlie."

While everyone applauds, I stare at Sam defiantly, daring him to look at me, to meet my gaze, to own up to the gall that he's at my home being rude as shit.

The light is cold and graying, but there's a slice of burnt sunlight that touches the edge of the tent.

I try hard not to let my eyes drop to Sam's throat or the weight of his shoulders or the slim brawn of his arms, which had once been skinny with no hope of a muscled future.

Gone is the boy I knew.

He's a stranger to me now, a man with a web of lines around his eyes, which have seen more than his years would suggest. A man whose nose is more defined, whose jaw is leaner, whose eyebrows are thicker, hooding his deep-set eyes more sharply than before.

He shifts on his feet. Clearly he's still a man not comfortable in the spotlight, a man who looks like he'd love to stalk off into the darkness of night and never look back.

As the applause continues, he smiles, a soft, maybe genuine smile. I can't tell. But his gaze never finds mine. It makes me feel triumphant, but I know I've won absolutely nothing.

Unexpectedly, Amanda hands him the mic. I don't know why but I feel a rush of panic. It's one thing to *see* Sam. It's another thing to hear the voice that once soothed me to sleep, the voice that spoke our dreams into existence, the one that was so very good at lies.

A small burst of winter air drifts into the tent. There's a hum to it, the sort of cold you feel in your bones right before the storm comes.

I wrap my arms around myself.

Sam's face is tense when he says, "You're all welcome to

visit the ranch out near Sirena Lake, about forty minutes from here," he adds, just in case people don't know he's referencing the lake that according to legend, was cried into existence by a brokenhearted woman who was transformed into a mermaid.

My entire body tingles with the memory of being the focus of his gaze, his smile. Of lying in those arms, of kissing that mouth. I shake the images away, feeling betrayed by my own mind and I choose instead to focus on the memory of his back when he walked away.

I take a sip of wine, twisting inside, wishing he'd leave now. Wishing he'd stop looking so goddamn good. Wishing...

Okay, maybe I've become a wisher.

"I'd like to thank the Estrada family," he says, the words cutting through me like a dull knife. I can't hear whatever he's thanking my family for, because I'm a mile under water, fighting my way up to the surface.

I blink and the party is back in full swing. Music. Chatter. Clinking glasses.

I'm buzzing with curiosity, desperate to ask Mom why Sam mentioned the family, but she's deep in conversation with someone and now isn't the time.

I was hoping Sam would vanish from sight, but the tent wall stays pulled back so that the horses are in full view and so is he. Stroking one of their manes, whispering into a perked ear.

I know what I need to do. I'm just too much of a chicken-shit to do it. But if I don't, I tell myself, I'll be a victim to this heartbreak forever. I need to prove to myself that the powerful memory of him, the one that my magic is no longer protecting me from, is an unwelcome monster that I no longer need to be afraid of.

Go back to the beginning.

I gulp down the rest of my wine and march toward him.

11

When I step outside, the full cover of darkness has fallen across the sky.

Pinpricks of light flicker in the distance and the moon hangs in a lazy half arc.

Sam is now nowhere to be seen. The man is a regular disappearing act.

I don't dare scan the area for fear he might see me and misread my interest as something it's not. When really, all I want to do is be rid of him, or at least prove to him he means nothing. Less than nothing.

The horses become more striking the closer I get. Their white coats glossy like winter moonlight.

I've never spent much time around the animals, far preferring human behavior that, to be honest, is much more predictable. One can never tell what a large animal is going to do when cornered, so I approach slowly, hands extended as if to say "I come in peace."

"Hello, beauties," I whisper, tracing my fingers over the

French lilacs circled around their necks, wishing I could smell their floral honeyed notes.

It's then that I feel his presence, a swell of energy that glides up behind me.

I turn to face Sam, waiting for him to say something—hello, hi, it's been so long. Something. Anything.

He merely stares down at me from his six-foot stature like I'm a new species of creature he's never seen before.

I force a lighthearted grin, one that tells him all the years have been erased and I'm so over it, over him, and doing swimmingly, thank you very much.

Lie. Lie. Double lie.

"Hey," I manage, doing my best to vanquish the small, unbearable silence.

When we were kids, we'd have staring contests to see who blinked first, and as we got older, the rules of the game changed. We'd sit face-to-face and wait to see who would cave under the heat of our gazes and touch the other first.

I was almost always the victor.

His lips part. "I…" He blinks. "I didn't know you'd be here." His voice, almost apologetic, cuts through the music as he shifts his weight from foot to foot.

There's no malice in his words, just fact, which I'm having trouble parsing out. *If I'd known you'd be here, I wouldn't have come?*

It's my turn to say something and I need to keep it light, nonthreatening. "These are your horses?"

His long arms shift awkwardly at his sides like he's not sure what to do with them. "Yeah, that one's Rainy and this one here is Blanco."

"Blanco." I huff out a small laugh. "Original."

He doesn't share my wit. His gaze tightens. He's uncomfortable and I find some delicious sense of power in it. "You own a ranch now?" I ask.

What happened to becoming a pilot? What happened to the sky being home?

"And you're a doctor."

That is *not* an answer, but I'm too lost in the fact that he knows this about me, which tells me (a) he's either asked about me, or (b) he heard word around Ventana, where gossip spreads like the flu. I manage a simple, "I am."

There's a war going on between Sam's scowl and an almost grin. The scowl definitely comes out on top. "You got what you wanted."

Did I? Not exactly, I want to say. Not because of the investigation but because I don't know if can ever go back to that life. I don't know if I trust myself. Every protocol, all my training, everything that I thought I knew seemed to evaporate into nothingness when Sarah died.

My colleagues told me that it happens eventually, that a patient dies on your watch, as if said eventuality somehow makes it bearable. But what if I'm not built that way? What if bearable to one person is devastation to another?

Sam rubs the back of his neck. A rebellious lock of hair falls over his left eye and I fight the urge to brush it out of his face. The lift of his arm reveals a tiny blue tattoo inked on the inside of his wrist, but he shifts so quickly I can't make out its details.

"I saw you earlier," he admits, "and… I meant…" He takes a small breath. "I should have waved." His eyes meet mine. "I was surprised to see you. I should have waved."

He was surprised?

"Sam, this is my house." His name on my lips feels so natural, so normal. Rainy snorts like she's on my side.

"Good point," he says, folding his arms stiffly. "I just didn't think you were in town." His words come out dry, maybe even annoyed, like he's on the verge of being harassed and he just wants to avoid the whole affair.

Me too, Sam. Me too.

It's so much effort to stand here, but the longer I do it without combusting the more powerful I feel. Like maybe the fear of seeing him again was never going to be as bad as the actual act.

Then, as if being summoned, a ripple of magic loosens from the soil. I can feel its vibration twist up my legs, reassuringly. Its warmth soothing my heart.

With a slight shiver, I gesture toward the tent. "Nice wedding."

He follows my hand, and for just a moment, his mouth looks like it might curve into a smile, but then he straightens it, forcing it back into line. When he returns his gaze, his eyes flick to my bare skin, as if he can see the goose bumps sprouting. They linger there, a hot branding iron, until he forces his gaze up at me and says, "Charlie's a great kid."

This is too weird, this whole interaction, standing in the dim light with Sam like no pain, no memories exist between us. How can we be reduced to small talk when our entire lives were so entangled it was hard to determine where one of us ended and the other began?

I have so many questions, the kind that are part of the natural flow of catch up between two old friends: *Where have you been? What have you been doing? Why, again, do you have a ranch?*

Sam was never the horse type. He preferred devilry like cliff diving and rock climbing. He was happiest when his feet were off the ground.

Back then, our personalities suited our goals, our plans.

I remember the day we outlined our future. We were seventeen, enjoying his uncle's birthday party at a beautiful winery not far from town. The mariachis were playing lively music for the enormous crowd. Hundreds of helium balloons were tied from the trees in bursts of colors that almost looked like floral arrangements.

The air was sweet, heavy with honeysuckle and roses.

Sam and I lay under a shady tree at the edge of the party, in silence. His arm was thrown over his eyes when he announced, "You're going to marry me someday, right?"

I whirled toward him, thinking he'd sit up any moment and laugh it off. But he didn't. He just kept enjoying the shade. I was both annoyed and entertained. "Please tell me that isn't a proposal," I said.

"You're right," he admitted, arm still draped over his face. Even with his eyes under cover, I knew he was frowning. "I'm terrible with words."

My heart fluttered because what Sam instinctively understood was what I really meant: I didn't need anything fancy, or over-the-top. I only needed him.

"I have it all planned," he said. "You'll be a doc. I'll be a pilot. We'll get a dog, a car, a house."

"Two dogs," I told him, thoroughly enjoying our pretend future.

Abruptly, he launched to his feet and reached for a balloon tied to the branch above us. He cut the string with his teeth, knelt, and tied it around my finger. "Promise me," he said.

We sat like that, staring into each other's eyes, daring the other to blink first when I caved. "I'll definitely think about it."

I wore that string for over two years before it fell off, lost to the memory of that perfect moment, and a perfect future that evaporated on the edge of five cruel words: *I don't love you anymore.*

Anger rumbles through me as I stroke the length of Rainy's nose, knowing full well Sam named her for the weather he loves most. Well, at least one thing hasn't changed.

"She's pretty," I say, satisfied that I did what I came to do, to show him (and maybe myself) that I'm not afraid to face him. That I'm still breathing.

That the echo of betrayal can maybe, finally be quieted.

"She's one of my most gentle," he says, inching closer.

One of? How many are there?

"She looks too strong to be gentle," I say. The magic within me intensifies, expanding up and up into my heart the way a beam of sunlight finds you on a cloudy day.

He dips his head, a boyish move that immediately infuriates me. "She's excellent with people's emotions."

I search his face for an ounce of regret, sorrow, something… but he's as unreadable as stone. "Like Amanda's?"

His full brows knit together like I've touched a nerve. "A lot of people find healing in horses."

"So that's what you do now? You—"

"I know it's surprising." He caresses Rainy's mane. "Hell, it was to me, too, but I guess life can be sort of…unexpected."

In a feeble attempt to hide my anger, I smile harder. Life can be unexpected? Is he serious?

"Well, I better get back inside," I say, because if I linger here one more second, my rage will fly to the surface and that rage will turn to grief and the grief will turn to tears and I swore to myself I would never *ever* let him see me cry again.

As I turn to go, he says, "Lily?"

I swear I can feel the thorns in my heart sharpening as I swing my gaze back to his. A distant hope rises, and I think he's going to ask if he can see me, or…if I want to go on a ride or check out the ranch. He's going to take this opportunity to tell me he's sorry for being such a prick all those years ago.

But no.

He smiles. It's genuine, tender, goddamn beguiling and it reaches his dark eyes. "It was good to talk to you."

All I can manage is a nod.

The tent flap closes behind me with a painful swish.

12

That night, I don't dream.

I fall asleep with magic bleeding into my heart, soothing me, making me feel less alone, but it does nothing to erase
this presence or the endless dark of Sam's eyes.

I chalk it up to the fact that as part of my magic, I have an
intense, emotionally detailed memory. One that can recall
entire pages of books after a single read, or the specific curve
of someone's face who I've only met briefly, or the collision
of lips that tastes like fire and metal.

For the next two days, I can't stop thinking about him.

*The heart you've been walking around with isn't natural. It's
magicked.*

Does that mean everything since hasn't been real? I refuse to
believe Lana's assessment, preferring to subscribe to my seven-
year-old self: *You have thorns in your heart. Thorns cause scars.*

At least thorns are sharp, violent little things that can be
used as weapons. Magic is something much messier.

This morning, I wake early.

My mind and body are buzzing with anxiety. I need to

move, to get the blood flowing. To get out of the dark corners of distant memories.

I slip on some tennis shoes and head out the back door.

The sky is laced with gray clouds, and an early morning mist hovers over the blooming landscape. I breathe it all in, the crisp air hitting my lungs as my feet pound the earth.

I push forward with no destination in mind.

I used to love running, but then medical school happened, demanding the high price of my well-being. I learned to live on chemically processed crap, cigarettes, and no sleep. A bullshit system for "health" care providers. Most days were just shapes and shadows of a pretend life that drifted in and out of my memory.

With each turn of my legs, I tell myself repeatedly and determinedly that Sam doesn't matter. That he was someone I once loved, and the world is filled with billions of lost loves. My heartbreak isn't rare. It isn't special.

Would I feel better if I could fill in the blanks, if I knew why he so easily and quickly locked his heart away?

And why did Sam give up his dream of becoming a pilot? Did he give up on it as cavalierly as he gave up on me? Is that what this is? A mercurial boy who couldn't decide what he really wanted?

A nagging feeling trails behind me as I run down the ditch bank, past a field of various shades of pink: gladiolas, hydrangeas, ranunculus, and azaleas. The irrigation system spits and sprays. Misty vapors swirl into the cool air, pulsing with hints of green and violet.

The muscles in my legs scream, my lungs revolt, but the pain of each drives me forward down the country lane, past the golden hillsides, beyond the grassy fields of goats and sheep and donkeys.

My chest lurches and my throat flexes as I collapse onto

the earth, desperate to catch my breath. Even after my pulse returns to mortal status, I feel a sharp ache in my bones, a weight that's been mounting for... I don't even know how long. Sometimes I think it's a permanent part of who I am, like another limb or organ but with no real purpose.

It makes me think about Mayahuel's song: *when all has been destroyed, the goddess shall rise.*

Is that what this is? The destruction of my so-called life? Which sounds so selfish because I'm still breathing, and Sarah... Sarah isn't.

I stare up at the endless expanse of pale sky, refusing to close my eyes.

I can't go back into that cold and sterile room with those cold and sterile machines and the cold and sterile voices.

My God, life is so much more than the science we're taught.

And while it's true that the human body is approximately 99 percent comprised of just six elements—oxygen, hydrogen, nitrogen, carbon, calcium, and phosphorus—there is another element that can't be measured or verified: the soul.

I rub my chest in slow circles, taking deeper and deeper breaths, trying to ease the ache.

It isn't enough.

I try the five-senses technique, but the effort seems endless, senseless when all I want to do is scream. The memory of Sarah looms, pacing at the farthest edge of my mind like the monster that it is. I fight it, force it back into the darkness, but it comes anyway—teeth and all.

The world around me bends, shifts, making space for all the grief and regret.

I can't outrun it. I can't pretend it away. And no amount of time will ever make it better.

We all have moments we'd rather forget, memories we'd rather shatter into a million unrecognizable pieces. I bet that if I asked twenty strangers on the street, they could immediately list each one because no one forgets the monsters that live under their beds.

It's impossible to slay them.

And maybe, just maybe you can coax them into the light. You can set them free.

But damn if that doesn't take courage, a level of guts I wish I had.

I guess in the end, I'm scared that the grief that's taken over my body will never let me go and that maybe this is my new normal.

Thorns and scars.

No. I can't accept that.

I stay like this for many more minutes, until the idea forms, until that intrusive voice inside my head, challenges me. *You don't have the guts.*

Yeah, well, I've got nothing to lose.

Slowly, I get to my feet, brush off my shorts, and walk down the scrubby hill into town.

This time, I know where I'm headed.

13

The only thing that ever changes in La Ventana is the light. The way it can slant or bend or smooth or erase. The way it breeds shadows that wedge themselves between hours.

All the other details, though, remain the same.

The way the ochre and crimson and azure buildings are bound together by rutted walls and locked behind mysterious gates with odd brass knockers like hands and screaming mouths and fury-filled dragons.

The way bougainvillea vines spill over the rooftops, serving up colorful glimpses of expansive gardens no one will ever see from below.

The way you always feel just one inch off-kilter when navigating the bumpy cobblestone streets, which have outlasted generations.

There's comfort in the sameness and the always.

Fifteen minutes after my near stroke, I walk down a steep narrow road, past a boutique hotel, a realtor's office, a few touristy shops, and several restaurants.

My phone rings.

I answer immediately because I learned quickly enough you should never ignore an eight-months-pregnant woman's call. "Hi, Har," I say. "Everything okay?"

"Good, you're there. I'm bringing Cam into the call."

"Wait…"

But she's already put me on hold.

"Hey," Cam says a second later.

"What's up, guys?" I ask, trying to rush this along. I have somewhere to be. That is, if I don't lose my nerve.

Harlow says, "Cam and I had the same dream."

"A dream about you," Cam adds.

There's a soft ping in my chest that tells me I'm not going to like what they're about to share When any two of us share the same dream, we know it's a powerful message for whomever we're dreaming of.

Steeling myself, I say coolly, "Lay it on me."

Harlow goes first, "You were in a cemetery but there weren't any headstones."

"Then, how do you know it was a cemetery?" I ask.

"There was a big stone sign with words carved into it," Cam says, "Where We Place Our Dead."

I twist my mouth and step into the shade of the panadería. Traces of cinnamon and chocolate float toward me and I feel suddenly nauseous. "Okay…was that the whole dream?"

"No. You had a shovel," Harlow says, "and you were digging into the earth."

"Great, so I'm a gravedigger now?" I tease, but it lands with a false note. My sisters must sense it because they go very quiet before I add, "So tell me, what did I dig up?"

It's Cam who answers, "Your own corpse."

The moment I walk into Pasaporte, rich java aromas flood my senses and conjure up memories of the hours I've spent in this coffee shop. My sisters and cousins and I would sit at the bar, drinking coffee, pretending to be adults with our *big* lives and make-believe problems.

Our family friend, Roberto, owns the place and also happens to be Sam's uncle. He's a man of many travels and tastes, and, well, women. The cafe has had a facelift since I was last here ten years ago. The once white walls are now a dreamy mocha color; there's a white stone fireplace, russet leather chairs and booths, and domed brick ceilings with windows that frame the sky.

I slip into a booth in the back of the café.

The table is stacked with journals. They're the brainchild of Roberto, who was intrigued by all of the conversations he had with travelers who passed through here, so he brought the journals in as a space for patrons to fill the pages with their travel memories. Everyone loved the idea of writing in the books anonymously, and soon, he added themed journals, ones for love, unsolved mysteries, and, a favorite, life's big questions, to name a few.

I mindlessly trace the various books' edges, thinking about my sisters' dream, which I've been trying to interpret for the last twenty minutes.

Harlow thinks it's a metaphor signifying a part of me that has died. Cam believes the corpse I dug up is merely a part of me that I buried long ago. Maybe they're both right.

But what I can't figure out is why there were no headstones, no honoring of the dead, no remembrance of life in any way. Only the words carved into stone: Where We Place Our Dead.

Our, not *the*.

The only other detail that emerged from their telling was the fact that the entire cemetery was blanketed with black nightshade, also known as Devil's Eye. The poisonous bloom symbolizes blemish, defect, and death. Not exactly heartening, except that the flower was an uncharacteristic shade of pink, a color that can signify renewal or hope.

Pushing the cryptic dream aside, I find a journal in the stack that I've never seen before, a black leather book with silver lettering: "Secrets and Confessions."

I almost laugh at the irony.

A server comes by and asks me if I'd like a drink. "Espresso," I tell her and then I wonder, "Hey, is Roberto here?"

"I'll send him over," she says.

The chickenshit part of me was hoping she'd say he was out of town on business, and then I wouldn't have to do what I came here to do. The other part of me is relieved that I can get this over with because the anticipation is always worse than the act.

Nerves twitching, I settle deeper into the booth and open the journal. I have to admit I feel a tad awkward, almost voyeuristic, to be reading about people's deepest secrets and confessions. Maybe I'll find a kindred spirit here, someone who's as messed up as I feel.

The first entry is by someone named Lucy who writes two simple but powerful lines.

I was the one who cheated. I don't love her anymore, but I don't have the guts to tell her.

When my espresso arrives, I take a sip of the dark and bitter brew and keep reading.

I slept my way to the top. Am I a monster?

And another.

Last year, my mom was sick. I didn't want to see her like that.

And I was busy with my own life, so busy that I missed the plane to be there when she died. Or at least that's what I told everyone. The truth is this: I missed the plane on purpose because I'm a coward.

My heart twists and sinks with each confession and secret I read. There's so much pain in this book, so much shame, and I can't help but wonder if any of these people healed. If they ever forgave themselves. If they ever slayed those demons.

I pick up the pen and with a trembling hand, I write slowly.

I should have paid more attention. I should have listened to my instincts.

I can't bring myself to write the entire truth. I close the journal and push it away, thinking I'm as big of a coward as the person who missed the plane.

"Lily?"

I look up to find Roberto.

His hair has thinned, but he's just as handsome as he was the last time that I saw him. Salt-and-pepper waves, smooth tanned skin, and a smile that very likely is his secret weapon in winning women over.

My own smile comes naturally as I slip out of the booth to hug him. He smells of spicy aftershave and freshly ground coffee.

"So," he says, as we both take our seats, "you have decided to drink my café again." His dark eyes glitter with mischief. Roberto never speaks frankly, usually preferring to skirt around an issue with clever niceties.

"I love your coffee," I tell him, sipping at my brew. "Life's just…"

"Busy," he fills in, stretching his arms out along the booth. "Ten years of busy, to be exact." And before I can defend the defenseless, he adds, "I've followed your career through your mama. Very impressive."

So that's how Sam knew. Does that mean he asked about me? *Oh my God, Lily—pull yourself together.*

"How's business?" I ask, thinking that's a nice butter-him-up topic.

"Bueno. Did you come here for the wedding?"

Not exactly, but I nod anyway. "We missed you."

"I don't attend bodas," he says with a rigidly straight face. "They give me a stomachache."

I laugh, glad this interaction is so easy, so natural. Sam never told his family anything beyond our friendship either, but Roberto has always been a special case. I wonder if Sam ever told his uncle about us, and our ending, which brings me to the reason that I'm here.

I have this sense that if I can fill in the gaps of Sam's life since we parted ways, it can be the first step in healing and just maybe I won't have to see him again and I can find some peace. Maybe that's what I was digging up in the graveyard—a past that's rotting in the ground but doesn't want to stay there.

Like the monsters under my bed.

All the Sam answers I could ever want are sitting two feet from me, and yet I can't find the guts to touch them. I can't find the right words. But then... I feel my memory magic shift. It curls and bends with a warmth that gives me a pinch of courage.

"Sam was at the wedding," I say as nonchalantly as I can, but the words sound false even to my own ears. Why is this so hard? There is nothing Roberto can tell me that will ever hurt as much as the night I lost his nephew.

Roberto eyes me. "You met the horses?"

Not what I was expecting, but okay. "Blanco and Rainy," I say.

"Those are just two of the many."

I feel itchy, like I want to step out of my own skin. "That's amazing," I say. "Never knew Sam liked horses so much."

"He's a natural. You should see the ranch. Beautiful. Maybe you could go out there while you're in town and go for a ride down to the river."

Another ping in my chest. "Perhaps." Nope.

Roberto rests his elbows on the table and stares at the book titled "Secrets and Confessions." "I never liked that one."

"How come?"

"Secrets are like devils waiting to burn you."

My neck and cheeks flush. He knows about me and Sam. I can tell by the way he's staring at me so intently. I can feel it in the heated rush of my magic now blazing through me. "But we all have secrets," I offer.

"Es verdad." Roberto reaches across the table and takes my hand. "Will you take some advice from this old man?"

I nod although it's not so much a promise as a signal that he can...should...go on.

"I have married four women," he says, "and loved the only one I didn't marry."

I knew he'd had several wives and countless affairs, but this is the first I've ever heard of love. It doesn't compute, and yet...

"Why didn't you marry her?" I ask.

"She wouldn't have me," he says, and there is a sense of longing in his voice that sort of breaks my heart. "I messed up. I let the devil in."

He doesn't need to explain. I get it. He cheated. "I'm sorry, Roberto."

"It was a long time ago." He drums his fingers on the table as I wait for the impending advice he promised. "Secrets should only be kept when absolutely necessary."

I lean against the booth trying to decide what he means and why he's telling me this. I decide to go all-in because I'm too tired to skirt the edges of the truth anymore. "Does this have to do with Sam?"

Surprise flashes in his dark eyes.

"Go see the ranch," he says, his gaze deepening. "Those horses are like the magic on your farm—they can heal anyone."

Is it that obvious that I'm broken?

"Why do I have the feeling you know something I don't?"

Roberto laughs. "I'm very old, mija. I know a lot that you don't."

He gets to his feet. "I'm already late." He glances at his gold watch before turning his gaze back to me. Many moments pass before he takes a long breath and says ominously, "If you want to uncover a secret, Lily, you must have the right shovel. Eh?"

I freeze. It's a coincidence that he's mentioning a shovel after the dream my sisters had, right?

Clearly, he's trying to tell me something without telling me. I can see it in the way he holds himself, tight like a violin string.

"Is that supposed to mean something to me?" I ask.

Roberto huffs out a laugh. "I'm just an old man with far too much useless advice."

"Why do you want me to see the ranch?" I ask.

He stares at me, studying me intensely or perhaps buying himself time.

"There are many shovels there."

If you want to uncover a secret, Lily, you must have the right shovel.

The memory magic hums through me at a pace that steals my breath. It speaks to me without words.

And in that single heart-stopping second, I understand. Harlow and Cam were wrong about the dream. I wasn't digging up a dead part of myself, or my past, or even my own corpse.

I was digging up a secret that was wearing my face.

14

I walk like someone waiting for lightning to strike.

Hunched against the unusually cold breeze and the glare of the leaden sky, pondering that damn corpse dream.

I've been in enough high-stress situations to know when a consequence is lurking in the shadows, waiting for just the right moment. And right now, that's what the dream feels like.

In my mind, I see myself in a graveyard, ankle-deep in Devil's Eye, excavating my own corpse.

A secret wearing my face.

What does it mean?

Secrets are like devils waiting to burn you.

I keep my head down, refusing to give the wind an inch as I reach the end of town and begin my trek down the country road toward home.

With each step, I remind myself that I'm a doctor, that I'm well trained in using the scientific method. That I operate in a field that requires objectivity. I will not be swayed by ethereal nonsense.

But I know better.

And as much as I want to apply science to magic, or say that a dream is just a dream, I can't. It never works.

Magic is this invisible, intangible thing, a nonempirical force that can never be measured. One that reminds you that no matter how much of it you possess, you're still just a grain of sand on the shores of enchantment.

Thunder cracks somewhere far away and the sky darkens ominously, reminding me of the words from the "Libro de las Flores."

I left my heart in the dark
And there it rusted, a decomposed box of memories lost in the cold. Until spring came. Until it emerged from a cocoon of dreams.

Spring.

Only a few months away and yet getting there suddenly feels more arduous than the titan Atlas bearing the weight of heaven on his shoulders.

By the time I arrive home, I have blisters between my toes and the backs of my heels. My legs ache and I feel like someone has driven a fiery stake between each shoulder blade.

The house is quiet, still.

The scent of burning cedar floats through the hacienda. Its aroma whisks me back to a moment with Sam and a starry night…which I promptly shut down in my mind because he doesn't deserve to linger in my consciousness.

I'm acutely aware of the power memories hold and the pain they can inflict. I know how they can feel tangible or imaginary, how they can fill a heart or drain it completely.

And as a wielder of their magic, I feel them, see them, touch them differently than others. Call it a sensitivity, an exposed nerve, an open wound.

Or a curse.

Whatever it is, there isn't any comfort in the telling.

But I'm tired and right now I need my mom's guidance.

If there is anyone in the world who can take a cryptic message and dissect, examine, and answer it, it's my mom. Her dream magic gives her the uncanny ability to analyze and interpret at the most sophisticated levels.

I kick off my tennis shoes, vowing to never put them on again as I go in search of her. I cruise down the winding endless halls that are filled with flower arrangements, some large and sumptuous, others tiny and skeletal.

The bouquets lean closer as I pass, a nod of solidarity and support, I think. And I'm supremely grateful for their empathy.

Just then my phone pings—a voicemail.

It's from the hospital. The call must have come in when I had my phone off earlier at Roberto's. Have they finished their investigation? Or do they just have more questions?

My nerves feel shaky, reminding me that whatever the findings reveal, they won't bring my patient, Sarah, back. They won't erase the horror of that moment or the cowardice of my actions afterward, which I can barely stomach.

Before I can listen to the voicemail, a text pops up on the screen from a colleague of mine in OB, Dr. Grace: Congratulations. And then more from others.

Such great news.

So happy for this outcome.

You're an excellent doctor.

Each message emptier than the one before. Anger swells inside of me, hot and wild.

Great news? Happy? How can they be so callous? I realize that they think they're supporting me, but truly? Their comments just feel like a thin veil masking their own rationalizations about an outcome they could all be confronted with at some point.

I listen to the voicemail, which is much of the same but more controlled and official.

You're not at fault.

The four words I've been longing to hear. I should feel some relief, some ounce of liberation, and yet I still feel a mountain of guilt.

Another text: time to come home

I white-knuckle my phone like a grenade that I desperately want to launch, but I turn it off instead.

A few minutes later, I find my aunt in the study, doing a crossword puzzle in front of a dying fire. "Hey, where's Mom?"

"We had an emergency at the shop." She looks up from her book with a devilish grin. "She lost the coin toss."

"Emergency?"

"Okay, sure, I should have used air quotes. It's just a plumbing issue, but you know how people are so dramatic these days."

I snort out a half-hearted laugh. "This family feeds on drama."

"The delicious kind," she agrees with a twist of her mouth. "Not plumbing." Her gaze tightens as she studies me. "Are you okay?"

I toss another log onto the fire, poking it relentlessly as the embers spark back to life.

"Fine."

Rosa taps the pencil against her chin. "Mmm." The low

hum comes slowly and tells me that she doesn't believe me. "You look like you've been swimming in a swamp."

"I feel like it," I say as I lean against one of the mantel's stone corbels: a carved dragon head, jaws open, sharp teeth exposed. I swear its beady eyes are glaring at me.

She smirks and sets down her crossword book with force, like she's about to begin an inquisition, but she doesn't get the chance because my mom sweeps into the room. "We have to close the shop for a few days," she announces, plopping into an overstuffed chair with a huff.

"Why?" Rosa asks.

"Apparently, old plumbing should be replaced and apparently no one told us and apparently the repairmen need to get in there and fix all of it which apparently is supposed to take a few days." She throws her head back and gazes at the timbered ceiling. "They had to turn off the water, which ended up blowing a fuse, and now the electrical is out as well. I rescued all the flowers, which are now in the barn cooler, but there are some deliveries I'm going to need help with tomorrow," she says, turning her gaze to me, a silent request.

"Sure," I say. I've got no plans and maybe delivering flowers all day will do me some good, offer me an ounce of normal. Get my mind off all this useless sleuthing.

"Anyone want a drink?" Mom asks with a sigh. "I could definitely use one."

The three of us spend the next hour in the south garden, drinking gin and tonics infused with our special brand of lavender. Lying back on a chaise lounge, with a blanket wrapped around me, I stare up at the slice of moon while my mom's and aunt's voices float in and out of my consciousness. Their distant chatter gives me an odd sense of comfort, as if this could be my real life if only I were able to erase certain memories.

I cling to the wish, imagining the peace of that kind of a

reset. I could start over and fall into trivial conversation with a drink in hand and the moon high and magic surrounding me on all sides.

"*Survivor* is on," Rosa announces, getting to her feet with a languorous stretch. "Anyone want to join?"

"You know all of that is scripted," I say teasingly.

Rosa waves a dismissive hand at me. "It's a *reality* show, Lily. They aren't trained actors. You should see the feats!"

Mom splutters out a laugh as Rosa heads inside singing, "You don't know what you're missing."

I sit up and turn to my mom, glad to finally have a moment alone with her. Before I have a chance to reconsider, I say, "I need your help."

"What's going on?"

"Cam and Har had a dream about me."

My mom nods slowly like she already understands what I'm asking of her. And after I tell her the dream's details, she's silent a moment, pondering. Her fingers tap the edge of her chair.

I wait for her wisdom, for a brilliant interpretation that is going to seem so obvious after she tells me.

"I already knew," she finally says.

"They called you?" No way. They'd never betray the sister code of secret keeping.

"No." She fixes her gaze on me. "I had the same dream."

"What?" I stiffen. "Why...why didn't you tell me?"

"You weren't here this morning, and I was at the shop and that isn't the point. Your sisters either left out a detail, or perhaps, it only emerged in my dream."

Wrapping the blanket tighter around me, I nod, waiting. "Okay."

"In my dream you weren't digging up your corpse," she says. "Your body was alive, eyes blinking. And you were saying something. Or at least trying to but the dirt kept pouring into your mouth."

Not exactly a comforting image.

"What did I say?"

"I couldn't make anything out."

"Mom, that isn't helpful."

"Lily, I don't want to pry, but I'm worried about you. This dream—it was so ominous, so incredibly sad. And I know it's what you're feeling too."

The garden seems to sigh—the roses tip closer and I realize that the longer you hold a memory away from the light, the bigger it grows and the harder the telling becomes. "I... I can't talk about it." I'm scared that if I do, I'll let the genie out of the bottle and there will be no putting it back inside. The memory will take on a life of its own. It will go from sleeping inside of me to living in the real world and that just feels too permanent.

Mom comes over and sits next to me. She doesn't ask for details, doesn't pry. Her very presence is enough.

"Did your sisters say how their dream ended?"

"Just that I'm digging up my corpse."

"So they didn't make it to the rain."

"Rain?"

She nods. "A storm came and washed away the cemetery, turning it into a river."

"Perfect," I groan. "The secret that's been buried is now drowning."

"What do you mean, *secret*?"

"I think Harlow and Cam are wrong," I say. "I don't think I was digging up my past or anything like that." I press my lips together. "I think I was digging up a secret with my face, a secret about me. Does that sound crazy?"

"Not at all," she says. "Dreams are best interpreted using instinct and sensitivity, so you should trust that."

"Well, I was hoping that you could interpret it for me. Like maybe tell me who's keeping the secret and why is it showing up now?"

And what does it have to do with putting myself back together again?

"Dreams are only guides, Lily," she says softly. "The work is up to you."

"You're the one with dream magic. And I'm tired of working!"

"The dream wasn't about me," she says. Then, as she gets to her feet, she adds, "You've always had a gift for resistance, for plowing ahead without so much as a glance over your shoulder."

"Because the past is gone and it does zero good to sit around thinking about it."

"Maybe." Mom sips the last of her gin and tonic. "You can keep fighting or you can surrender to whatever the magic is trying to tell you."

"The magic is being cryptic and it needs to be clearer." And truth be told, I don't want to heed Roberto's advice. I don't want to go to the ranch. And even if I had the capacity to appear that pathetic, what would I say to Sam? *Hey, want to tell me the secret you're keeping?*

The air suddenly feels crisper, colder. I don't tell my mom that I wasn't made to surrender. Ambition and determination are immune to it. She knows this about me, and yet here she is, asking me to go against my nature. To abandon the parts of me that only know how to bulldoze ahead. Or at least that used to.

After we go inside, I go upstairs and take a shower, letting the hot water cascade over every ache and pain. For the briefest of moments, I let my memory go blank as the steam rises all around me.

I feel like I'm part of the mist, floating up effortlessly.

Deliriously.

After, as I'm drying off, I hear a knock on my bedroom door, followed by Mom's voice. "I'm going to leave the delivery list for tomorrow on your nightstand."

"Okay."

"Good night."

"Night," I call out as I wrap myself in a robe and step out of the steamy bathroom. Exhausted, I collapse onto my bed and close my eyes.

Congratulations.

You can come home.

My colleagues' hollow words make me feel restless and tense, and as much as I want to ignore them, I know that I have to return the hospital's call. I have to let my attending know when I'm coming back.

First, I should probably listen to the voicemail. I grab my phone off the nightstand, and when I do, the delivery list flutters to the floor.

I gather it up and give it a glance.

Six names. Six addresses.

When my eyes land on the last one, I stop breathing.

Samuel James.

This is a joke, right? The magic or fate or whatever are playing mind games. They're forcing my hand.

But none of that matters, because there is no way I'll be making this delivery. I'm not game for more suffering; I'm not stepping foot on that ranch.

And absolutely nothing will change my mind.

15

My mind was changed at exactly 10:31 a.m.

It happened when I removed the day's deliveries from the barn cooler and set eyes on Sam's gratitude bouquet, an assortment of Bellflowers and bluebells, along with a thank-you card from Amanda and Charlie.

First, I felt guilt. Which quickly turned to irritation.

Why shouldn't I deliver these? Why shouldn't I help out my family?

My self-righteous indignation was empowering, but that isn't what changed my mind either. It was the nagging idea that the secret was related to Sam, coupled with the memory of Roberto's words: *those horses are like the magic on your farm—they can heal anyone.*

What if that were true? What if Sam's horses had the power to heal my broken, magically unveiled heart? What if the steeds could help me forget? Is that where my magic is trying to lead me?

The bitter irony that the man who broke my heart could

also be the one to help heal it is another reminder that magic has a cruel sense of humor.

After I load up the flowers into the back of the van, I head out.

Baseball cap pulled low. Sunglasses hovering at the tip of my nose—just covering as much of my face as possible without looking like a total bank robber. Left leg hiked up onto the driver's seat. The only thing missing is some good music, but the rickety van's speakers blew out a long time ago when some overzealous employee rocked out a little too hard.

The van creaks and moans as I drive over the uneven roads, making my deliveries: anniversary, new job, just because.

I love seeing the joy in people's faces, the sheer delight that brightens their eyes as I hand over the flowers. I try to refuse the tips, but no one will allow it, so with a pocketful of pesos, I hop back into the van and grip the steering wheel, trying to prepare myself mentally for the last delivery of the day.

"You are not a chickenshit," I tell myself aloud. "You made it through medical school and residency. You've been screamed at, belittled, put through impossible tasks, and seen things no one should ever have to see."

With each word, I feel the bravado expanding.

"So yes, you can deliver a bouquet of fucking bluebells."

The flower is symbolic of gratitude, truth, and luck. A bloom attached to a story I vaguely remember. Something about your true love returning to you if you can fold the blossom inside out without damaging it.

With a disgruntled snort, I pull onto the road.

I check Google maps on my phone every few seconds and watch myself drawing closer and closer to Sam's ranch. A right turn down the next road.

Four miles.

My heart is flip-flopping, being way too dramatic.

Three.

My stomach twists.

Two.

The van makes a ghastly sound, then stalls.

"What the…?" I press my foot to the gas pedal forcefully, but the engine is dead.

I coast to the shoulder of the road, kill the ignition, and turn it again, but there is only the grating, painful sound of a very deceased engine.

"Shit!"

Then, as if the gods haven't had enough entertainment for the day, I see that I now have no cell service.

I'm officially stranded on a long country road with no residences, no traffic, no businesses in sight. Because why not?

Or maybe this is a sign that I shouldn't be going to Sam's ranch after all. I should have listened to my instincts, I should have…

Ugh!

I've got a choice. I can hoof it back to town which is a good ten miles, and the blisters on my feet are already screaming in mutiny, or I can walk the remaining two-ish miles to Sam's, hoping he has a phone, or at the very least, a pigeon carrier.

I slide out of the van, grab the gratitude bouquet, and begin the trek to the ranch. Maybe if I'm lucky, Sam won't be there, and some nice ranch hand will give me a lift back to the farm.

A few minutes in and I begin to walk with a slight limp thanks to my messed-up feet.

If it weren't so unfortunate, it would be epically comical.

Me, hobbling down the side of the road, in the middle of nowhere, carrying a *thank-you* bouquet for the man who dumped me a decade ago.

I feel the sweat start to gather on my brow. The air is warmer today, but the looming clouds promise rain.

I swear to God, if it starts to rain, I'm going to throw these flowers into a ditch and bury myself next to them.

At the same moment, a car pulls up alongside me. A red truck, dented and rusted, way worse off than the van.

The passenger window is rolled down and I pull my dark shades lower to get a better look. Before I see who it is, I hear his voice, "Looks like you could use some help."

Sam.

To prove that his sudden and unexpected appearance doesn't unnerve me in the slightest, I casually lean into the window. "I have a delivery for you," I say, offering up the bouquet.

His mouth curves into an infuriating grin. "You're bringing me flowers?"

"Yes. No. I mean, they're not from me. They're from Charlie and Amanda. A thank-you bouquet." Why am I rattling on?

He stretches across the bench and opens the passenger door. "I'll give you a lift. Get in."

"Um, I can just leave these here with you." I extend the now-droopy flowers into the truck, setting them on the tattered seat.

"And then what?" he asks. "Walk all the way to your broken-down van? I saw it a mile back."

"That's the plan."

"Well, there's no service out here, so it won't do you any good. Come to the ranch. I've got some tools. I can head back and take a look at the engine."

My mind shuffles through all the possibilities, landing on what I perceive as the best one. "Or maybe you could just take me home."

"Can't do it," he says. "I've got an important appointment in—" he glances down at his watch "—five minutes."

I look left, right, down the long empty road. Thunder

booms in the distance as if to say, *get in the damn car*. Reluctantly, I do as the thunder commands.

The cab smells like freshly turned soil and old leather.

Sam pulls back onto the road, and I feel lightheaded. How did I end up in this small space with Samuel James and only a bouquet between us? I glance quickly at his left hand, looking for a ring. Am I really this pathetic?

Unexpected relief ripples through me when I don't find one.

"Why are you limping?" he asks.

"Oh, uh—I went for a run yesterday and I guess I overdid it."

"You're still a runner," he says. And I realize that the decade between us has shorted out his references to me. He remembers nineteen-year-old version of me and knows nothing of who I am today. It feels both bizarre and incredibly sad.

I simply nod because I'm not in the mood to explain that I gave up running on account of a ruthless life and schedule, and he wasn't there for any of it.

A minute later, we turn down a twisting road lined with walnut and encino trees, their branches sloping dangerously low like they might snap any second.

Beyond are wide-open alfalfa fields, wooden fences, grazing horses. In the distance is a rundown barn in desperate need of a paint job. Or at least that's what I thought until I catch sight of the house perched on a hillside nearby, a white structure with a pitched roof and long porch dotted with a pine table, some mismatched dilapidated chairs, and various tools leaning against the pitted walls.

Sam says, "It doesn't look like much yet, but…"

"It's amazing," I whisper so quietly I'm not sure he hears me. It's then that I realize I'm smiling. This place is so quintessentially Sam.

Yes, it's a mess, and damn if I don't love it. There is a reassuring energy here, an audacity to be so authentic, as if this place knows exactly who it is and won't apologize for it.

Sam parks in front of the barn, and we exit into a cloud of dust. A trio of chickens run in the other direction, clucking murderously as Sam reaches back into the truck for the flowers.

A gray dog tears through the commotion, racing toward Sam like the pup hasn't seen him in forever.

Sam smiles and squats in his worn jeans and even worse-off boots. His dark almost wavy hair hangs messily around his face. "Bullet, this is Lily," he says, rubbing the dog's ears. "Lily, this is Bullet."

The dog sits at attention, eyeing me like she already doesn't trust me.

"Nice to meet you, Bullet," I say, extending my hand slowly to see if she'll let me pet her. I look up at Sam. "Bullet?"

"She's silvery gray and a speed demon. Get it?"

Bullet sniffs my hand and I must pass her inspection because she collapses dramatically and rolls onto her back, dark spotted belly exposed. Sam chuckles. "And she's a real killer."

I bend down and rub her soft tummy while her eyes go soft with immense pleasure.

Sam says, "She showed up a couple of years ago."

And of course you let her stay, I think.

"I think she's part wolf, or at least she thinks she is."

"Is that true?" I ask Bullet. "Are you part wolf?"

Bullet jumps onto all fours and barks as if to say, *Can't you see the resemblance?* Then she takes off running toward the barn and Sam follows.

"I thought you had a meeting," I say, trailing behind him.

"I do."

We head into the barn, which is stacked with hay bales, tools, bits of old furniture, and numerous odds and ends. Bullet turns in bouncy circles, waiting for us to catch up.

"Do you want me to wait somewhere?" I ask. "I don't want to interrupt..."

Sam glances over at me, still clutching that damn bouquet. "You're not interrupting."

We slip through the barn and exit on the other side.

I nearly gasp.

It's as if we've stepped from one world into another.

Before me are the most exceptional-looking stables I've ever seen. Not that I've ever really been anywhere near stables, but these look like they should be in a how-to-run-a-perfect-horse-farm book. White. Pristine. I can practically smell the fresh paint.

"I just finished construction," Sam says, as if he can read my thoughts, and all I can think is how typical *Sam* it is that he perfected the horses' home before his own.

He was the kid who shared his lunch, who adopted any stray animal on the side of the road. He'd give you his umbrella during a summer storm and his coat in the winter. And the worst part? He'd do it all with damn smile.

"Did you...build all this yourself?" I ask, remembering how handy he was, how he made birdhouses and feeders, repaired fences, constructed desks and coffee tables out of old wood, even tried welding. And once, when we were ten, he built us a fort deep in the woods where no one would ever find it.

The windowless space was only five feet wide. The structure was barely standing and to any passerby it would look like an abandoned shack, but to us, that fort was the best hideaway in the world.

I wonder if it's still there.

"I had a great crew help me," he says, "Took almost two years, but we got it done."

He opens the stable's massive wooden doors and Bullet races ahead. "How long have you had this place?" I ask.

"Five years and two months."

So, what were you doing the other four years?

"Want to know the best part?" he asks.

"What?"

"I won it in a poker match," he says, grinning. "Imagine."

I frown, not sure if he's teasing. "Seriously?"

Bullet's caught the scent of something, because she's sniffing like a wild animal on the trail of her next meal.

"It's a great story," Sam says, but he doesn't elaborate. And I don't ask because I'm so taken with the way the structure is flooded with light from the countless windows. The wide center aisle is lined with gray brick pavers, leading to at least twenty stalls, safeguarded with sliding wood doors.

Giant ceiling fans turn above us, circulating the air, which offers an unexpected aroma, like a river snaking through the countryside. Natural, earthy, pleasant. Not at all what I imagined a stable to smell like.

Sam stops in front of the second door on the right, pushes his hair back, and slowly opens the door. Bullet sits attentively at his heels as if she knows not to enter.

"Hi, girl," Sam says softly, tugging some cubes of sugar from his pocket.

Drawing closer, the black horse grunts out an exhale. Her shiny coat glistens in the afternoon light and I can tell even from where I stand that she's expecting.

"This is Lady," Sam explains. "She's ten months pregnant."

"Ten months?!"

"Mares carry for a good eleven to twelve months."

"That's horrid."

"It's nature," Sam says, never taking his eyes from the mare.

"*This* was your meeting?" I ask.

He nods as he strokes her ribs with his free hand. "Lady is

annoyingly picky and expects her treats on time." He hands me a cube. "Want to try?"

I place the treat in my palm and before I know it, the soft fuzz of her lips nuzzles my hand as she licks up the sugar.

"She likes you," Sam says.

"Or she likes sugar," I say, smiling. "She's beautiful." I run my hand over her soft mane, marveling at the calm that washes over me. Maybe Roberto was right. Maybe these horses *are* like magic.

We stand in the quiet light with Lady for minutes, minutes that could turn to hours and I wouldn't notice because the moment is so perfectly silent and calm. Until Sam steps back out of the stall and stuffs his fists into his jeans pockets. "We should look for those tools," he says so abruptly I stiffen.

Right. The van.

"I can call a mechanic," I say. "I don't want to inconvenience you."

Bullet sits between us, looking back and forth with her tongue lolling to the side and her tail whipping excitedly.

"Lily."

A pulse of heat moves through me at the sound of my name on Sam's lips. "It's no trouble," he says. "If I can't fix it, I'll give you a lift back home and then you can call a mechanic." His dark brows rise into a gentle arch. "Okay?"

"Okay." I stroke Lady's mane, gently twisting her hair between my fingers. "But first," I say, "you have to tell me about this poker game."

With a half-hearted chuckle, Sam shakes his head. "A friend of mine got sick and asked me to sit in for him. Things got heated, money ran low, and before I knew it this place was put up for grabs."

"And?"

"And before you ask," he adds, "it was total destiny. I still stink at cards."

It's because he's a terrible liar or, at least, has a terrible poker face.

"What was the winning hand?" I ask.

Sam smiles. His teeth are perfectly straight with the exception of his right incisor, which turns slightly to the left. He lost his retainer on a hike when we were fifteen and never replaced it. I told him to get a new one, but he said he hated perfection and that flaws make for the best kinds of stories. "Royal flush."

"Impressive."

Bullet barks and takes off outside, leaving us alone in the quiet of the stable, which suddenly feels unnatural and overwhelming. "Did you ever think to sell the ranch?" I ask. It's a leading question, one I hope will tell me the how and why behind him giving up his piloting dreams.

"No way," Sam says. "There had to be a reason for that hand. Plus, this place was a war zone. The house and barn were barely standing. And the plumbing? A corroded disaster."

Samuel James, the boy who always believed in signs and destiny and fortune. Every time I told him that we carve our own paths, he'd remind me of my penniless great-grandmother who met a goddess on a moonlit trail and left with magic in her pockets.

Maybe that's why Sam abandoned his dream of becoming a professional pilot—because fate gave him a winning hand that changed his future.

"And people like Amanda," I say as we step out of the stall, "they come here for...?"

"Everyone has their reasons..." His voice trails off before he picks it back up. "It started with helping one person at a time and it's still a pretty small operation, but somehow, the people who need to find us do." He closes Lady's stall door and turns back to me.

I nod, wanting desperately to ask the one question that continues to hover above us like a lightning bolt ready to strike: *Why?* A word that carries the weight of years and simply lands on *why did we ever let go?*

Instead, I say, "Roberto says this place is as magical as the farm."

"That's a stretch," he says with a grin, "but the horses do have an unexplainable way of fixing people."

I want to tell him I need fixing, but how can I when he's no longer my friend, when the trust we once had was destroyed a decade ago?

Sam's eyes meet mine and before I can respond, a scrawny older man carrying a pail and wearing a straw hat enters the stables. "Alonzo," Sam says before introducing me to the man in Spanish.

Alonzo smiles, removes his hat, and shakes my hand. His dark eyes are rimmed with a pale blue that softens his rough appearance. "Are you here for healing?" he asks.

Yes! Please. Now. "Oh...no, I'm...just..."

Sam puts in, "Lily is a friend."

Friend. God that sounds so wrong.

Alonzo smirks. "You have friends, boss?"

Sam pats the man's back, driving out a false chuckle as Alonzo turns his gaze to me. "I'm always telling him to get out, mingle with the *gente*, but he'd rather hang out here with an old man and some horses."

Ah, yes. Sam the loner. I knew him well.

Caught up in the banter, I blurt, "He'd rather pitch a tent under the stars than go out." I'm immediately filled with the dreadful and sudden awareness that I've overstepped my bounds. That this simple sentence lays a trail to our past.

I know Sam senses it, too, because for the briefest of moments, his eyes find mine and I see something there—a flicker of doubt or regret or...

"We should bring in the herd, Alonzo," Sam interjects, his tone suddenly serious. "It looks like it's going to rain."

Alonzo winks at me as he places his hat back on his head. "You got it, boss." And then he's gone, leaving me alone again with Sam, who looks like he's wrestling with an idea. I've seen it before—the tilt of his chin, the roving eyes, the twitch of a restless hand.

"So, the tools," I say, reminding him of why I'm here.

He snaps his fingers like he'd forgotten. "Right. Right."

But then he says nothing else—just glances around like he's looking for something.

"You okay?" I ask.

He turns an unsure gaze back to me. "Are you in a hurry?"

His words take me by surprise. I know I should tell him that I'm needed back at the farm. That I'm incredibly busy with the remains of my disintegrating life.

I should tell him that standing this near to him, and looking at his excruciatingly pleasant face and the way he keeps pushing his damn hair back from his eyes, is too much to bear.

I nod, but the words that climb up my throat betray me. "No, I'm not in a hurry. Why?"

A near grin. "Because I have something to show you."

16

My nerves are firing warning shots, telling me this is a bad idea, screaming, *this guy lied to you. He broke you.*

But I'm already walking alongside Sam and he's already pointing out the wash stall, the tack and feed room, the bridles, saddles, blankets, brushes, and all the other horse equipment.

It's all very safe and easy.

A ranch tour for an old friend.

I have an odd suspicion that this isn't what he wants to show me. If I still know him at all, he's just warming up. I feel jittery and am worried it shows, but what if the something he wants to show me is the secret that the dream and Roberto were pointing to?

From the corner of my eye, I see Sam leaning against the door jamb. I can feel the weight of his gaze on me as I wander about the tack room, wondering what this is all about. Wondering why we keep making pit stops on the way to whatever this big reveal is.

I say, "This place is as organized as the OR."

"I bet you're a really good doctor."

A brush falls off the wall, startling me. I'm glad for its interruption because I do not want to talk about medicine. And I for sure don't want to fill in the spaces of the last ten years with niceties that make him feel more like a stranger.

This was a mistake. I shouldn't have come here.

With a shrug, I turn to him. "Is this what you wanted to show me?"

Sam runs a careless hand through his thick hair, making me want to murder him. "Oh," he says like he'd forgotten we were on a mission. "No—just a pit stop really and..." He shakes his head and grunts out a small laugh. "Maybe I oversold it."

Folding my arms across my chest, I say, "Now I'm even more curious."

Sam's mouth curves ever so slightly. "It's nothing earth-shattering."

Perfect, I think, *because I'm not in the mood for* anything *shattering.* "You're really selling this," I tease. "Is it another horse?"

"Nope."

"The deck of cards from the poker match?"

He rubs his jaw, and frowns, making a show of looking perplexed. "Why didn't I think of that?"

I walk over to him, keeping a safe distance. "Fine. Show me this non—earth-shattering *something.*"

We walk outside where the air is crisp, cool.

It doesn't take long before we fall into step, stride for stride, past the pasture and barn, toward the dilapidated house that I'm dying to get a look at up close.

Sam and I were always so good at silence, at reading each other's eyes and body language, but now it just feels awkward.

As we trudge up a dirt hill, Sam says, "The guy who lost this place in the poker game never lived here. Didn't even spend any time here. Can you believe that?"

He says these things like he wants me to share in his astonishment over a man who didn't appreciate what he had.

"Why do you think he kept it, then?" I ask.

"He inherited it," Sam says. "I asked him if he'd miss any part of the ranch and he looked at me like I was crazy. Then I came out here." Sam stops and looks up. "And I saw this sky and the land and thought he was the crazy one."

I watch Sam stare at the sky. I feel a sharp ache in my chest at the way his eyes linger on the horizon—a wishful, hungry, defiant gaze that reminds me of the boy I used to know. The one who had planned to spend his time up there with all that mystery.

"You should see the stars at night," he says. "No light pollution, no…" He stops short. "Not too different from the farm."

In the fading light, he turns to me, studies me as if he's trying to read my face, as if he can glean a past that he wasn't a part of. And just like that, the years are erased and the man standing before me is the boy I fell in love with. He has no wrinkles, no worries in his eyes. He's made up of possibilities and adventure and risks worth taking.

And maybe, if I look deep enough into *his* eyes, I can find the answer I'm searching for. *Why did you leave me?*

No, that's not the right question. It's more like *How could you leave me so easily, so callously?*

And I realize now how much I need to know the answer so that I can finally move on.

My pulse pounds in my ears as a fresh anger expands inside of me, and I want to kill the silence between us just like I want to choke all the years we lost. Because of him. Because of five words: *I don't love you anymore.*

Damn you.

His phone buzzes.

He looks down at the screen, staring a second too long, like he can't decide if he should answer it or not. By the pained look on his face, whoever is calling isn't someone he wants to talk to.

I think he's going to ignore the call but then he says, "I have to get this." He paces several yards away, creating enough distance for at least some semiprivacy.

I turn toward the pasture and watch Alonzo leading a spotted horse back into the stables. He's talking to the animal, smiling and laughing, animating wildly with his free hand like whatever story he's telling is the most entertaining of all time. It makes me like him even more.

When I return my attention to Sam, he's pacing, speaking into the phone. He pinches the bridge of his nose and closes his eyes.

What I wouldn't give to be a lip reader.

Sam ends the call and I avert my gaze quickly.

When he returns, there's a restless energy vibrating off him.

"Everything okay?" I ask.

"Listen," he says almost distractedly, "I need to take care of something. Alonzo can take you back to the farm and then I'll check on the van later."

A wall goes up inside of me. I hate that he's shutting me out again. It feels all too similar to last time.

"No, it's fine," I say coolly. "I'll call a mechanic."

"Lily," he says. "I said I would do it."

Does he not see the irony of that statement? That his privilege to make promises to me died ten years ago?

In the end, I give in because I know it'll be a losing argument.

He texts Alonzo, then walks me to the truck and opens the door gallantly, another infuriating move. I step inside as he looks around uneasily, shifting his feet. "So, uh, thanks for the flowers," he says, closing the door.

Bullet comes rushing toward us, stirring up clouds of dust and barking wildly.

Sam play wrestles with the pup, then turns to me and says, "Do you mind?"

I'm not sure what he's asking until he adds, "Bullet loves to ride in the truck."

"Oh—of course," I say opening the door and scooting over so Bullet can leap inside and settle between me and Alonzo with an exaggerated yawn before she rests her head on my lap.

Sam chuckles.

Suddenly, I don't want to leave. I want to hear more about the poker game, the colorful details, not the sterile summary. I want to see the house and more of the farm. I want to see that *something he mentioned*. I want to sit on that porch and actually confirm if the farm has the same view, because I don't believe him.

I think his patch of sky is bigger and brighter.

Minutes later, the ranch is in my rearview, a still-life painting seared into my memory.

A part of me is glad to be alone with Alonzo. It'll give me an opportunity to ask questions that I might otherwise never get the answers to.

"So, tell me," I begin, as I stroke Bullet's long nose, "how long have you worked on the ranch?"

"Many years," he says, tapping his fingers lightly on the steering wheel to the beat of a song that isn't playing. "Long before Sam won the place."

"And you just decided to stay on?"

He tilts closer to the windshield to survey the darkening sky. "The horses needed me and so did Sam."

Now we're getting somewhere. "How so?"

Alonzo side-eyes me like he's on to me. "How long have you been friends with the boss?"

"We were close as kids," I say, deciding to indulge him. "Then we..." We what? Fell in love? Vowed to grow old together? Swore we'd be together forever until forever turned out to be shorter than I thought?

"You what?" he asks.

"We fell out of touch and, um, went our separate ways." This is coming out all wrong.

Bullet's ears perk like she can hear the lies coming out of my mouth.

"So you are no longer friends," he says with a period. A finality that hurts.

I shake my head. "Not really." Not at all.

Why is Alonzo looking at me like that?

"You should keep your eyes on the road," I tell him, twisting in my seat.

"You look very familiar."

I shrug and stare out at the darkening world whizzing past.

"Well," Alonzo says, "even if you and the boss aren't friends, you can still come back to the ranch and let the horses help you."

Specks of rain begin to tap the windshield. Bullet sits up and looks out the window.

"Oh...no..." I chuckle nervously. "I... I don't need help."

Alonzo smiles at me like he can see right through my lies.

When we get to the hacienda, I thank Alonzo for the ride, pat Bullet's head, and start to get out of the truck when he says, "Now I remember!"

I stare at him blankly.

"Why you look so familiar," he says, grinning. "I've seen your photo."

Confusion winds through me. Where could he have possibly seen me before?

"In the photo, you were younger," he says. "But it's the same eyes and smile and..."

"Where did you see my picture?" I ask, heart slamming violently.

"When Sam moved in," he says. "I found it in a box. A little, gold, dented frame. You had on a white sweater and jeans and were laughing."

I remember the photo—Sam took it a week or two before we broke up. I was exhausted from a bad night's sleep and complaining about something when he took out this disposable camera he'd found that still had some film left.

I threw up a hand and turned away. "Sam!"

"You're beautiful when you're grumpy."

"I'm not grumpy."

"But you are beautiful."

I laughed then and he snapped the picture. I didn't know he had ever developed that film, never mind framed it.

"I wasn't sure what to do with it," Alonzo goes on, "so I set it on a bookshelf, thinking I'd ask him about it later, and when I did, he told me nada. He can be very tight-lipped, you know, and since he didn't seem very interested in the picture, I put it back in the box."

Something painful twists inside of me. "Thanks again for the lift," I say, wishing Alonzo had never said anything. That he'd never drawn up a memory I had actually managed to forget.

"Funny thing is," Alonzo says, tipping his hat back, hesitating like he isn't sure he should say anything else.

"What?" I ask.

"Do you promise not to get me in trouble?" he asks like a man with a delicious secret he can't wait to share.

I nod, barely breathing. "Swear."

"Your photo wasn't in the box the next day."

Bullet lets out a little whine, dancing on her paws like she wants out of the truck.

"I'm sure Sam didn't even remember he had it," I say, making excuses to save my pride. It was probably some artifact he'd forgotten to throw away after the breakup.

"Later," Alonzo continues, "I found it back on the shelf. Tucked behind some others. And it's been there ever since."

A tremble works through me, cold and spiteful. *You must be mistaken*, I want to tell the man. *You aren't remembering correctly. Sam left me. He broke all his promises to me. He was unexpectedly harsh and cold and...*

I don't love you anymore.

Alonzo gets out of the truck and comes around to open my door. "Don't forget your promise," he reminds me. "It's our little secret."

"Of course," I manage. Bullet barks and I kiss the top of her head before stepping out.

Then, before I turn to go, I ask Alonzo, "Did you know he wanted to be a pilot?"

Alonzo's deep-set eyes soften. With a nod, he says, "Life had other plans."

I lie awake all night, tossing and turning, shutting out Sam's damn face, lying to myself about how much he still affects me—it's the same lie billions have told themselves throughout history, a lie that's so much easier than the truth.

I can't stop wondering why my photo is on a shelf in Sam's house. Could it mean he still cares? I follow this thread of hope for a breath, maybe two, before reality slams into me. Sam is easily distracted. He sets things down without realizing it, loses everything from his sunglasses to his keys.

To make myself feel better, I fall asleep imagining him in a moth-eaten sweater with a week-old beard, putzing through a dusty, debris-filled labyrinth, making promises he'll never keep.

Somewhere around midnight, a sound startles me awake.

An engine. Wheels crunching along gravel.

I rush downstairs and look out the kitchen window where I see my van's taillights.

A jolt of adrenaline pumps through me. Sam's here.

The anger grips me with surprising force. What's the big deal? Sam fixed our van like he said he would.

Like he said he would.

And there. It. Is.

The clarity is excruciating. Sam will keep his word most of the time, except the one time it mattered most.

I curse my brain for conjuring an image of him out on the road at night with a flashlight, probably humming along to some George Strait song, entirely out of tune, while Bullet danced around his feet. Then I imagine him driving the van back to the farm while I slept, and parking it exactly where it's supposed to go because he of course notices these small, inconsequential things.

He's an insider, a confidante. Someone I trusted with my family's most valuable secret.

I don't know what comes over me, but I'm tired of the guessing and wondering and conjuring and fantasizing.

I bolt outside, grateful for the garden lights to guide my way.

He must hear my approach because he spins to face me like a prowler caught in the act. "Lily. Wha...what are you doing out here?"

I freeze up. I hadn't thought this through enough to plan what I was going to say or how I was going to say it, and now here I am, wearing only a white T-shirt that barely covers my ass, standing in the freezing cold face-to-face with the man I clearly am not over.

Damn him!

Before I can respond his gaze drops to my legs, then whips

back up to my face and I swear I see an apologetic expression flash across his face. I'm not sure if he's apologizing for looking or for getting caught. "It's freezing out here," he says, fumbling with his words. "You should go inside."

I tug my shirt lower, fidgeting like a kid awaiting their punishment in the principal's office. "You fixed it?" I ask.

"The starter just needed some adjusting."

It's an effort to hide the shivers, which are evident in my voice when I say, "Thanks."

"Lily," he says gently, "please go inside."

The conversation I really want to be having is on the edge of my lips: *Why do you still have my photo?* Except I promised Alonzo I wouldn't rat him out. "How are you going to get home?" I ask, teeth nearly chattering. "Do you need a lift?"

Sam stiffens like I've hit a nerve, but all I did was offer to get the guy home. "Alonzo's waiting out front," he says, jabbing his thumb over his shoulder. "So, uh, I better go."

A feral energy slides through me, eviscerating all common sense, and as Sam makes a move to pass me, I do the most unexpected thing: I grab hold of his arm. He might be able to hide certain emotions on his face, but he can never hide the feelings coursing through his blood.

He stops, looks down at me, frozen like a rabbit caught in the headlights. I swear a feel a tremble work through him.

It's then, in that single heart-stopping moment, that I search his dark eyes. And there in the faintest of light, I see it—the love that used to burn so brightly.

Sam clears his throat, and I don't know if I let him go or if he breaks free, but before I know it, he's just a long shadow trailing away into the night.

The next morning, I find a note stuck under one of the windshield wipers.

As promised. S.

17

I know what I saw.

Sam still loves me.

The first few hours after I climbed back into bed, I considered that I might be delusional. But there was no denying the glimmer in his eyes. The warmth that radiated off him like freshly lit kindling. And there was no denying the gravitational pull between us.

Is that it? The secret he's been harboring?

Why, then, did he leave me? Could there ever be a reason good enough to be forgivable?

For the next two days, I stay busy, helping to prepare for the annual Celebration of Flowers, which suddenly feels around the corner. With all the frantic setup, I mimic the pace I'm used to at the hospital, allowing my mind to shift into neutral and my heart into the shadows.

While I hoe and tend and plant, I don't think about Sam, or the truth he can't hide anymore. I don't wonder why he hasn't texted me to invite me back to show me "something" at the ranch. I just use my hands.

It's such a precarious balance, trying to reconcile the hope of his love with his abrupt departure from my life. It was too final to not mistake it at the time for what it was—a man who didn't want to be with me anymore.

I turn the earth over and over and over. Until sweat drips down my neck, until my back aches and blisters form on my fingers.

This is what I'm exceptional at. Work. Focus. Determination.

Pushing through the pain.

Tilting up my sun hat, I tighten the scarf tied around my ponytail, take a breath, and step back to admire the fifteen-foot circle of white daisies, golden yarrow, and pink azaleas I've planted. The azalea signifies passion, the daisy, beauty, and the yarrow, love.

The circle represents the promise that my great-grandmother, Margarita made to the goddess to always protect passion, beauty, and love.

Ultimately, that's what our family's magic does. And while an applicant's request might be packaged in something else, *inside* it's always about an iteration of those three.

I hear footsteps and spin to see Lantana walking toward me. "Surprise!" she announces, and before I know it, she's scooping me into a giant hug and I'm giddy with an odd sense of relief that she's here.

"Lana!" I squeal. "What are you doing here?" No one is set to arrive for another five days.

Lantana, several inches taller than me, pushes her auburn hair over her shoulder. She's wearing silk cargo pants and a halter top that shows off her long, lean arms, which look like they've spent the last year in the gym.

"You needed me," she says with a small grin that makes me love her more than I already do. "And it's way easier for me to help you if I'm here. Plus, you know I have my best epiphanies thirty thousand feet in the air."

Lana has always been like a summer breeze—there's levity in her very presence, which makes everyone wish to be in her orbit.

She's a lithe and graceful creature reminiscent of a ballerina, even though she's a klutz on the dance floor. And while I might be the shortest in the family, at least I was born with moves.

"What was the epiphany?" I ask, hoping against hope that she's arrived with an armful of answers.

"So I was on the plane, staring at some hideous cardboard chicken that was not passable for food, which I'm writing a complaint letter about, by the way, and it hit me. I needed to be here in the flesh for several reasons."

"Okay?"

Lantana glances around at the flower circle I've created. "First, to offer support," she says. There's a dangerous twinkle in her eye that's making me nervous. "Second, to talk to the flowers and get to the bottom of this. And third, to tell you, face-to-face, that you need to open up about this guy. I think the secrets you're keeping are messing with the spell's release, and if you ever hope to be free, you have to go all-in, bare the soul and throw caution to the wind." She says this last part with wildly gesticulating arms.

"Did they teach you all those idioms in law school?" I tease.

"And a few legal skills too," she says with a smile. "Now, quit stalling."

"So, you want me to tell you about him."

"Or tell someone. Preferably me, since I'm so excellent at keeping secrets and I did just fly over a thousand miles." She takes a breath. "Okay, I'm ready. Go ahead."

"Lana."

"Lily."

"I'm not going to do that."

"Look," she says, "I'm not asking for a play-by-play or even his name, just the usual generalities. I mean, it's worth a try, don't you think? Or you could drown in the not knowing and be miserable and walk around with a spelled heart that is likely to lead you to ten cats and a canning hobby."

I roll my eyes. "Canning can be very practical you know."

"Lily."

Maybe she's right. Maybe speaking the experience into existence will help unmask my heart so that I can finally begin to heal. And not just from Sam, but also from my patient's death, which started this all. Isn't that what therapists all over the world say? It's cathartic to talk about an experience? But where's the proof?

I press my lips together as I stare across the circle of blooms that I spent all day planting. What better place to spill my guts than surrounded by love, beauty, and passion. "Okay," I say, clenching and unclenching my jaw. "What do you want to know?"

"First, can we go to Lupe's for some tacos al pastor? I've been dreaming about them all day," she says, rubbing her stomach.

Suddenly, I'm famished, too, and within thirty minutes, we've driven into town and are seated at the bar of Lupe's, a dark, divey café that only locals frequent. The kind of place that feels both seedy and safe, where corner corruptions are just as frequent as town gossip.

Gripping the bar, Lana takes a dramatic whiff of the scent of grilled beef. "This is heaven."

"In all of Dallas, you can't find a good taco?"

Lana scoffs. "I live in gringo land, Lil. No one does al pastor like Lupe!"

I'm relieved we're the only ones sitting at the bar, and after we order and our drinks arrive, a Manhattan for Lana and a beer for me, she swivels her stool to face me, knees bumping my own, and says, "Okay, Let's hear it."

There's a low, bluesy song drifting from the jukebox to mask the secret I'm about to spill to my cousin. "I'm not sure where to start."

"Let's start small," she says, like she's coaching a client for a deposition. "How about you tell me about him. Basic stuff—age, height, etcetera. Kind of like a warm-up."

I blow out a long breath and shake out my hands to lessen the nervous energy pulsing through me relentlessly. "We were both nineteen. I don't see why it matters how tall—"

"So I can picture him, Lil. Jeez. Haven't you ever told a story before? I know you're a doctor, but can you at least try to paint a picture?"

"Fine. He was six-one-ish."

"*Was?* Did he die?"

I huff and take a swig of my brew. "*Is*, I guess. And he was so…"

"Sexy?"

I throw her a glare. "Thoughtful. The kind of person who rescues abandoned animals, and he overtips, and he'll buy whatever someone is selling on a street corner even if he doesn't need it." The more I talk, the more I fall into a rhythm that I can't slow down. "Oh, and he has this annoying habit of always looking at both sides of things even when you want him to just be on *your* side."

"A regular saint," Lana snorts as she traces her fingers over the rim of her glass.

"Hardly. He lives in his head a lot and you have to be able to read him to know what he's thinking, which is…was so infuriating."

"Where did you meet?"

We've entered a danger zone, so I keep it simple. "Here in La Ventana. We were friends and then it grew into this other thing. I just, I don't know how you can possibly explain love, Lana."

Our plates arrive, and Lana shifts her attention briefly to take a huge bite of her taco. Tender pork pieces fall out of the corn tortilla. "Oh my God," she says around a mouthful, "this is all a person needs to be truly happy. I'd move here just for these tacos."

"And give up your career?"

"For sure."

"What about Tara?" Her girlfriend of eight months.

Lana dabs the corners of her mouth delicately with a napkin and sighs. "I guess she'd be pissed if I chose tacos over her."

"Good guess," I say with a chuckle.

"Okay, back to mystery man," she says. "Did he love you too?"

I nod and begin picking the onions out of my taco. "I even thought he might have loved me more, or at least he loved me first. And everything was perfect. We mapped out this whole future and made all these dumb plans."

Lantana goes quiet for the first time. Then, "Lily, did you think you were going to marry him?"

I hesitate. If I'm going to tell the truth, I need to stop censoring every word that comes out of my mouth. "Yes."

"Oh." She takes a long pull of her Manhattan. "Wow."

"We made promises, and it wasn't some kids living in a fantasy, you know? And I didn't care if we ever made it legal or not, as long as we were together."

Lana ponders a moment before she asks, "Do you have any idea why he ended it?"

Tears prick my eyes. I realize I've opened a door that can't be closed again. Keeping this secret hasn't protected my memory of him, or of us; it hasn't given me ownership of my past. All it's done is left me alone, grieving in the dark.

Like the heart from the libro.

My inability to share for so long only reminds me of the night my patient died, and the words that I couldn't bring myself to say. And I realize I don't want to be that person anymore. The one who believed she didn't need anyone else to make a life, to heal, to be happy.

I take a shaky breath. "I want to tell you who it was, but only if you promise not to judge or…" I rethink my position. "No, it doesn't matter. You can think whatever you want."

"Lily, I won't think anything, or judge you. I mean unless—" she chuckles, lifting the moment "—you fell in love with Satan."

"It was Sam," I blurt. "Samuel James."

Her head is bobbing up and down as she says, "Ohhh."

"Oh?"

"I'm mean, I'm not surprised."

"Why not?"

"In some sense, we all knew, Lil—not that you were in love with him but how much he meant to you. I mean you spent every waking moment of every summer with him." She gets the bartender's attention and orders another round of drinks. "Bring her a filthy martini, please."

"I'll stick to beer," I say.

"You need something way stronger."

The heavily tatted girl tending bar nods, and as she turns back to work, I lean closer to Lana and say, "Seriously, you knew?" I'm not sure if I feel offended or incensed or something else entirely. "And you didn't say anything?"

"We didn't want to put you in a weird place. You've always been so private and secretive."

"We…"

"All of us, Harlow, Cam, Dahlia, and me," she says. "Don't

you remember I asked about him once? It must have been the summer you broke up. You were so cavalier, saying you guys had grown apart and lost touch. And then you went on to tell me about some new guy you were dating."

Right. One of the many faceless figures of my dating history.

"It's why we agreed to never ask about him again," she says.

The darkness of the bar wraps itself around me in an oddly comforting way. "I saw him," I say, "Sam. At the wedding." Then it dawns on me. "Is that why Mom and Rosa didn't mention that the ranch belonged to him? Did they know too?"

Lana's face falls into a pitiable pout. "Don't be mad. I'm sure they thought they were protecting you."

I bark out an annoyed laugh. It would be just like my mom to not interfere, to allow magic or destiny to guide the process.

I swallow my frustration for the moment and go on to tell her about the ranch fiasco, and even the photo Alonzo mentioned. Each word more freeing than the last.

The bartender delivers our drinks and I take a swig of the filthy martini, wincing at the salty olive flavor that burns my throat.

"Lily," Lana says, "that doesn't sound like a man who stopped loving you."

"I know."

"Wait." Her eyes narrow. Her mouth parts. "What do you mean?"

"I know he still loves me." Is it pathetic that this simple sentence sends my heart soaring?

"You didn't lead with that?"

"You didn't ask."

"Explain."

I tell her about the other night out at the van, adding, "I caught him off guard, I think, but it was obvious. If there's one thing I know in this world, it's Samuel James in love. But here's what I can't figure out. The Sam I know would never make up the fact that he no longer loved me. He'd never lie about that."

"That's why he still has that photo," Lana says, pouring more salsa onto her taco. "You owe it to yourself to find out what's going on. So, this is what you're going to do," she says, clearly in lawyer mode as she licks the salsa off her fingertips. "You're going to go back to that ranch and confront him. You're going to get the whole truth."

"I'm sure you're joking," I say, imagining myself marching up to that porch and banging on his door like some kind of unhinged ex. "You want me to tell him I saw the love in his eyes, like some kind of loon?"

"Well, he does know you're magic."

"I'm serious, Lana."

"So am I," she insists. "Look, even the magic is pointing you in this direction. Please tell me you're not willing to give up the love of your life because of your pride."

"He made that choice for both of us," I groan. "If he had wanted to reach out, he's had a decade to do it. So no, I am not going to demand anything from him. Jesus, the first breakup was awful enough."

"Then, do it for yourself, Lily. So you can finally move on."

"I have moved on. I've built an entire life!"

"Have you?"

I feel a sharp ache in my chest. "What's that supposed to mean?"

"Working like a dog and serial dating gorgeous men isn't building a life, Lil."

I start to argue, but I've got nothing. She's right, and all this time, I thought I could hide behind my accomplishments, behind an ego that encouraged the lie.

I feel an irrational fury building inside of me.

I've spent so much time trying to forget Sam, his damn dark eyes and long, lean body, even his calloused hands, which always seemed to smell like diesel or sawdust or turpentine from God knows what. And then there was the charming drawl he would get when he drank too much or got too sleepy.

Sometimes I think it was all a dream, those summers spent with him. It was as if nothing could touch us. As if the grim reality of life didn't exist, and now I wonder how we could have been so reckless.

"Want me to go with you?" she asks. It's a rhetorical question, I know, but it does its job in consoling me just a little.

"I'm not going."

"You're being a child."

"I'm being safe."

"Yeah, well safe is boring." Lana flings her napkin at me. "How about this? I came all this way to ask the flowers for some guidance. So let me do that and then we can set our course."

"Our?"

She offers a devilish smile. "You should finish that martini first."

"You think I need to be drunk to hear what the flowers have to say?"

"No," she says, "I think it's a perfectly good drink that shouldn't go to waste."

I feel a shift inside, a shift of magic, telling me that if I do this, if I ask the flowers for the truth, I might not like what they have to say.

I down the rest of my martini, for courage, for strength, for bitter warmth.

As we step into the glaring light outside Lupe's, I try to ignore the nagging feeling inside me. It was Sam who threw the first stone. He made the ripples that became the moments between now and then.

And all my wanting, all my reckless hope, even the fact that he still loves me isn't going to change the sickening truth.

Samuel James is a liar.

18

When we arrive at the farm, Lana leads me back to the circle of daisies, yarrow, and azaleas. Newly planted flowers are always more willing to talk than well-established blooms, which can be stubborn little devils.

"If they tell you something really bad, maybe keep it to yourself," I say.

She exhales dramatically. "Why do you always think the worst? That's such bad vibes."

"Because it's usually true?"

She rolls her eyes and begins to walk the circle in silence, slowly, methodically, waiting for an invitation to sit. A moment later it comes, and she takes a seat in front of a cluster of yarrow.

I've witnessed this ritual a million-and-one times, the way Lana and my aunt wait to be invited into the world of the blooms. I don't dare even utter a word while the golden yarrow tilts closer to Lana as she whispers, then listens.

I'm painfully curious at the tilt of her head, the graceful movement of her fingers as she brushes them over the flowers. What does it all mean? What are the flowers telling her about me?

I look around the circle I've created: beauty, passion, love. A promise of protection I never agreed to. Would I have done the same thing as my great-grandmother? Would I have said yes to the magic to escape a life of misery and dread?

A few moments later, Lana gets to her feet.

I'm so jittery, I can barely ask, "Well?"

"Well, the flowers spoke to me all right."

"Lana," I say, growing impatient. "What did they say?"

"Sam was here."

"I already told you that. At the wedding and then when he brought the van back."

She shakes her head. "He was here today."

My brain goes into logic overdrive. "Maybe he was checking on the van or…"

"He was here to pay his respects to Mayahuel. Apparently, he was at the agave."

The place where my great-grandmother struck the deal with the goddess. "But…" The martini is mercilessly working its way through my bloodstream and I suddenly feel lightheaded. "Why would he do that?"

It isn't uncommon for my family to leave a flower, stone, or some other trinket for the goddess, but Sam's never done it before. No one outside my family has. The flowers must be wrong.

"Did you ever show him that spot?" Lana asks.

"We walked past it all the time," I say. "He knew that we would leave gifts for the goddess. Sometimes I'd find an interesting-looking stick or oddly shaped leaf and I'd tell him it was for Mayahuel, but…" I take a breath, trying to pull my thoughts out of the haze as I begin to pace.

Lana closes the distance between us. Her expression is one

of concern, or maybe even pity. "You have to find out what this secret he's keeping is."

I don't know how long I stand there, staring at my cousin, grappling with the words that have spilled from her mouth like water.

Except that there is *no* secret big enough, powerful enough that would have ever kept me from Sam, so even if the flowers are right, it doesn't matter and it doesn't change anything.

"Like what?" I ask Lana, my voice a few notes from panic. "Do you think the secret is he still loves me?"

"Honestly? I don't know. This is why you need to confront him."

I take off running.

Lana shouts after me, but I don't stop. I don't slow down. I run hard and fast until I reach Mayahuel's mystical agave, the plant that has defied time, the one that symbolizes the promises my great-grandmother made to the goddess.

The large silvery cactus rests at the north side of the farm near the edge of a small orchard. Its six-foot-long leaves are lined with teeth sharp enough to draw blood.

There is no disturbance of soil, no footsteps on the dirt path, no clue to tell me Sam's been here.

And then I see it. A single bluebell set beneath the thorns.

Why in the hell would Sam come here? Why would he leave a flower that symbolizes both gratitude and grief? A flower that, when worn, will compel someone to tell the truth.

Everything feels askew, as if the world has been shoved onto its side and I'm in danger of falling off the edge.

In a fumbling rush, I reach for it, catching my arm on a spine that slices open the skin. Blood erupts.

"Shit!"

Setting the bluebell between my teeth, I tug the scarf from

my ponytail and tie off the stinging wound with a wince and a few more choice curses.

Then, as if the entire world has gone still and silent, a sweet aroma drifts up to meet me. Subtle at first, but with each breath, I'm sure. I can smell the delicate green honeyed scent of the flower.

I pluck it from my mouth and take a long whiff to make sure I'm not delusional. That I'm not dreaming.

"Lily?"

I whirl to find Lana, sweaty and looking mildly annoyed. "Jesus, you could have waited," she says, panting.

"I can smell the flower!" I shout. My heart pounds with furious optimism.

Lana's eyes drop to the scarf tied around my arm then back to my beaming face. "You left before I could tell you. The heart-masking spell's been broken. That's why you can smell the bluebell." She isn't smiling when she says this, and her expression is one of cautious hope.

"Why?" I ask. "How?"

"Because you told me a truth. Because you opened your heart."

But I didn't tell you everything, I think as the memory of my patient floods my mind and heart.

An ice storm is gathering strength with each breath. A warning: *some truths should stay buried so deep no one will ever find them.*

What exactly is the truth? That I'm a monster for what I did? Or *couldn't* do?

"Can I tell you something else?" I ask Lana.

She nods.

"Remember I told you something happened at the hospital?" I don't wait for an answer. "A patient died." But that isn't entirely accurate. I clutch my stomach and swallow past the aching lump in my throat. "I killed her."

The words I haven't spoken aloud, not even once. I thought they might offer an ounce of freedom, some sort of exoneration from the tangled web I've woven over my heart, but all I feel is the same wretched cold, and the optimism I felt only moments ago has nearly dissipated.

God, why do I feel so weary?

"Lil," Lana whispers, drawing closer. "What happened?"

I step back, holding my trembling hands out to stop her advancement. "I still can't talk about it. So please don't ask. Not yet."

Her expression is one of pity, love, and all I want to do is tell her everything, fall into her arms, and let her comfort me, to tell me lies that would create a different reality, but there's a feeling gnawing its way through me, telling me that I don't deserve it.

"It was Sam." A small, exasperated sound escapes my throat. "He helped me that night after I left the hospital, after I dragged myself home. It was his voice that rang through me—*It's going to be okay. You're going to be okay.* I mean it wasn't real. It was a memory."

But God, it felt like he was in the room with me. Maybe it was my memory magic's way of offering me an ounce of comfort, but I never considered, until now, that it was Sam who helped me that night.

Some memories spark to life like that. They can illuminate the dark, or punctuate a moment with such vividness that it's like living it all over again. For months—or, let's be honest, years—after Sam left me, I would call up certain memories, ones so vibrant that I could smell the mint on his breath, I could taste the sun on his skin. As pathetic as it was, those recollections kept him alive—they made him real. Even if the intensified masking spell protected me from feeling too deeply, from drowning in the emotions. There was something comforting about being able to keep him close without the intense pain.

"What was the memory?" Lana asks.

I tell her that when we were thirteen, I bet Sam that I could climb the cascadas higher than he could, to prove to him that I was just as brave and risky and fearless as he was.

Halfway up, he said, "You win." Then he climbed to the ground and stared up at me. "Come down, Chapulin. You're going to fall."

I didn't listen. I never listened.

A minute later, I reached for a narrow ledge, miscalculated, and came tumbling down, an injured bird falling from the safety of her nest. Thankfully, Sam was there to soften the landing.

Lana waits a few more beats as if she isn't sure the story is complete. When I take a breath and look away, she says gently, "I get it now. You needed to free your heart of this spell, of the secrets you've kept so that you can really heal from whatever this hospital trauma is. And I think..."

"What?"

"Sam is part of that healing."

His horses. *They can heal anyone.*

Even if that were true, how can I reconcile that Sam left me—he lied to me and fractured our lives—with him also being the potential answer. "What could he possibly be keeping from me?" I ask.

"Maybe the reason he left you."

"He already told me the reason."

I don't love you anymore.

"Then, the real question is, why did he lie?"

"What if he won't tell me?" I ask, wondering if I'm even bold enough to confront him.

"If anyone can beguile and charm, it's you."

With a not so confident nod, I cling to Sam's flower, to its secrets and promises. "Lana?"

"Yeah?"

"I'm going to need another martini."

19

That night, I do the first hard thing.

I call my attending to discuss my return date. After niceties and congratulations (which seem so painfully misplaced), we agree that I'll come back eight days from now. That'll give me three days to unwind after the Celebration of Flowers, which was part of my planned leave anyway.

When we hang up, a thick and cold silence wraps around me.

I feel numb.

No shiny afterglow of absolution, no boundless relief that I can return to my job, to my life.

My life.

Those two words spark a surprising ache. Why do they make me feel so empty?

When I finally fall asleep, the nightmares come. Vicious and glaring.

All shadows and echoes of those horrific moments in the operating room. Faceless figures, clawlike hands gripping the instruments, sickening ghosts with endless maws wailing into the darkness.

I wake in the morning, clinging to my pillow like it's a life raft. Clinging to Mayahuel's ideals of love and passion and beauty. The very foundation of my family's magic.

Of *my* magic.

I gave them up, I realize. I gave up love, passion, and beauty to protect my heart from ever being eviscerated again. I closed myself off, cut off the blood supply. I let the cold in.

Suddenly, I feel like that fragile bird again, falling from her nest.

And I've been falling ever since Sam left me. I thought that if I was successful enough, respected enough, smart enough, tough enough…if *I* was enough, that maybe, just maybe I could grow wings, but all I grew was an impenetrable armor that's been suffocating me for almost a decade.

I know deep down that this is not the case of a scorned woman who can't move on. It's rather that I've never been able to accept how abrupt Sam was, how indifferent he seemed. This was a man who had turned into a stranger overnight. I can't reconcile that with the boy I knew and loved.

I've been a prisoner of the past for too long, searching for reasons, creating scenarios and truths but always coming up short. Only one person can give me what I want, and after all this time I realize that I'd rather risk humiliation and rejection than die with all these questions.

That afternoon, I boil some garlic and chives and down the brew. Both are known to give courage and strength. The only downside is I smell like a pungent pasta dish, so I pop some cinnamon gum into my mouth and slip out of the house while my family is busy planning the details of the Celebration of Flowers.

It'll take an hour or so for the courage spell to work, and

even then, it will only take the edge off, but I'll take whatever nerve I can get.

Despite my heart thrashing like a wild beast and the ominous gray sky, I drive down the road with determination and speed.

For once, I have no plan, no rehearsed monologue, no expectation of how this might go. For once, I surrender to the mystery.

I make a vow to myself though. A vow that no matter what, I'm going to be okay. I'm going to re-create my life and it's going to look vastly different from the tower of success I've spent so many years building.

I pull down the ranch's long tree-lined road, park the car, and begin to march up to the house, with a sense of bravado I wish was bigger, when I hear, "Lily?"

I spin to see Alonzo with a rake in one hand and his hat tipped back.

"Hey, Alonzo," I say with a small wave. "Is Sam here?"

He closes the distance, shaking his head. "No, he had to leave town briefly."

I feel my heart dip. Shit. "Oh...when will he be back?" Because I might never reach the heights of this bravery again.

"Tonight."

It's none of my business, but I ask anyway, "Where did he go?"

Bullet comes racing out of the barn, bounding toward me like she hasn't seen me in years. I cup her gray face, rubbing circles behind her ears with my thumbs. "Hey, Bullet. Are you holding down the fort?"

Bullet let's out a bark as her tail spins in wild, joyful circles.

"Do you want something to drink?" Alonzo asks and I realize he hasn't answered the question about Sam's whereabouts. I'm about to tell him no when I realize that this might be an opportunity to get inside that house, to see my photo up close and personal, and perhaps do some shameless digging.

"Sure." I follow Alonzo and Bullet inside.

Based on the tangled mess of the porch, the home's interior is not what I was expecting.

The living room is tidy, minimal in its appearance with two deep-green sofas and a glass coffee table with only a small bowl filled with dice and matchbooks. The empty walls are a pale blue color in desperate need of a refresh, and the wide-planked oak floors are scraped and worn.

To my right, a rickety wooden ladder leans against the wall, and each rung holds a folded blanket. Next to it is a coat rack where a flannel shirt hangs on a hook alongside a few baseball caps.

The entire scene is one that screams *simplicity*, a canvas just waiting for the right artist.

Alonzo clears his throat and moves toward what looks like a small dining room, which is just as sparse as the living room. "Have a seat. I'll be right back."

But I don't want to sit. I want to explore. I want to see every inch of this place that Sam calls home.

Bullet looks up at me with her soulful eyes, soft pools of brown that say, *I'm game if you are.*

I hear Alonzo clanking around what must be the kitchen as I head down a small narrow hall with rutted walls and impossibly low-timbered ceilings. Bullet strides ahead like she wants to be the tour guide, glancing over her shoulder every few strides to make sure I'm following.

There are three doorways off this hall.

The first leads to a guest room. There's a twin bed draped with a blue-and-gold quilt and a crooked window that frames the ever-darkening sky.

The next door opens into a surprisingly large room complete with an unexpectedly small stone fireplace, stacks of fire-wood, a couple of worn leather chairs, old baskets filled with blankets and discarded socks. There's a dark wooden book-case lined with various odds and ends, a few books, and several framed photos.

My heart begins to thud dramatically, so loud I can barely hear my own thoughts as I rush over to see if this is the book-case where my photo lives.

"Lily?" Alonzo's voice echoes down the hall.

I stop in my tracks.

Bullet looks up at me with guilty eyes before leaping onto a chair where she curls up as if she's already bored of our little scavenger hunt.

I decide not to act like a snoop but instead as if cruising around Sam's home is the most natural thing in the world. But before I can call out to Alonzo, he's already in the doorway, holding a glass bottle of Jarrito's orange soda in one hand and a bottle of Modelo in the other.

"It's a little early for beer," I say, hoping to earn a smile that might erase Alonzo's frown.

"Soda then?" he asks, and his face brightens enough to loosen the knot in my chest.

"Thanks." I take the bottle from him and twist off the top before taking a syrupy swig. "I hope it's okay I'm taking a look around," I say. I hate to admit it but I'm actually quite adept at asking for forgiveness, not permission. I wouldn't survive as a physician if I wasn't.

"Por supuesto," Alonzo says, his eyes flitting to the book-case. He knows why I'm here, what I'm looking for.

I follow his gaze to the photo that I missed on first glance. It's not tucked behind the other photos of Sam's mom, or some beach photo, or Bullet. It's lined up with them, a declaration that I, too, am part of the family.

The four-by-six dented gold frame with nineteen-year-old me, laughing, is just as Alonzo described. I feel a shift of energy as I take the frame in my hands. A wave of memory magic pulses in my toes and winds up my legs, and for the briefest of moments, I catch a bright green scent, woody pine and lilacs. I hear Sam's voice so clearly, it's as if he's in this very room: *you're beautiful when you're grumpy.*

My pulse is a wild, untamable thing no matter how many deep breaths I take.

A crack of thunder makes me jump.

I return my attention to Alonzo who's gone over to the window where he's gazing at the darkening world beyond. With his back to me, he whispers something I almost don't catch. "Storms like these are never an accident."

Alonzo clears his throat and turns to me. I almost ask him what he meant, but there's another question burning its way out. "Has Sam told you anything else about me?" I realize it's an unfair question and one the poor man probably has no response to. He likely doesn't even want to be here having this awkward conversation with a stranger.

"Boss doesn't tell me much about his life before."

"You mean before he won this place?"

Alonzo gives a half-hearted nod that doesn't quite answer the question. His mouth is pressed into a tight line as if he's afraid he might say something he shouldn't.

Rain begins to pound the roof, hard and furious. Bullet looks up through slitted eyes, yawns, and tucks herself into a tighter ball.

"I should go and check on things in the stable," Alonzo says. "Do you want me to tell Boss you're waiting here for him?"

If Sam isn't expected until tonight, I might as well leave, but why waste this amazing opportunity to check out the entire hacienda. "I'll just finish my soda before I take off. If that's okay?"

Alonzo dips his hat lower. "Holler if you need anything."

Just as he leaves, I say, "What did you mean that storms like this aren't an accident?"

With a tender smile, he says, "I think you were meant to be here." And then he vanishes back through the doorway.

20

I spend the next hour wandering the home, which in my estimation is an amalgamation of many additions over the years— It's obvious by the way some corners and walls don't line up, the way some rooms extend beyond others like afterthoughts.

And then I find myself in what must be Sam's bedroom.

It's a large space at the back of the house, with two windows that frame what I guess is a wide-open field, but it's hard to tell because the rain is falling with such ferocity, everything is a blur.

The iron bed looks like something he welded himself. I can tell because the seams are imperfect. When we were teenagers, he took up the art of welding as a summer hobby, but he could never get the beads right. He'd usually ask me for help, saying my hands were steadier, reminding me that, "You are going to be a surgeon, after all."

It's a bitter irony to me that my dream to become a doctor is also the thing that saved me—the grueling hours, the relentless challenges. All of it kept me moving forward, steering me away from my own heart.

I stare now at Sam's mismatched linens and overstuffed pillows, which give his room an unexpected cozy vibe that makes me want to nestle in. The thought conjures images of Sam curling up with me, and I curse myself for letting my imagination wander.

There's a stone fireplace near the bed with a stack of books on the mantel—all nonfiction, including a fly-fishing guide, grilling cookbook, and a couple of American presidential biographies.

I imagine Sam sitting in front of a fire, flipping through the books until he drifts off. He never could drag himself to bed, preferring to fall asleep wherever and whenever the mood struck him.

Lightning flashes, illuminating the dusky room, followed by three rounds of thunder that are so violent the walls tremble.

Bullet pads into the room, sits at my feet, and begins to lick her front paw.

"How was the nap?" I ask as she rubs her face against my leg, begging for an ear stroke, which I happily oblige before she leaps onto the bed.

There's a collection of black-and-white photos on the wall opposite the fireplace—running horses, birds taking flight, a placid lake with sun glistening on its surface so vividly it's as if I can step into the photo.

Sam's world, I think.

This is what he's built—a home, memories, a life filled with the things that make him tick. Even his scent is everywhere—campfires, churned earth, flannel in the winter, and cotton in the spring.

I consider my own apartment back in LA. Blank walls, sterile rooms, a nondescript, utilitarian space that could only be described as a lifeless, joyless box.

I get a text from Lana. **Are you okay? Terrible storm.**

Fine, I text back.

How's it going?

He's not home.

Argh. Ok well don't drive in this. Just wait it out.

I send her a thumbs-up as the rain continues to batter the roof. Storms like this usually blow over in minutes but this one seems to be out for revenge, as if the sky has too much ammunition in her stores.

An hour later, I've wandered through every room of the house, and with each step, I feel a deeper sense of comfort—there's an ease here, an uncomplicated simplicity that feels like the building blocks for another life, one that I was supposed to help create.

I chastise myself silently. This is not my life or my home or my dreams. I don't even know Sam anymore. I don't know the friends he's made along the way, the experiences he's had, the people he's loved.

Has he loved someone else?

And so what if he still has my photo? So what that he brought an offering to Mayahuel? So what that he maybe, probably still loves me? Maybe it's just because I was his first, and something like that has lasting effects. It doesn't mean he wants to be with me *now*.

A chill works its way through me, and I suddenly feel like an intruder. I shouldn't be here.

I say goodbye to Bullet and start to head out when I see

Alonzo running up to the porch. He shakes off the rain, removes his hat, and hurries into the house, water pooling at his feet.

"The roads are a mess, Lily. Up at the fork, it's all washed out, so you'll need to stay here awhile longer."

"Stay? I was just leaving."

He's already shaking his head. "No way you're getting through."

Which means Sam isn't either.

"Isn't there another way, another road?" I ask. I can't be stuck here. This feels like a cruel cosmic joke.

"Only one way in and out."

"Well, how long do you think until the roads clear?"

"No idea. Won't know until this storm stops," he says. "I'll put your car in the barn."

"Thanks."

"Would you like me to start a fire for you?"

"It's okay," I tell him. "You've been so nice. I can do it. But what about you? How will you get out?"

"Oh, I live on the property. I have a house at the north edge of the ranch."

He's turned to leave when I ask, "I guess Sam can't get home tonight then either?" There's no hiding the disappointment in my voice.

Alonzo barks out a laugh. "Boss will hike through fifty feet of mud if he has to."

Of course he will.

After Alonzo leaves, I wander into the kitchen and peer into the fridge where I find half a bowl of fresh eggs, a moldy loaf of bread, leftover spaghetti, and a few half-filled jars of salsa.

I glance down at Bullet, who is sitting at attention, ears perked. "Sorry, girl," I tell her. "There is nothing you'd want in here."

She barks and races over to a tall cabinet, which reveals shelves and shelves of dog treats.

"Perfect," I say. "More food for you than Sam, huh?"

I offer Bullet a few cheese bones, which she gobbles down like a hungry wolf. Next, I find a bottle of Chardonnay, pour myself a glass, and head into the living room, where I build a small fire.

"Okay, Bullet," I say. "I didn't see a TV, which how is that possible? Maybe we can find a book that isn't about the outdoors or some dead white dudes?"

My search yields nothing, but then I spy a stack of Moleskines on a side table. When I flip through the first one, I see that it's a jumble of messy sketches—the barn, the house, a new fence, etcetera. Sam's made notes here and there about types of wood, the flooring in the barn, and dimensions of various places around the ranch.

The next journal is more of the same and so is another.

I don't know why, but these notations, these dream sketches, make me feel closer to Sam. I take the books, play some moody tunes on my phone, and settle onto the sofa in front of the fire.

The rain is relentless in her pursuit to flood the world, but I'm safe inside of Sam's house, curled up with Bullet under a cozy blanket, sipping wine, reading Sam's future plans.

I can feel my muscles relaxing, my body unfolding in the most luxurious way. I can't remember the last time I felt this tranquil, this at ease. I can't remember the last time I felt a moment of such bliss that it was worth sinking into.

I must sink too far because before I know it, I've fallen asleep.

Footsteps rouse me.

I'm blanketed in darkness except for the last glow of the embers crackling and smoldering in the fireplace.

It takes a moment to remember where I am, and then I see Sam's form in the shadows. He's standing by the dying fire with his back to me, clearly unaware that I'm here.

I lie still, afraid to breathe or move or explain my presence. Bullet rises with a languid stretch, hops off the sofa, and goes over to meet Sam.

"Hi, girl," Sam says as he begins to peel off his soaked shirt.

Oh God. I should say something, announce myself, but the moment has passed. And now I'm lying here watching Sam in a flawless afterglow, when all I want to do is slink into the night unseen. Okay, maybe I also want to watch him a few more seconds, minutes, hours. A lifetime?

His shoulders are broader than I remember, and his back is roped with muscle he didn't have ten years ago.

My heart is racing to the furious rhythm of the storm. Maybe I should make a noise, clear my throat. My eyes land on his left shoulder blade where he has a tattoo of a black bear paw no bigger than my fist, claws extended.

"How was your day?" Sam asks Bullet. Maybe he'll go into his bedroom, and I can slither away into the rain-soaked night, and he'll never know I was here. But that defeats the purpose of why I came to his house in the first place. I have to confront him. I have to get answers.

Although I'd so much rather watch him in the firelight with his soaking-wet hair, and leftover rain dripping down his back. Did I mention the hard line of his muscles?

I begin to sit up when he begins to unbutton his jeans.

Jesus.

My whole body freezes. My pulse is pounding in my ears. My mouth has gone dry and my skin is prickling from head to toe and all I can think is, if he strips naked in front of that fire, I'm going to die right here on his couch.

He begins to pull his jeans down when I manage to clear my throat.

He whirls toward me. An astonished sound escapes his body,

and just as I smile up at him as innocently as I can, he wrestles to right his jeans, trips over the stack of Moleskines I left near the hearth, and crashes to the floor with a violent thump.

21

"Sam!"

I rush over to try and help but he's waving me off and stumbling to his feet.

"Lily!" My name is nothing more than a groan as he buttons his jeans. "What the hell. What are you doing here?"

What am I supposed to say? *Oh well, I'm here to interrogate you because the magic says you're a liar. And I know you still love me, although that doesn't necessarily mean you're in love with me, so give up the secret already.*

I can hardly find the words because he's shirtless, standing in the radiance of a dying fire with his dark wet hair hanging around his face like some kind of goddamn sculpture and I have the sudden and equally painful urge to kiss him. To fall against his broad chest and feel his heart thrumming against my body.

"I came by to talk to you," I manage. "And this storm and the roads and I fell asleep and…"

I take a breath and only now notice the streaks of mud across his cheeks, which are also splattered all over his hands and jeans. They're a welcome distraction and stop me from staring at his chest and its various planes, both deep and shallow.

"Yeah," he says, "roads are a mess."

"You hiked through the mud," I say, trying not to smile.

Sam looks down, then as if remembering he isn't wearing a shirt, he steps back, too fast, stumbling into the pile of his journals again. He glances up at me with a question burning in his eyes: *Why were you looking through my things?*

"You don't have a TV," I say by way of explanation. "And your other books are boring"

"Boring?"

I wrinkle my nose. "Who wants to read about the dead presidents, Sam?" *And for the love of God, can you please put on a shirt?*

He stares a little too hard as if he's just now realizing that I've been in his bedroom, which means that it's likely I have been in every room and have therefore seen my photo. If he's unnerved, he doesn't show it.

His body is rigid as he inches away, more carefully this time. He grabs the flannel shirt (mercy) on the coat rack and puts it on. His expression is one of both warmth and confusion, and I can see him warring with both emotions. "I didn't see a car," he says.

"Alonzo parked it in the barn," I tell him. "But the fire— didn't that tip you off that someone was here?"

He shakes his head. "I thought Alonzo had done that for Bullet."

At the sound of her name, Bullet lets out a small whine. Sam squats and kisses the top of her head. Then, looking up at me, he exhales. "How long have you been stuck here?"

"Since around one. What time is it?"

He stands and looks at his phone, which he must have set on the mantel. "Close to midnight." He clears his throat and glances around like he isn't used to people appearing on his sofa at an ungodly hour, especially his ex. Then comes the most unexpected question. "Did you get anything to eat?"

"Oh, uh, I wasn't hungry." *You had nothing edible in your fridge.* "I opened a bottle of wine. I hope that's—"

"Help yourself to anything you want."

Well, Sam...what if what I want, I can't have?

"You must be starving," he says, now actively avoiding my gaze. "Problem is, I've got nothing great to eat, but I could whip up a couple of sandwiches or maybe some eggs or..." He snaps his fingers. "I might have a frozen pizza." He deadpans, "You'd have to pick off the mushrooms though."

He remembers I hate them. This tiny thing feels like such a victory right now.

I realize I haven't eaten since breakfast, and suddenly, I'm ravenous. "Sounds perfect."

He nods once and presses his mouth into a straight line like he isn't sure he heard me right. "There's a big wash out at the fork, so you'll have to stay the night. I've got a guest room. It's nothing fancy but it's all made up."

Sam, you don't have to sell me on sleeping at your cozy house with your perfect dog and your empty refrigerator and your books filled with dream sketches.

"Will I be able to get through in the morning?" I ask, wondering how it came to be that I'm here with Sam discussing a sleepover while a storm rages on outside. "Without hiking?" I throw in with a small laugh.

"I'll get you home," he says. "No hiking. But right now..." He glances down at his jeans, then back at me. "I'm going to take a shower."

I feel like I should make myself useful. "Can I help?" Wow—that didn't come out right. "I mean, want me to put the pizza in the oven or maybe..."

Sam's eyebrows knit together in a surprising frown. He

turns his head to the left and then there's a flicker of a smile as he leans closer, so close I think he's coming in for a hug.

Shit. Shit. Shit!

He stops short, takes a slow, deep breath. "Lily?"

"Yeah?"

"Why do you smell like garlic?"

The fucking courage spell.

My cheeks flush. A laugh bursts out of me and just like that the uncomfortable moment evaporates like mist.

By the time I hear Sam's footsteps approaching, the pizza is nearly ready, the storm is still stirring, I've had a second glass of wine, and Bullet has wandered off into the living room for another snooze.

For the last five minutes, I've debated pouring Sam a glass of wine. Is it suggestive? Is it rude if I don't?

Sam waltzes in, immediately halting my train of thought because now all I can think about is how good he looks after a shower. Wet hair. Glistening skin. Heated cheeks. Although, to be honest, muddy Sam isn't half bad either. All Sams occupy my thoughts, I guess—every last variation of him.

He begins to poke around in some drawers, pulling out forks.

"I already set the table," I tell him.

"You found everything?"

I nod, searching for conversation that's more than a few words, the kind that will lead to the secret he's keeping. I'm not here to eat pizza and drink wine and shoot the breeze, Samuel James.

I need you to tell me your secret.

"Wine?" I ask.

"How about—" he heads over to a cabinet, opens it, and tugs free a bottle of scotch, which he promptly opens and pours into a short tumbler glass "—this?"

He offers me the half-filled glass. I shouldn't. I've already reached my self-imposed limits of two glasses of alcohol, and I really should stop while I'm ahead, but I don't have to drive tonight. Plus, that first glass of wine was forever ago and maybe this will take the edge off.

I take the glass from him and as he pours his own, I take a sip, forcing my face into neutral, but obviously failing, because Sam laughs. "It's kind of strong," he says. "I got it in Scotland a few summers ago."

My heart dips and soars at the thought of Sam in Europe. Who did he go with? How long was he there? Did he like it? God, how many countless moments are there in both our lives that remain unknown to the other?

"Scotland, huh?" I ask. "How was it?"

"Cold and rainy," he says as he takes the pizza out of the oven. "Have you been?"

I shake my head. "Someday."

Holding the pizza in an oven-mitted hand, he stares at me for a second too long, like he might say something else, but instead, he glances up at the ceiling and lets out a low whistle. "I've never seen this kind of storm."

And just like that my memory is jolted and I remember what my mom said about the corpse dream.

A storm came and washed away the cemetery, turning it into a river.

Coincidence? Is it some kind of omen, or am I reaching here?

"It's a wild one," I say.

I take another sip of the scotch, letting its heat spread down to my toes as I search Sam's eyes for that same flicker I saw the other night. How will I ever get the truth out of him? It's not like I can come out and accuse him of holding a secret because the flowers said so. Nor can I just blurt that I know he still loves me, because what if I'm wrong? What if the love I saw burning in his eyes was some kind of leftover emotion?

A minute later, we're in the dining room. Me picking the mushrooms off my slice of pizza, him smiling as I do it. "I'll never get over how anyone can not like mushrooms."

"You mean fungi?"

"Semantics."

For the next hour, we eat and drink and touch on all the safe topics—the ranch, horse behavior, the treachery of medical school, his travels, my grueling schedule. It feels good. Necessary. And yet…we never once venture into dangerous territory.

Sometime after 1:00 a.m. I realize I'm a little drunk. The glowy, soft kind of buzzed that opens your heart and mind and gives you more courage than any spell could.

I'm watching Sam talk with his hands cradling the back of his head as he tells me again about the winning hand at the poker game that earned him this land. His eyes dance and his face brightens in the most alluring way.

"I guess it was meant to be," I tell him.

He crosses his arms over his chest and narrows his gaze, smiling like I'm the most entertaining person in the world. "You don't believe in destiny."

I pour a bit more scotch, even though there's a voice in my head telling me to stop. After a long pull, I prop my elbows on the table and with the straightest expression I can manage, I tell him, "Yeah, well, sometimes things change."

My voice is north of suggestive and now my cheeks are burning with a blush that's nearing humiliation, but Sam just laughs it off.

You were meant to be here.

Alonzo's words swim in my head, and for a nanosecond, I wonder again if this storm is the goddess's way of forcing my hand. Forcing me to stay the course and confront this man once and for all.

Sam threads his fingers together and stretches his arms upward. "I'm beat."

"Yeah, we should get some sleep." But I don't mean it. I don't want to sleep. I want to spend every waking moment talking to Sam, soaking up his energy, his soothing voice.

We stare at each other for a moment longer than is comfortable, a game of chicken to see who will make the first move.

"Okay," he says. "Uh, let me make sure you have clean towels."

Feeling deflated and maybe even dejected, I stand, holding the table for balance.

Sam leaps to his feet like he might need to catch me. "Easy, rider."

I wave him off, but by the time we get to the living room, the world is spinning, and my head feels like it might float off my body. Woozily, I drop onto the sofa. "Maybe I'll sleep here."

Sam looks like he's going to argue. I sink lower into the couch just as the lights flicker, once…twice, and then we're plunged into darkness.

"Hold up," Sam says.

I nearly laugh. Where does he think I'm going to go?

I hear him walk away and I expect some banging around, but there is only the fall of his confident footsteps across the oak floors. A drawer opening. The strike of a match.

When he comes back, he's holding a small candle in the shape of a 5.

"Is this from a birthday? Did someone turn five?" I tease.

"Not exactly," he says with a chuckle. "We apparently celebrated five years here, so Alonzo got me a cake and made this whole deal about it."

Sam's face is caught in the candle's golden light, and for once, he doesn't look tired or worried or uncomfortable. He looks like Sam.

I start to get up but the effort hardly seems worth it, so I curl my knees into my chest and gaze unblinking at the glowing embers. "The fire's dying," I say so low it's a near whisper.

Sam doesn't hear me. He's too busy tossing the candle into the hearth and sucking on his finger. "Is it true that mustard is the go-to for burns?"

"No scientific evidence," I say. "Do you have aloe vera or coconut oil?"

"I don't even have a stocked refrigerator."

"Good point," I tell him. "Want me to look at it?"

"It's only a tiny burn, Lily."

"Then, why did you ask about the mustard?"

"I was curious."

Sam begins to poke at the wood with an iron and soon the room is illuminated in a soft golden glow, the scent of piñon fills my senses as Sam takes a seat on the other end of the couch.

Why does this feel so dangerous? Sitting here in the dark, with Sam in front of a fire, with Bullet curled into a ball at our feet, while lightning flashes and the rain continues to batter the roof.

Sam's arm is draped over the back of the sofa casually. "You said you came here to talk to me."

"You said you had something to show me."

A slow grin. "It's too dark now."

I tug the bluebell out of my pocket and set it on the sofa between us. "You were at the farm yesterday."

Even in the dim light, I can see a muscle jump in his jaw. I wait for the lie, for the excuse. "Yeah, I was," he says.

His candor throws me off, but I decide to match it.

"Why did you leave this for Mayahuel?" I ask.

"Is that why you came here? To ask me about a flower?"

I shake my head. This is it. This is my chance.

"Then, why?"

His eyes are so dark in this light, endless black holes I would happily be pulled into.

All the love I have for Sam seems to fill the room, threatening to break down every wall, shatter every window. The impulsive, overwhelming enormity of it is too much for me to hold alone anymore. "Sam..." My body is leaning closer. A tired sigh falls from my mouth. I've reached the upper limits of lightheadedness of my drunkenness or maybe it's my proximity to Sam. Either way, I realize this man and alcohol do not mix.

My hand is reaching for his, grabbing it tightly—all its contour and curves. All its warmth and possibilities. He doesn't pull away. He doesn't hold on either.

"I forgot how nice your hands are," I say, studying his long fingers in the firelight. I realize it's too much honesty, but I don't bother to correct myself. The scotch has mixed with the courage spell and I'm feeling too light to extend any clarifications or apologies.

He looks down at his callouses and says, "Yeah, you're definitely drunk."

My eyes meet his. It feels like an eternity that we sit like that, staring at each other, calculating next words or moves, trying to read the other's past or maybe present. "Why do you have my picture, Sam?" I whisper.

He looks like he's been struck with a hot poker iron. "Lily..."

Tears prick my eyes, but I don't even try to hide it anymore. What's the point? "Tell me the truth."

He's still staring at me, his hand still resting in my own so naturally it almost hurts. He begins to shake his head, to pull away. But he keeps his hand pressed into mine like some kind of anchor.

His thumb makes a single, small, barely there circle across my palm.

"Sam?"

Silence.

The dam breaks.

"Why…why did you give up flying and why…?"

"Lily, don't."

My next words come out in a sob I can't control. I've worked myself into a frenzy, a river of emotion that won't stop flowing. "Why did you screw everything up and don't tell me you don't love—"

And then Sam is on me. He's kissing me. His mouth parts my lips. His hands are on my face, in my hair, gliding the length of my body with the fervor of a man who's never touched the ocean and I'm the ocean.

There's nothing gentle or loving about it. It's as if years of anger and frustration are spilling from his mouth and I have no choice but to swallow it all and I do.

Desperately, I do.

My arms are around him and we're tangled up and he's pressing into me harder and harder. There is no end or beginning to any of it, to him, to me.

To all the pain in between.

I fold into him like this was how it was always supposed to be, like no time has stood between us. No secrets, no lies.

And nothing matters because I have Sam in my arms and

his body is communicating how much he wants me. How much he needs me.

I feel the warmth of his hands moving up my shirt. Caressing my skin as I bask in the sheer delight of his fingers slipping beneath my bra.

My own hands are tracking the lines of his back, the bear claw tattoo I now know is there.

The rain lashes harder and faster.

His name escapes my lips in a heated whisper.

I arch into him, wrapping my legs around his solid body, pulling him closer with each breath.

Then, in an abrupt and cruel move, Sam pulls back.

He sits up, catching his breath. His lips are swollen. His eyes are glazed over. "I'm sorry," he says, shaking his head. "That was selfish."

"No, don't do that," I say, reaching for him, desperate to find our way back to only a moment ago.

But he's already on his feet, dragging a hand through his hair, like he doesn't know what else to do with his hands. "Look, we're both a little drunk and—"

"That's why you kissed me?" I stand. "Because you're drunk?" It's not a question, it's an accusation and he knows it.

"Maybe," he says so stoically I want to punch him in the face.

I back away angrily.

He grabs my arm and pulls me against him.

I try to struggle, but I'm too exhausted, too sad to fight anymore, so I relent like a newly broken horse. This time there is no kiss. He just holds me. His chest moves up and down, and soon my own heartbeat matches his, both thrumming wildly.

"You're right," he says, breathing into my hair. "I'm not going to blame the scotch or anything other than…"

"What?" I don't dare look at him. Instead, I close my eyes

and press farther into his chest. *Please, Sam. Please just tell me the truth.*

I feel the tension in his body as he lets me go and backs away, leaving me cold. "We should talk in the morning, once the storm clears and we've gotten some sleep."

"Why won't you let me in?"

"I don't want to hurt you again, Lily." His voice is hot and raw and all I can think is, *you just did.*

"But…" I blink up at him. "I know. I know you still love me."

There. The words I came here to say are floating between us like spirits from another life.

I watch as his Adam's apple bobs up and down. I watch as the agony slides across his face like a shadow.

"Am I wrong?" I ask, forcing his hand.

"You know I'll always…"

"That's *not* what I'm saying, and you know it."

"I let myself get carried away." He runs a hand down his face. "Jesus, I'm such an asshole."

His demeanor, his tone are so reminiscent of the night we broke up. And my entire being feels the rejection and grief of it as my memory magic expands, swirls through me achingly, compelling me to remember when all I want to do is forget.

Attraction is not the same thing as love.

The lights flash back on.

Sam looks like a man who's just been delivered the worst news in the world. He's wearing an expression of intense anguish and disbelief.

"I should never have let that happen," Sam says evenly, with a level of control that makes me hate him.

The pulse of my blood pumps to the rhythm of the rain. Years of restraint, of unanswered questions, of heartache and sorrow explode out of me like an atomic bomb. "You're right,

Sam. You are an asshole." I bolt into the guest room and slam the door.

Sam's footsteps never pass down the hall. I spend the next hour waiting for them, waiting for him.

He never comes.

Of course he doesn't.

23

When I wake at 8:00 a.m., the world is a foggy, silent haze.

And if my heart wasn't aching and my ego wasn't so bruised, I might lie here and enjoy the stillness of it all.

I might pretend that I live here with Sam and Bullet and the chickens and the horses and the wide-open skies. Our mornings would be calm, quiet things. Sam and I tangled between the sheets, luxuriating in each other's warmth and love. He'd make coffee and we'd sit on the porch and shoot the breeze about nothing. Our entire future would be a long straight path before us, and all we'd have to do is place one foot in front of the other with ease.

There's an afterglow to the fantasy, so warm that I can almost feel it, almost taste it. And as I close my eyes and take a deep breath, my memory magic awakens, a warm tendril of energy that only intensifies last night's kiss.

I can still taste Sam on my mouth, still feel the heat of his body against my own. I can hear his breath and feel his pulse, a hurried passion that forces me to remember what it felt like to be loved by Sam.

Like the sun was small enough to fit in the space between us.

But all the pretending in the world isn't going to make any of it true.

It's never going to erase the fact that when he ended things, we became two points on the map and the distance between us grew so vast, nothing could close it.

He's just an impossible, beautiful memory, and that's all he'll ever be.

I throw off the covers, pad to the window in the guest room, and press my forehead against the cool glass. My head is throbbing, which is my own fault. I've never been able to handle liquor and maybe if I hadn't drunk so much, I wouldn't have accepted Sam into my arms. I wouldn't have yielded so easily, so quickly.

Or maybe the alcohol had nothing to do with it.

Maybe I'm doomed to love a man who will never love me back in the same way.

Closing my eyes, I take an unsteady breath, and with painful focus, I still my memory magic. I imagine its tendrils vanishing like mist until it goes quiet.

Washed-out roads or not, I'm determined to get back to the farm this morning, back to my family where I feel safe.

Away from Sam. And all his bullshit excuses.

And I'm going to begin to heal, to peel back the layers of guilt and anger and shame.

After I make up the bed neatly, I slip out of the room like a mouse. The wooden floors creak beneath my feet as I tiptoe down the hall, holding my breath, praying I don't run into Sam.

That's when I hear someone whistling, banging pots around in the kitchen. My pulse quickens.

As I reach the front door and clutch the knob, I hear Alonzo's voice, "You're awake!"

I steal a glance at the man who's beaming at me from the hallway now, holding a cup of coffee.

"Oh, hey," I croak, before clearing my throat.

"Coffee?" he asks.

I'm already waving him off. "Gotta go."

"I checked on the roads this morning," he says, looking woeful. "Still impassable."

"I'll hike." I'm not going to be stuck here another second. And where the hell is Sam? No way is he still asleep—he was always a rise-at-dawn kind of guy. That annoying person who wants to suck the marrow out of life and thinks sleeping is only for the dead.

Alonzo nods thoughtfully, although his scowl tells a different story, and I don't know him well enough to recognize if it's worry or frustration.

He walks toward me, stopping near the fireplace, which is now filled with cold dark ashes.

"Boss asked me to make sure you had breakfast," he says.

Sam's audacity is so over-the-top it takes every ounce of control to not explode right there in his living room. But Alonzo doesn't deserve to be caught in the cross fire of Sam and my ill-fated love affair.

I look around for Bullet, realizing she's likely with Sam.

"I'm not hungry," I tell Alonzo kindly, "but thanks."

"Will you let me drive you then? I have a lot of experience navigating these muddied roads."

I'm about to agree when I realize that I'd have to come back for the truck eventually, and that sounds like an exercise in torture. "I'll be okay, really."

Alonzo lifts his coffee mug to his mouth for another sip. His eyebrows come together in a tight frown. "I might get into a lot of trouble if anything happened to you."

I'm not a goddamn damsel in distress, I want to shout. I can hike through mud, and I can get myself home and I can rid my heart and memory of Sam, if given enough time.

"How about this?" he says. "I'll follow you, make sure all is okay."

Alonzo seems so kind and patient. Although, I can see how he could just as easily shift to a man of insistence, a man just doing his job. The last thing I want to do is get him into any trouble, so I agree because what's the harm in letting him follow me just in case the roads are still impassable.

A minute later, we're heading out to the barn. Across the way, the fog floats over the grassy pasture, where I can make out the outline of several horses grazing. The moment could be a photograph, a snapshot of a memory that would never fade.

A lot of people find healing in the horses.

That might be true, Sam. But I also think the healing is in this place—in its empty and silent spaciousness. It's in the wildness and in the way the old trees shift and sway. It's in the scents of earth and green and memory.

I can feel them. The memories. Like a vibration that sweeps through me, soft and fading.

People were happy here once, babies were made and born and raised. There was sorrow and loss but also laughter and love.

Alonzo follows my gaze. "Did you know a horse's first defense is to run?"

I shake my head as the vibration of another time evaporates. I understand why Sam made this his home. This place is haunted by love and joy, so far removed from the world's glossy veneer of achievement and success.

"But if cornered," Alonzo adds, "a horse will bite and kick and fight to the end."

"I can't imagine a horse fighting anyone or anything," I say.

"Ah, but this is the natural world," he says. "And animals will do anything to survive."

Alonzo talks like a man who was born and raised in the wild and I realize I know nothing about his story.

I turn to him. "You said you were here before Sam. How long have you actually lived here?"

Alonzo considers the question or perhaps how he wants to answer it. "I came to work here when I was fourteen," he says, "and I've been here ever since."

A lifetime.

"What made you stay all that time?"

He lets his gaze drift. "It's the land," he says. "It tells you how small you really are. It teaches you lessons, maybe even welcomes you, and if you're lucky, it opens your eyes to the truth."

"Truth?"

A small chuckle floats out of the old man. "That we are all just specks and not nearly as important as we think we are."

When I get to my truck, Alonzo hands me the keys. Then, as I'm about to open the door, he says, "Boss went on a ride this morning, left before dawn, something about fixing a fence."

I feel a ping in my chest. Why is he telling me this?

"I bet he just needed to think," he goes on. "He always goes on long rides when something—" his eyes flick to mine "—or someone is on his mind."

I'm about to inform him that as much as I appreciate his romantic notions of me and Sam, they are entirely misguided, but his phone rings and before I know it, he's tugging it free from his pocket and telling me, "Wait here. I'll just be a minute."

I watch him exit the other side of the barn as he takes the

call and I'm guessing it's Sam, probably checking on his prisoner. A heated anger rises in me all over again.

Quickly, I get in the truck, start the engine, and pull out of the barn before rushing down the muddied drive.

At the end of the road, I bring the truck to a stop when I see the horse gates are closed.

Shit.

Maybe they're manually operated, I think as I get out of the car, stepping into the slippery mud.

With my arms extended for balance, I trudge a few feet when I hear, "You're wasting your time."

I whirl to find Sam.

He's dismounting a gray spotted horse which he lets run off into the pasture. His hair is a tousled mess. His shirt is wrinkled, and his face is only a few hours from shadows, and yet he's still agonizingly attractive.

"Open the gates," I tell him.

"You'll never make it through."

"Sam, open the gates."

"Lily. Just hear me out first."

"You had that chance last night." I get back into the truck and slam the door, gunning the engine, a threat that I'll knock down the damn gates if I have to.

Sam positions himself between the vehicle and the exit, arms crossed over his chest. "Get out of the car, Lily."

I ignore him, narrowing my gaze.

With a grunt, he walks over to the driver's window, talking through the glass. "Fine. You want to do this here?"

"There's nothing to say. You made it clear." I clutch the steering wheel, wishing I didn't sound so petulant. "Can you please," I say, softer this time, "just let me go?"

He opens the door and leans in. "Just give me five minutes."

Five minutes? How can anything of substance or value be

said in just five minutes? This is ridiculous. I refuse to be held prisoner a second longer. I jump out of the truck and shove past Sam.

He's two steps behind me. "Lily, where are you going?"

"I'll walk home if I have to."

"Let me drive you."

I don't answer. Just keep slogging through the mud, thinking this is probably not the soundest of choices, but who ever made a good decision when their heart was breaking, and their adrenaline was soaring?

"You're being ridiculous," he says.

"That's rich, coming from you."

"It's too far."

I ignore him, keeping my focus on my willful anger. It's the only defense I have against this man.

I feel his hand grab my arm. He's spinning me to face him, and as much as I try to break free, his hold on me is too strong.

Fury building, I lash out, "Let me go!"

"Goddamn it, Lily." His grip tightens. "I love you!"

24

My heart gives a violent lurch.

I have so many things to say, so many words to launch at him: *If that were true you would never have left me.* Or *there is no world where I would have left you, no reason big enough,* but my head is swimming and I'm drowning in Sam's presence, made even worse when he pulls me closer. When he takes my hand in his, I feel a tremor of warmth radiate through him and my memory magic ignites, making it impossible to think clearly.

"I've been trying to clear my head, to…" His gaze drops to the ground. "Last night was…" He clenches his jaw, and I can see the struggle in his demeanor, I can hear it in his voice. "I have some things to tell you."

His secret. I wait silently.

His gaze drifts back up and pins me in place. "I love you," he says again, this time more gently. "I never stopped."

I thought hearing Sam admit his feelings for me would fix everything, but all it does is leave me feeling hollow. And I realize it's not enough. It doesn't excuse how much he hurt me. It doesn't erase the ten years we can never get back.

And yet...

My body responds to his in ways I'll never understand, and it's no use for me to fight this force—I will always lose.

Summer memories ripple across my mind like desert mirages. Fragmented and distant.

My magic wraps around each, holding Sam close.

"Then, why?" My voice is small, unsure, teetering on mistrust.

He exhales, shakes his head slowly. I can see the pain on his face, the agony of indecision or maybe regret.

"Sam?"

"It's...complicated."

I feel suddenly tired. Tired of this charade, tired of trying to read him. Tired of holding on to something that maybe I should have let go a long time ago.

I wait another few beats to see if he'll add to the *complicated* BS, but he doesn't. He just stands there looking like a man lost in the wilderness.

"I didn't have a choice," he finally says. "You have to know that."

"Yes. You did," I say, and there's no masking my anger.

"Things got messy, and it was the only way."

I want so badly to run, but I can't seem to get my body to listen. "You're talking in circles, Sam. What could have possibly been so complicated?"

He looks defeated before he even begins. And then, in an unexpected move, he wraps his arms around my waist, and when I don't flinch, he pulls me closer, sliding a hand up my back as he presses his forehead to mine. "Isn't it enough that I love you?"

Tears burn my eyes and my entire body trembles with the memory of Sam.

Everything around us fades. This moment is all there is. All that matters. And in the next breath, I lose all sense of time and reality and I'm floating, longing, tilting my face so that my lips are now brushing against his.

I try, oh how I try to resist, but I'm dizzy with the nearness of him. And he's holding me up, pressing into me, deepening the kiss slowly like he's asking for permission.

Lost. I only want to be lost in Sam. And yet I can't leave with lingering question marks, with answers that aren't answers.

"I need the truth," I manage.

He's nodding, holding me closer, breaking through my armor with a single touch. "Let's go back to the house. I'll tell you everything."

Silently, we make our way back to the truck. I scoot across the bench as Sam jumps into the driver's seat, turns the ignition over and begins to back down the driveway but the truck doesn't move—the engine screams and the wheels spin, kicking up mud.

"We might have to walk back," Sam says as he turns the wheel left and right to no avail. "Or I could get the ATV and come back for you."

"Sam, I was willing to walk all the way home," I say with a chuckle. "Pretty sure I can make it back to the house."

He offers a skewed smile, narrows his eyes, and says, "Would you really have tried to walk home?" Before I respond he shakes his head and adds, "Never mind. I know you would."

He steps out of the truck and extends his hand to help me as I slide toward the driver's door, but I can't find purchase because Sam is blocking my way. He's still holding my hand, taking hold of my other, threading his fingers between mine. "I don't want you to hate me."

My heart skips a thousand beats. *I won't. I couldn't.*

Suddenly, I'm afraid. Afraid to know the truth. Afraid that his reasoning will be unbearable, unforgiveable.

And if that's true, this could be my last time with Sam. The last time we touch, or kiss or...

Fuck reality.

I press my mouth to his, half expecting resistance. It never comes. Sam leans against my body, kissing me with a feverish want, inching me back and back until I'm lying on the seat and pulling him down on top of me as he awkwardly closes the door behind us.

My mind is whirring with justifications and rationalizations. *This is wrong. This isn't the answer.*

This is the goodbye I never got.

"Sam." My voice sounds scraped and raw, and I don't know why I say his name out loud. Maybe it's to convince myself that this is okay, that all that matters is this moment and that Sam's right here, in my arms.

I can feel the attempt at restraint in his limbs. It's barely controlled, like he's one breath away from losing himself to me, to this moment, a man holding back a passion that could burn me alive.

I thread my fingers through his thick hair, sinking into the heat of his touch. Begging him silently to never stop.

But he does.

He pushes himself up. Hovers, staring down at me, chest rising and falling with a desperation that nearly breaks me. "I'm sorry." His voice is a whisper now.

I begin to shake. He presses a hand to my sternum. The gentleness of his touch makes me want to cry. "I'm so sorry," he says again.

This time he's looking into my eyes, and I see all the unrelenting anguish of a man who left me. Somehow, this feels dangerous, reckless.

But I'm tired of being logical and reasonable. I'm tired of following all the rules, of controlling my emotions. Emotions that have been too tightly contained for too long.

Can't it just be enough that Sam still loves me?

I rest a hand on each side of his jaw and draw him closer. "Please stop talking."

A ghost of a smile tugs at his lips. His eyes go soft as he lowers himself. As we kiss. As I cling to him. As I let his hand slide across and down my body freely, exploring every curve and contour like he's never felt them before.

My own hands wander under his shirt, down his back, trailing the waist of his jeans. He lets out a raspy moan, and I can feel his body retreating. "Lily."

"Please, don't ruin this."

"Are you sure?" he whispers.

"Yes."

I half expect Sam to finally let go, to unleash the passion I can feel pulsing in his blood, but his strokes are tender, patient. Like we have all the time in the world.

"Boss?" Alonzo's voice is a shout coming from what sounds far away.

Sam and I freeze.

"Shit!" he says. And then he sits up. "Give me a minute."

He clears his throat, tucks in his shirt, and runs a hand through his hair before opening the door and stepping out.

"What's up, Alonzo?" Sam asks. There's a hitch in his voice that I adore.

"It's Lady," I hear Alonzo say. "She's had her foal."

25

When we get to the stalls, Lady's foal is lying next to her. A filly with glossy black legs curled beneath her thin, lithe body, and a mother nosing her newborn with so much tenderness, so much hope you could almost believe that nothing could ever be bad again.

No one opens the stall door or makes a move to get any closer, and when I ask why, Alonzo responds with, "It's best to give them space to bond."

"The foal should stand soon," Sam says, his gaze pinned on mother and baby with a look of such pride it melts me.

Bullet races in, tongue hanging out the side of her mouth, tail wagging, and as she approaches, her demeanor shifts, as if she knows this is a sacred moment. Sam reaches down and pets her head.

Then, a few minutes later, the foal struggles to get to her feet, awkward, jerky movements that leave me holding my breath, rooting for her silently.

And when she stands, when she balances on those long

skinny legs, we all cheer, lost in this moment of celebration. Of life.

Sam hooks an arm over my shoulder and damn if it doesn't feel like the most natural thing in the world. With a gentle squeeze that pulls me closer to him, he says, "Do you want to name her?"

I wince a little, unsure I'm up to the task. "Really?"

Sam's smile is so endearing I can't say no. I stare at the newborn, considering her spunky energy, her spiritedness and determination. And then it comes to me. "Spirit."

"Excellent," Alonzo says with a wide grin.

Sam seems to approve, too, because he nods confidently and says, "Welcome to the world, Spirit."

Back at the house, Sam builds a small fire and asks if I want anything to drink. "You're stalling," I tell him, taking a seat on the couch. My chest flutters in the silence. What if his excuse is terrible? What if this doesn't bring any sort of closure?

Bullet turns in circles, finally settling into a big gray ball while Sam rubs the back of his neck and eventually relaxes on the other end of the sofa, turning to face me.

I wait.

He studies his fingers, takes a deep breath, and then in an admirable show of confidence, he looks up at me and says, "I was sick."

I feel like someone's punched me in the stomach. "What do you mean?"

"I was diagnosed with Hodgkin's lymphoma."

I can't believe the words coming from his mouth. He was only nineteen. It's not possible. Sam was always so vibrant, so full of life.

The fire sparks and crackles, sending tendrils of smoke curling up the chimney.

"I had to do chemotherapy." He grimaces, exhaling a long breath through his mouth.

I'm lost, unsure I can fathom what he's telling me, unsure I can find the right words. "Wait. How…? Why…?" I'm trying to process the fact that Sam was ever sick, never mind had to undergo something as brutal as chemotherapy. "Why didn't you tell me?"

"I couldn't put you through that."

It takes me a moment to digest his words, to try and understand what he's telling me.

"You couldn't put *me* through that?" I recoil as Bullet takes her leave, like she doesn't want to be here for this conversation. "Don't you think I could have made that choice on my own? I would have stayed by your side. I would have…"

"You would have dropped out of college, risked medical school, and the thought of you giving up your life to save mine…"

My body moves on its own volition. I wrap my arms around him, resting my chin his shoulder. The tears come without warning, and for once, I don't hold them back. We stay like that for a while, breath for breath, heartbeat for heartbeat.

Sam was sick.

Sam had cancer.

The one thing that always kept me going was knowing that he was out there, living, breathing on this shared plane of existence. To think he was dangling off the edge and I never even knew it.

He pulls back. "Do you understand? I didn't want you to see me like that."

I rest my hand on his forearm. Sam, this man I've loved, whose memory can never be erased, he'd carried this burden alone. As lost as I was in my own grief and loneliness, his had to have been a million times worse.

"But you got better," I say as he wipes a tear from my cheek.

"It took some time, but yeah." He smiles softly, but it doesn't hide the pain that flashes across his face, "I got better."

"So then why didn't you call me?"

"I did."

His words tighten the knots in my stomach. And then I remember that I changed my number after a year of checking my phone every minute of every day, hoping Sam would reach out. When he never did, I realized with certainty that he was never coming back, and that it was time to let the dream of him go.

"I even came to see you in L.A. about six years ago," he says, "after all the treatments, when my hair grew back, and I was in the clear. I thought maybe I could explain. That we could pick up where we left off."

I'm still processing this as Sam continues. "You were with someone else."

My heart takes a nosedive. "Wha…what are you talking about?"

"I flew out there," he says. "I mean, after I asked your mom for your address."

"Wait, you asked my mom? She never told me!" Why didn't she tell me? And then the answer comes with a painful truth: *because she didn't know what he truly meant to me.*

Sam runs his thumb over my knuckles, staring down. "You weren't home, and I had these wildflowers that some lady was selling on the street corner." He barks out a small, humorless laugh. "Imagine that I thought flowers were going to win you back."

A single petal would have won me back, Sam.

"Then what happened?" I ask as if the telling has some kind of power to rewrite history. To stitch back together all the lost years.

"I waited outside of your place for a while, then figured I'd come back. I'd keep coming back until I caught you."

"Why didn't you just ask my mom for my number?"

His jaw muscles jump. "I realized that I needed to do this face-to-face. So, I drive down the street. And I stop into a bar for a drink when I see you and this guy." He shakes his head. "Of all the bars, right?"

"So?"

"So you looked very cozy." He glances up. There's no malice there, no anger. "You were kissing him and..." He pauses, swallows. "You looked really happy, Lil, and I thought what kind of a selfish bastard breaks someone's heart and then tries to waltz back into her life years later?"

If he only knew that I can't even recall the man, the moment, the bar.

"Sam, no one else has ever mattered." I sit up and face him. "I was trying to move on, to get lost in anything, anyone else, but it never worked. I was always missing you!"

"You don't have to explain." His entire expression softens. "You deserved to be happy."

"Jesus, Sam. This is so absurd. You quit everything just because you saw me with one person, one time?"

His expression withers. "That, and I heard through my uncle that you had a boyfriend. I wasn't about to be the dick who messed that up."

"But you could be a dick when you broke up with me, especially without telling me the full story?" I don't mean for the words to sound so harsh, so unforgiving, but I'm furious.

"Exactly! I think playing that shit role once was enough for a lifetime."

I scoot back out of his reach. The reality of his words, the devastation of it all lingers between us and I don't know what to do with all the emotions warring within me right now:

resentment, hope, regret, love. "You decided for both of us," I say. "All these years... I thought... I *believed* that you didn't love me."

Your identity changes when someone stops loving you because you're not *that* person anymore. You're left with only the crumbs of what was instead of what will be.

Sam leans closer, running a hand through my hair. "It was the only way to get you to let me go. Don't you know how much it killed me?"

"We could have found a way. I could have taken care of you and just postponed everything."

The words feel wrong in my mouth, half-truths that even I don't believe. Sam's right. I would have sacrificed it all to be with him, to support him, to love him through the agony.

"I was just a kid." Sam drags a hand down his face. "I really thought I was doing the right thing."

A small pause affords us both some breathing room, some contemplation.

"This is why you didn't pursue a pilot's license," I say, putting the pieces together.

With a slight shrug, Sam says, "After I got better, I was different. The things I thought mattered didn't matter so much anymore, and then I won this place. I was planning on selling it, but when I came out here something changed for me."

He scrapes a hand over his jaw, working it back and forth like there's too much tension. His gaze meets mine and his voice changes, not to one of pleading or convincing, but to one of utter surrender. "This place was the first time I felt peace since the night we broke up, and I felt like if I couldn't have you, I could have a different life, one that could still make me happy."

I stare openly, adrift, and so confused.

Sam squeezes my hand. "What are you thinking?"

"That I really want to punch you right now."

With a playful smirk, Sam says, "That's fair."

There's no logic to the emotions blazing through me, there's no space to shelve them. I fall against his chest, listening to his heartbeat, a constant steady thrum.

"So you aren't going to hit me," he teases.

I make a pathetic attempt at a lighthearted smack to his ribs. A small, tender laugh bubbles out of Sam before he goes still.

"I can't ask you to forgive me," he says, wrapping his arms around me. "Because I'm not sure I could ever…" His voice breaks and I find myself looking up, into his golden-brown eyes framed so perfectly by his dark eyebrows. For someone who puts zero effort into his appearance, how can he be so perfect?

"Sam, I do. Of course I forgive you. I just wish…"

He strokes my forehead and I know without words how deep his love is, how much this must have destroyed him, how lonely the last ten years have been for him too. But I don't have to think about that right now because we're together now. And all I want to do is sink into this fragile moment.

Into him.

Slowly, I begin to unbutton his shirt. It isn't a sexual over-ture. I just need to feel the warmth of his skin. He relaxes into my touch as I part his shirt and press my hands against his stomach, trailing my fingers up his body.

"I've missed you," I say.

"Lily."

His eyes are wet, and I'm not sure if I'm seeing some emo-tion that isn't there, because my own vision is blurred by left-over tears or if…

"Sam?"

"You have to know something else."

26

In the span of five minutes, my emotions have gone through the extreme highs and lows of the past, of Sam's admissions. I could dwell on them, but I know I need to focus on the future, on moving forward, on the fact that Sam still loves me.

I can forgive him, and we can pick up where we left off and nothing needs to change.

"There's a chance I might be sick again," he says.

My world comes to a grinding halt. I stare, unblinking, unwilling to acknowledge the cruelty, the impossibility of his words.

"Might...?" I begin to tremble all over. "What do you mean?"

"I went for testing—that's where I was yesterday." He squeezes my hand, but it does nothing to comfort me.

This can't be true. None of this can be true. It's just some sick cosmic joke, right?

"Lily, when I saw you at the wedding," he goes on, "I knew that I was still just as in love with you as I've always been. If I hadn't just been handed this shit news, I would have told you right then and there, I would have begged your forgiveness, I would have spent forever making it up to you." He draws in an exhausted breath.

"But you don't know for sure," I say, going into doctor mode. "I mean, how do you even know?"

"A routine scan found a shadow on my liver."

Liver cancer. My memory reaches for my oncology rotation. To survivability rates, treatment, but all I find are fragments of useless knowledge.

"A shadow that could be nothing," I insist.

"Right. Or it could be—"

I press my hand to his mouth. "Don't say it!"

This is why he took the flower to Mayahuel.

It was a prayer, a plea.

Gently, he slides my hand away. "Lily, I need to be realistic."

"Fuck reality!" I launch to my feet and begin to pace in front of the fire. "No! You're fine. Everything's going to be okay." I've seen this reaction before—family members, loved ones who refute the existence of any danger, of any risk as if clinging to denial can change the truth.

A painful silence settles over us. There's nothing to say to make this moment anything other than what it is—agonizing.

My churning thoughts turn desperate. "Maybe Dahlia can—" I stop midsentence because I know that even her magic can't fix this.

Dahlia's powers can't heal physical disease. What good is my family's magic if we can't use it to save those we love?

"I want to see your records," I demand, even though I'm not an oncologist. "Do you have the scans and who's your doctor? Have you gotten a second opinion? Are you seeing someone here or in the US.? I can talk to a colleague and..."

"Lily." Sam's on his feet but I'm still pacing, lost in my own mind because it's a safer space than my disintegrating heart.

Medicine makes sense. Science makes sense. I simply need everything to make sense.

Sam folds me into him as if his role is to be the consoler. "I'll get the results next week. And I understand if…"

I can't seem to get enough air as I press my cheek into his bare chest, biting back the tears. "No *if*," I say, unrelentingly. "I'm here. I'm not going anywhere."

Sam pulls back and brushes a strand of hair from my eyes. He smiles tenderly like this is a happy moment, like we've just shared a wonderful memory. "I know" is all he says.

We stand like that, clinging to each other. His hands slide up my back, a nurturing caress that asks so many questions: *Will you love me? Will you forgive me? Do you still want me?*

I peel his shirt off his shoulders to get a better look at the man before me—the planes of his chest, the lean muscles that only scream health and vitality.

He's everything I remember and nothing I remember.

Sam watches me stare, watches as I glide my fingers down his torso. I want to memorize him, every freckle, every line, every curve. It's then that I allow my memory magic to awaken, warm wisps of energy that radiate through me, promising that I'll never forget a single detail of this, of Sam.

"Lily."

My eyes flick to his.

And then he's leaning, drawing me up and up until his mouth is on mine. Until I'm parting my lips, kissing him deeper.

This time Sam shows no restraint.

Our bodies collide, a reckless, hungry longing, wild and heedless. There is no before, no after. There is only now, this moment.

Quickly enough, our clothes are on the floor.

When Sam leads me to the couch, I'm shaking from head to toe as he lays me down, never taking his gaze from mine.

I want, I need, this man more than air.

He pauses for the first time, studying me, his eyes roving the entirety of my body. He doesn't need to say anything. It's all there—the love, the regret, the desire.

Then slowly, he lowers himself on top of me, achingly so. Dark hair spills around his angled face as I slide his hand over my breast, down my stomach, to the inside of my thigh.

His hand travels freely, exploring all of me.

I can't breathe, can't see anything but Sam intertwined between my legs, gliding his mouth across my body, leaving me longing for more.

I trace my hands down the length of his lean, muscular form. Beneath all of it is the boy I fell in love with a lifetime ago.

There is an urgency to my movements, to my breath and desire. He pins my hands in place above my head as he continues to trail kisses down my neck, my breasts, my stomach.

"Sam..."

I feel his body vibrate with a silent laugh.

"Something funny?" I manage.

He brings his lips to my neck again and in a willful whisper, says, "So impatient."

I push him back, force his gaze to meet mine. Then, with a wicked smile, I reach down, wrap my hand around his member. His breath hitches. A muscle jumps in his jaw.

"You don't make the rules anymore," I say, pressing my mouth to his, wrapping my legs around him, taking the fullness of him.

We move ravenously, outside memories and betrayals and secrets.

There is nothing more than this.

Nothing more than Sam moving inside of me, taking all that I offer. All that I have, until moments later, we collapse into each other, quivering, breathless, spent.

I hold him close, twisting my fingers in his hair, feeling his pulse slow against my chest. The fire flickers. Shadows dance across the walls and floor.

I don't know how long we stay like that, silently in each other's embrace, the contours of our bodies connected like we're two pieces of the same puzzle.

It's not enough. It's never going to be enough.

We make love again on the floor in front of the fire. This time more slowly, more patiently. Then again in Sam's bed. And again in the kitchen when we come up for air to eat leftover pizza and Sam lifts me onto the counter, dissolving into me like it's the first time.

Some say pleasure and pain are close cousins, and now I understand the analogy.

When we're deliriously exhausted and lying in his bed, tangled up in each other, and the darkness is sliding across the sky, I close my eyes. As I drift off, I tell him quietly, "I love you."

And for the first time in ten years, I fall asleep in Sam's arms.

27

I dream of Sarah.

Of her bright smile and wide, curious eyes.

It's a dream that takes a dark turn into a morgue.

The sound of a slow-beating heart echoes across the cold, chemical-smelling space. *Thud. Thud.*

And then, from inside the walls, Sarah's voice finds me, "You're here."

In a fit of panic and desperation, I stumble over to the drawers, opening each, peeling back sheet after sheet, searching for her, but all I find is one cadaver after another.

The floor begins to melt like hot wax, and I'm sinking, groping for purchase.

Sarah whispers, "You can't save me."

I can. I can!

Gasping for air, I grab hold of a metal table for balance and leap on top of it as the floor disintegrates into an endless abyss. There's a body beneath this sheet.

For a dark moment, I sit frozen. Ragged breaths escape my

lungs. Then, with clumsy fingers, I reach for the sheet and lower it.

It's not Sarah.

It's Sam.

I open my mouth to scream but nothing comes out. The only sound is Sarah's hushed voice, "It's too late."

I wake with a start. I'm alone, naked in Sam's bed.

It was just a nightmare, I tell myself. That's all it was.

Turning, I touch the space Sam occupied—it's gone cold, which tells me he's been up for a while. But I'm not ready to face the day. I want to luxuriate in his bed, wrapped in the memories of everything we did here, the pleasure he gave me, that we gave each other. The way his body felt against mine. The way every kiss, every touch comforted me, made me believe in whatever he wanted me to believe in.

My eyes flick to the window.

Outside, the sky is a patchwork of pale blue and stormy gray. More dark clouds amass in the distance, headed in our direction.

It's not too late, I tell myself. Sam's fine. He's going to be fine. *And if he's not*, a sinister, unpleasant voice whispers at the back of my mind, *what are you going to do?*

Just then the door inches open and Sam pokes his head in. When our eyes meet, he smiles. "You're awake."

Bullet bolts past him and hops onto the bed, rolling over, begging for belly rubs, which I oblige.

With a laugh, Sam tells Bullet, "Go finish your breakfast, Bull."

The pup's ears perk up at the word *breakfast*. She leaps onto the floor and runs out of the room.

Sam comes in and sits at the edge of the bed. He's wearing faded jeans and a T-shirt, and smells of pine soap. "Sleep okay?"

With the sheet pulled over my chest, I sit up and nod. "You

snore," I tell him playfully. He didn't used to, and it makes me wonder what other things have changed. What other discoveries am I going to make about this man?

His expression is a mix of frowning and grinning. "Seriously?"

I do my best to reenact the blustery breaths, which earns me Sam's hearty laugh. "Sorry 'bout that."

"My own little noise machine," I tell him as I run my hand over the stubble on his chin.

"I know. It's getting out of control."

"Don't you dare shave."

"Lily," he says, "I'm going to look like a grizzly bear if I don't."

"I love grizzly bears." I close my eyes, wishing I could make this moment last forever, but with each breath, I can feel it slipping through my hands. "You were up early?"

"Checking on Spirit."

The image of Sam at dawn, strolling to the barn with Bullet running alongside him warms me all over. "How is she?"

"Perfect." Sam kisses the top of my head. "You up for a ride?"

I feign a coy smile, running my hand down his chest. "What kind of ride?"

Taking my hand in his, he chuckles. "I meant a horse ride."

I've only ever been on a horse once or twice, far preferring my feet on the ground, where I can control things.

"I still have that something to show you," he says, his tone cheerful.

I drop my head onto his shoulder sleepily, thinking I'd much rather fold myself into the dimensions of Sam's warm bed. "Is it good?"

"Define good."

"Mmm, last night was very good."

Sam pulls back to meet my gaze. He's grinning when he says, "Last night was exceptional."

We dance around the potential illness, pretending it doesn't exist. Maybe if we can make love enough, laugh enough, touch each other enough, this demon threatening our joy will vanish and this perfect bubble we've created can last forever.

"True," I say, curling into him. "But is this *something* worth getting out of bed for?"

Sam's body vibrates with a chuckle that makes me smile, makes me love him more. "I think you're going to like it."

"Okay," I say, curiosity piqued. "Let's go see this mysterious something." I drop the sheet and get out of bed.

Sam eyes me hungrily.

It strikes me that he hasn't seen me naked in the morning light in ten long years.

Sam clears his throat, tugging me onto his lap. "It can probably wait."

I'm drunk on the way Sam looks at me, the way he touches me like he can never get enough. *We* can never get enough.

But, like everything else, *enough* always ends.

There's always a last kiss, last embrace, last goodbye. And so often we don't know when it's coming. Sarah's son had no idea that when he brought her to the hospital it was their last morning together, their last words. He couldn't have known that he'd be going home without her.

Which begs the question: Should we reach for the big and the bold at every turn or is there something worthwhile in the small, simple moments, those seemingly insignificant glimpses of this life that radiate true joy?

Sam trails light kisses down my neck.

I exhale gratifyingly as we fall onto the bed, entwined in each other as if time doesn't exist outside this room.

Afterward, he holds me. A tremble works through him.

"We're going to need sustenance," he says, stroking my back in gentle circles.

"Sustenance sounds very good," I say, deliriously contented, thinking this is it—*this* is all I'll ever need.

"Coffee?"

"I thought you'd never ask."

In the shower, it occurs to me that this incessant need for us to be close is about more than lust and passion. Not that I'm not fully subscribed to the idea of insatiable desire—I am. But truly? I think this is about Sam and me trying to touch those places in each other that have been cold for so long.

Which makes me wonder how many women Sam has bedded in the last ten years.

Not that it's any of my business. I've had sex with my fair share of men, but that's all it ever was. A physical transaction between consenting adults. One that made me feel powerful, in control.

But, of course, I could never fill the void Sam left.

The idea of other women in his bed conjures images I'd rather not entertain. Still, I can't expect that he's been chaste, and if that's true, did he ever have feelings for someone else? Has anyone mattered to him?

Did he ever unleash the kind of desire he showed me last night?

I let the hot water cascade over me as I consider the fact that he walked out of that LA bar without a word, without giving me a chance to decide. I'm not even sure how I would have reacted, to have been on a date only to look up and see Sam.

Would I have run into his arms? Socked him in the jaw? Told him to go to hell?

After the shower, I dress in a pair of Sam's sweats and an oversize gray sweater before I find him on the porch. Bullet's curled up on the bench too, eyes half slits like she isn't sure if she should sleep or if she should keep watch just in case something is about to happen that she doesn't want to miss.

I take a seat next to Sam and his dog as he wraps a thick blanket around me, then hands me a mug of coffee. "One sugar, right?"

I smile, tucking my feet under my body. "Right."

We sit like that, staring out across the pasture where three horses graze. It's one of those perfect moments you wish you could wrap in a silk box and carry with you forever. And for me, that's possible, but for Sam, this will fade like so many of his other memories that will never wash over him in the vibrant colors I experience.

I quell the memory magic shifting inside of me.

Not because I don't want to commit every detail of every second spent with Sam, but I've collected enough memories in the last twenty-four hours to last a lifetime, and maybe it's okay to let some fade into the recesses of my mind and heart. Maybe that makes the others even brighter.

I sip at my coffee, appreciating how Sam and I don't need to talk.

We're comfortable in the silence, one that allows me to live fully in the present. To admire the ranch's impossible green fields and ageless trees, a ranch he won because he was lucky. I pray his luck hasn't run out, that Mayahuel will take notice of his gift, that somehow, someway, Sam's healthy and whole. And the shadow is merely that, a tiny thing not big enough to intrude on our lives.

After my last sip of coffee, I ask the question that's been gnawing at me, "Has there been anyone else?"

Sam visibly tenses, throwing me a side-glance before he clears his throat. "Other women?"

I nod, suddenly wishing I hadn't asked. It doesn't matter. Does it?

He leans forward, plants his elbows on his knees. His gaze narrows as he stares into his empty mug. "No one that's mattered." He looks up at me. "You must know that."

I go over, sit on Sam's lap, and rest my head on his shoulder. I love the way his scruff feels on my cheek. The way his arms automatically encircle my waist. The way his heart belongs to only me.

"Well," I say, grinning, "I am pretty extraordinary." I'm teasing of course, but seeing myself through Sam's eyes makes me feel beautiful, invincible, like the version he sees is who I truly am.

Sam laughs, signaling his agreement. Then, without warning, he stands, spilling me off his lap before catching me and pulling me into his chest. He kisses the top of my head and says, "Let's see how extraordinary you are on a horse."

28

An hour later, Sam's saddled two mares.

"This is Sadie," he says, stroking the black mane of a reddish horse with white markings—one on her chest looks like the shape of a star. "She's slow and old and won't give you any trouble."

"Hi, Sadie," I say, petting her nose in long, admiring strokes. "Don't listen to Sam. He's a barbarian who doesn't understand that you never call a woman old or slow."

"Sorry, girl," he whispers in Sadie's ear. "What I meant was that you're sure-footed and would never hurt Lily."

Sadie curls back her mouth to show us her big teeth before letting out a snort, and the last word on the matter.

Sam tries to help me into the stirrup when I shake him off. "I can do it."

"Still stubborn?"

I laugh. "Still independent." I settle into the saddle and after a two-minute tutorial on how to use the reins and how to position my feet, we head out.

Bits of sun poke through the gloomy clouds as we stroll side by side down a trail and into a thicket of trees.

Sam asks me questions as if we aren't intimately acquainted, but his inquiries are fair. He wants to map out the last ten years in a straight line he can follow. *How was medical school? Have you traveled? Do you like Los Angeles?*

Brutal, but doable. Not as much as I want to. Everything but the traffic.

For fifteen minutes, we make small but necessary talk, Sam leaning into every detail of my life, all while I try to circumvent the topic of medicine. I don't want to think about his potential prognosis or Sarah.

You can't save me.

Sadie is as sure-footed as Sam promised, to the point where I feel a connection to her that breeds trust and respect. There is something emboldening about riding a nine hundred–plus-pound animal—a powerful creature that could throw me or trample me anytime she wanted to, and yet her strength is in her gentility, in her graceful stride.

I can see why people feel healing here. It's not just the horses or the beautiful surroundings—it's also Sam, his effortless, calm, and confident demeanor that would sell for millions if he could bottle it.

"You're a natural," Sam says, staying close.

"Sadie's the natural one."

"So, you like it?" There's expectation, a certain sort of longing in the question. He wants me to love what he loves.

I pat Sadie's muscular neck and sigh. "It's actually relaxing."

"You sound surprised."

"I wasn't expecting—" there's a sharp pain in my chest and it makes me wonder if all these emotions, all this clarity has to do with breaking the spell that unveiled my heart "—to feel so connected to her."

"Horses are natural teachers," Sam says as we cross a churning creek. On the other side of the bank, the trees thicken, obscuring the sky.

We continue in silence another few minutes before I ask, "Is it enough, Sam?"

He gives me a quizzical look.

"I mean, this place. Is it enough to forget flying?"

Sam's eyebrows come together as he contemplates, never one to utter an unmeasured response. "It's not a comparison," he says. "I love all of this, Lily. But it's different." He shakes his head and rebalances his weight in the saddle. For the first time, I realize how damn good he looks on that horse, so natural, so open. So much a part of this landscape. "I still want to get my license," he goes on. "I just don't need it as a career anymore."

This is what Alonzo meant when he said *life had other plans*. And while most people struggle against the tide of life, Sam rode the wave.

I admire how he can switch gears and find new and meaningful joys without resentment. It makes me think about my own career, about how far away I've gotten from the reasons I went into medicine in the first place—to make a difference.

But the stress and pressure and capitalistic bullshit has eroded that intent.

And then there's Sarah and how much her death has changed me. It's as if a door inside of me was opened, one I didn't know existed, and I'm discovering new things about myself, softer, gentler places that I want to know more about.

We come to a steep, rocky trail that winds to the right, and just as I'm trying to figure out how the hell the horses are going to make that climb safely, Sam says, "We need to walk the rest of the way."

He quickly dismounts and I follow his lead, waiting as he ties the horses to a branch.

As we hike up the rock-strewn path, Sam breaks the silence. "Is being a doctor all you thought it would be?"

I knew this question was coming eventually, and I don't know if it's the fading light or the fact that these woods feel like their own private world, but the words work their up my throat and out of my mouth with surprising ease. "I killed someone, Sam."

He stops, turns to me.

There's concern in his eyes, a fiercely protective gaze. He wants to reach for me. I can see that. But he doesn't say anything. He doesn't need to. He's giving me the space to tell him more if I choose.

I continue walking and he follows, slowing his pace to match mine as I tell him about Sarah. As I draw the memory so close, I can smell it, taste it. I can touch the instruments, so cold and hard in my hand. I can hear the voices echoing through me. I don't diminish, I don't retreat.

I allow the memory magic to ebb and flow like ocean waves, and when I get to the end, to Sarah's last breath, I realize I'm crying.

Sam pulls me close, forcing both of us to a stop. His chest rises and falls with a sort of desperation that nearly breaks me. He says nothing because, of course, what's there to say? That it's okay, even when it's clearly not?

"I couldn't save her," I tell him through a sob.

He strokes my hair. "Lily, it wasn't your fault. The hospital even said so."

"Fault doesn't matter when someone is dead, Sam."

I lift my face to see him staring down at me. His eyes hold all the love and protection I'll ever need. "Lily," he whispers, "I'm so sorry."

A shiver works its way through me because I know what comes next. I'm going to tell Sam the secret I've been carrying for too long. I know it's the only way to reclaim myself, my truth.

"And when it was over," I say, choosing my words carefully, so as not to paint myself the victim. "I couldn't... I couldn't even find the courage to tell her son. I chickened out—I asked my attending to do it. I should have told him myself, Sam. She was *my* patient. I should have had the guts to own up. I ran. I ran into a stairwell and sat there blubbering endlessly."

Sam glances up to the top of the hill several yards away, then back to me. "I guarantee you," he says, "that man was in so much pain he wasn't paying attention to who told him or how it was said. And even if you had been the messenger, it wouldn't have changed anything."

"I owed him that," I argue. "It's my job."

He strokes his thumb across my chin. "You didn't kill her, Lil."

"But I couldn't save her!"

And I can't save you.

Fresh tears spill down my face, and as sick and tormented as I feel, it's also cathartic to admit these truths. To bring them into the light of day, to see that I'm still here. I'm still breathing.

"We can't control everything, Lil. I know you want to. Hell, you've always wanted to."

"Why can't we though?" I say, sniffling like a child.

A gentle breeze sweeps past us, rustling the trees' leaves.

"When I got sick," Sam says, "I figured some things out."

"Please don't tell me that life isn't fair."

A sad smile plays at the edges of his mouth. "I was going to tell you that life is a long string of surrenders and learning to let go."

The enormity of those simple words lands with a weight that feels too burdensome to shoulder. And yet I know it's true.

Surrender.

Whether it's people, places, our youth, our health.

Our hearts.

We're always in the process of letting go of something or someone that matters. And no amount of fighting, no amount of willful determination can ever change that.

"Like you let go of me." The words come without warning; they sound bitter without me intending them to.

Sam offers me a blank stare, one that tells me *I had to, I never wanted to.*

It was such a lousy, unfair thing for me to say. And just as I'm about to apologize, he takes my hand and guides me the last few yards to the top of the ridge. "We're here."

I look around at the shaded woods expectantly. "Okay?"

Sam's smiling when he walks me through a grove of trees that leads to a small grassy clearing. Five stone columns, about four feet tall, are constructed in a circle, and atop each, flowers—single stems, bouquets tied with string and velvet, each fixed with a pile of rocks. "What is all this?" I ask.

"I was hoping you could tell me," he says. "I think the flowers are from your farm."

I start to go over to check out things when Sam grips my waist from behind and whispers in my ear. "And for the record, Lily, I could never let you go."

29

The moment I step into the circle of stones I feel a familiar vibration—a pulse of energy that confirms Sam's guess—there's magic here.

At the first column, I find a single withered daisy fixed beneath a stone, but it's not enchanted so I move to the next—a few dried roses and then a trio of daffodils. None hold any magic.

Then I come to a small bouquet of four dried flowers tied with a tattered velvet ribbon. The moment I touch the blooms, I feel a silky thread of magic weaving between my ribs.

"It's a dream bouquet," I utter as I bring the delicate arrangement closer to my face.

"For what though?" Sam asks, but I'm not sure I can give him an answer.

Each enchanted spray is vastly different and arranged in a very precise way, an alchemical process to produce whatever results the person desires. And that's what Sam's asking—*what's the purpose of this specific dream bouquet?*

I study the pink impatiens, the white peony, the red poppy, and the single pinkweed stem, an odd choice for dream magic.

"Impatiens are for ardent love, and they also mean tired of waiting," I say. I trace my fingers over the paper-thin peony petals. "This is for protection and prosperity, but also beauty and anger."

"Isn't the anger part kind of contradictory?" Sam asks. I don't respond. I'm too lost in the magic of these dried-up blooms that, in my estimation, are likely decades' old. While many flowers would have disintegrated in the elements, our family magic protects them from that fate, preserving them for many years.

"The pinkweed is for restoration," I add, "and the poppy is used to answer a perplexing question."

"How so?" Sam asks.

I stretch my memory, wishing my mom was here. She's the dream expert, but I know enough to remember that "If you write down a question on a piece of paper in blue ink, fold it into the seedpod, and then place the poppy under your pillow," I say, "you'll get your answer."

Sam stuffs his hands into his jeans' pockets. "So, someone was tired of waiting for an answer and dreamed one instead?"

"Someone in love," I offer. I can feel traces of memory in each petal, each stem: the hope, and joy, and then the utter disappointment. "But whoever used this, didn't like the answer they got."

Sam looks disappointed. "Are the flowers always right?"

I nod, lost in my own thoughts. "Maybe they were in love with someone who didn't love them back or…" My voice trails off because there's no way to guess what the question was, only that there was magic in finding the answer.

"But it couldn't have been too big of a question," I go on,

"because only one poppy was used, and a true divination requires way more than that."

"I thought divination was against the rules," Sam says.

I twist my mouth to the side, considering. "It is. That kind of power can deplete our crops, which is why none of us try to see the future."

Sam slides behind me, wraps his arms around my waist, and rests his chin on my head. "Why do you think someone left the bouquet here?"

"No idea." But inside a voice is escalating. *This isn't a wish. This is a memorial.*

Beauty. Anger. Ardent love. Protection. Tired of waiting.

My memory magic twists around my heart painfully, until I feel the anger in this bouquet, the desperation, the tenderness. Each aligning with my own intense love for Sam, of anger that he could be sick again, of utter desperation to save him.

My insides burn and my palms turns sweaty.

Sam releases me like he can sense all of this. "You okay?"

"I can feel their sadness," I say. "Not completely, more like something way off in the distance."

"Jesus, I'm sorry."

I force a breezy smile. "I mean, you couldn't have known, but how did you guess that these came from my family?"

Sam reaches into his pocket and produces a card from our farm. There are no words, no phone numbers, only an illustration of the agave plant, the symbol my family has used for generations. "I found this here."

A stream of sunlight pokes through the clouds. Shadows fall across half of Sam's face, worn with time and worry. And I wasn't here for any of it.

All the years I thought he didn't love me dissolve into a faraway past that suddenly feels like it never existed but for my nightmares.

Which only remind me of my dream of Sam's corpse. Of Sarah's voice. *You can't save me.*

A challenge from the grave, one that breeds new fury. That's when the idea takes shape, nibbling at my conscience.

Growing in its defiance and boldness.

Maybe it's always been there, something hungry in the shadows. But I've refused to feed it, afraid to even think it. And as much as I try to ignore it, it's already here, forcing itself into the world.

You can save him.

These four words send my pulse soaring. And suddenly I feel like I'm drowning in *what ifs*. What if it doesn't work? What if things go wrong?

It's too dangerous. Too risky.

But this is Sam. My Sam. And if there's even a chance…

He sets a warm hand on the small of my back, a tiny gesture that makes me ache all over. I lean into his touch, wishing we could stay in these woods forever, terrified that the moment we leave, everything could come undone.

I pluck a single enchanted peony petal before he notices and place it in my pocket.

As I set the flowers back onto the column, their last traces of *desperation* cling to me.

I know what I have to do.

30

By the time I get back home, it's dark.

I hated leaving Sam this afternoon, which was made worse when he pulled me into the shower with him to "get the horse stench off." And then again when we lay naked in his bed afterward, watching the last of the day's light vanish into nothingness, when he traced his fingers up and down my body like I was a map he was desperate to read.

"I need to go," I told him, laughing.

He pulled me on top of him. "Okay."

"This isn't fair," I said, pressing my hands into his solid chest.

"I thought we established that life isn't fair."

"You're a smart-ass."

He grinned. "When will you be back?"

"Tomorrow."

"I'll make sure to have groceries by then."

"Good because I can't eat spaghetti for breakfast again."

Sam laughs. The sound of it fills me up. "And maybe a few pounds of green grapes?"

My smile comes quickly. He remembers my childhood obsession with them, as if the world couldn't turn unless I had a handful of grapes.

I wish I could make this last—the banter, the humor, the ease of conversation without the black cloud that is always hovering over us.

A cloud I could dispel.

Maybe.

I thought about it all the way back to the ranch, examining my memories, the intense magical process required. I tried to talk myself out of it, but the moment I realized that there was a chance to save Sam's future, I fell deeper into the possibilities.

Yes, I could wait for his results, but it would be too late by then. If the cancer is back, that knowledge, that trauma would interfere with my memory magic, and for this to work, everything must be pure.

There is zero room for error.

"Will you do something for me?" I asked Sam earlier, knowing the second I did this, there would be no going back.

"Name it."

"I want to memorize you."

I saw the dawning over his face before he said, "You mean..."

"A complete memory we can relive together." A suffocating guilt came over me as I spoke the lie into existence.

We would never live this moment together.

This memory is for another purpose, and once he understood, once it was all said and done, he wouldn't hold it against me. I hoped.

I held the peony petal, clinging to its meaning, *ardent love.* My magic usually requires creating a concoction to be inhaled or ingested, but that's only if it's for others.

Sam brought his thick brows together, and with the sincerity of a soldier going off to war, he said, "Okay, what do I do?"

"You don't have to do anything," I told him. "Except don't distract me."

"Um…"

"Yeah, I know. Impossible."

A teasing smile tugged at his mouth. "I'll do my best."

I tried to record a memory for Sam once, but I wasn't practiced, and it wasn't as complete as I wanted it to be. What I've learned is that shared and amplified emotions are the key for the memory to be perfectly preserved.

Still, once I used this moment for my plan, it would be erased from my own mind and heart, a tangible thing I will have given away.

A small price to pay.

Effortlessly, naturally, we began to make love.

I called on my magic, allowing it to weave between us, through us. It emerged with unrelenting passion to witness the way Sam held me with his gaze, the way his warm, calloused hands clung to my body, the way I opened myself to him. We moved in blissful synchrony—the scent of wood and flame floating across the bed.

How we collided in pleasure just as he called out my name.

And when we were done, I kissed him goodbye and took the memory with me.

Now as I drive the last mile toward the hacienda, I feel a hollow cold spreading through me, luring me into the painful past.

It reminds me of Sarah, of how I failed her, of a career where I'm confronted with both life and death.

There's no rhyme or reason as to why some souls are granted access to this world and why others leave too early. And anyone who's experienced the latter knows the painful unanswerable question that always follows: *Why?*

As I pull down the long drive and park the car, I repeat the same mantra over and over. *I don't want to ask why. I don't want to ask why.*

I won't. I have a plan.

"It's about time!"

I startle as I glance out my window to see Lantana standing there in a long black T-shirt that barely covers her ass. She's rubbing the chill off her arms. "A little faster?" she says.

I open the truck door and slip out. "Well, maybe you should wear more than a T-shirt in January."

"I never get to be a grub. Not all of us have pajamas as our uniform, so cut me some slack."

She hooks her arm in mine, and we make our way inside where a fire is already blazing in the main living room. "Where's Mom and Tía?" I ask.

"Out to dinner," she says, getting comfortable on the sofa. She pats the cushions. "Tell me every single detail and don't leave anything out."

"I might need a drink."

"Way ahead of you." She grabs a bottle of tequila off a side table and pours us each a shot. "To love," she says, raising her glass. "And great sex." She raises her eyebrows inquisitively, a gesture that asks me to verify.

"I can neither confirm nor deny," I say with a small laugh that earns me a dramatic eye roll.

We each take a shot, and when my bones are warmed and my skin feels buzzy, I tell her everything, minus the intimate particulars. She listens with rapt attention, nodding at all the right places, gasping at others, and smiling when I reach the end. But I can't tell her it's a happy ending. Not yet.

"So," she says, "you've forgiven him."

I nod. Then reach for another shot of tequila.

"Well, how is this going to work?" she asks, eyes wide with curiosity and delight. "If he's here and you're in LA."

My insides coil tightly. I frankly hadn't even thought that far. All I want to do is make sure Sam *has* a future. And I'm going to need Lana's help and I'm not sure she'll give it. Not when I tell her what has to be done.

With the memory petal in my pocket, I hug a cushion to my chest. "I need something from you. Something you're not going to want to give but—"

"Shit."

"Hey! I haven't even asked yet."

"I can tell by your face and all that magic buzzing around you that it's a terrible idea, whatever it is."

I sit up, fixing my gaze on hers. Her auburn hair looks warmer, deeper in the firelight. "I love him, Lana."

These four words work like a spell, changing her expression almost immediately. She goes from adamantly closed off to soft and open.

"And," I add, hating that I even have to say the words, "he might be sick." I tell her what I know, and with each word, she deflates more and more.

I can see that she's crushed for me, for the potential destruction of the elusive happily-ever-after. "Lil, no."

Tears prick my eyes but I refuse to be swallowed by my pain. There is too much work to do.

She places her hand on my leg, gently. "It might be nothing." And while her words say one thing, her tone says another. She knows that clinging to hope isn't enough to make it reality.

With a shuddering breath, I say, "I… I can't lose him again."

She's nodding. "So what do you need my help with?"

"I want to do a divination."

Her hand withdraws immediately, like I'm a flame about to burn her. "Lil." She pauses, a beat and then another. "You know how dangerous that is. It could deplete the magic in the crops, and with the celebration coming up... If anything went wrong all those hopes and dreams—"

"Would die." I feel sick saying the words, but what choice do I have if there's a chance that I could save Sam?

"We'll do it right," I insist. "Nothing will go wrong."

A harsh whisper surges inside of me. *Like nothing went wrong in the OR?*

I ignore it, shoving the wicked thought deep into the darkest recesses of my mind.

Lana says, "What good does a divination do you? It'll only tell you his result a week early."

Here it is. The moment of truth. "Lana, I don't want to know the results. I want to change them."

She stiffens, and just as she opens her mouth to ask what I know is coming next, I add, "I need to do a memory divination."

She shrinks back, looking horrified as shadows dance across her glass-like skin. "Lily," she whispers. I see the gears in her mind turning. I wait for the dawning, for that moment when she realizes what I'm asking. And if it were anyone else, I'd expect them to leap off the couch, to go into a bit of hysterics, but Lana is steadfast, a master of emotion. She closes her eyes, takes a long, deep breath and says, "You want to infuse a divination with a memory strong enough to manipulate the future."

"And I need your help to do it." It's Lana who must select the blooms carefully before asking their permission. The power is in the flowers' consent. "If I can use a moment with enough love and abundance," I add, "then the energy, the essence of that can be his future. Not sickness. Right?"

"Technically, yes." I see the war going on behind her eyes, her desire to help me, and to also keep me safe. "Jesus, Lily. It's...it's..."

"Risky, I know, but we'll do it right. And all you need to do is give me the right flowers."

"Except that we've never performed that kind of a spell. I've only ever read about it."

Same. When I was a kid, I used to gather up the old journals of my ancestors and read through their spells, their successes, near misses, and utter failures. "Lana, I know I'm asking a lot."

"You could lose your magic," she reminds me.

"I know."

One of the consequences of doing something this forbidden is the possibility of losing our own connection to the magic we've been gifted. I can't imagine a life without it, but more importantly, I can't imagine a world in which Sam doesn't exist.

We sit in silence. The only sound is the crackling fire and some slow music someone must have left on in a faraway room.

"Are you sure he's worth that?" she asks.

"Yes." There's zero hesitation. "I'd give up my memory magic and more if it means Sam lives."

Lana gets to her feet gracefully, goes over to the fireplace, and leans against the mantel, keeping her back to me. I watch her lithe form, her shoulders rise and fall with quickening breaths. I expect for a truckload of logic to be hurled at me full force. For the list of convincing reasons that this is a worse than bad idea.

But logic and reason have nothing to do with love.

She stares into the flames as if there are answers to be found there, or maybe she's remembering what I already know, that divination requires fire and pain.

I hold my breath, twisting my fingers, wondering how I could ever pull this off without her. The answer comes swiftly: *you can't.*

Finally, Lana turns to me. Her gaze locks with mine.

"We'll do it tonight."

31

It's close to midnight.

The time Lana and I agreed to meet at the barn. A terrible guilt grips me, making me nauseous and clammy. How can I do something this risky, this forbidden while my mom sleeps totally unaware that I'm breaking a cardinal rule?

For Sam, I remind myself. I'd feel infinitely worse if I did nothing. Besides, there is power to movement, to keeping my focus on the task at hand, to stop me from thinking too much or maybe feeling too much.

It's the only way I know to fix what's broken.

Just as I'm heading out to meet Lana, my phone vibrates with a call.

It's Harlow.

My first thought is an alarm bell—*she's having the baby*—but the words that come rushing out of her mouth are "What in the hell is going on with you?"

I pause. I feel the blood drain from my face.

She knows. Shit! She knows.

She's somehow figured out the divination plan. How can

that be? Our typical sensory connections all but dried up the moment Harlow got pregnant.

"Hello to you too," I say.

She exhales loudly. "I had a dream, and when I woke up, I could feel that something was up with you, something painful and also lovely and...hold on." She lowers her voice, and I can hear her feet hitting the floor. She whispers, "I don't want to wake Ben."

Boundless relief spreads through me. Okay, she doesn't know anything. Or at least nothing damning. "Can we talk later?" I ask her.

"We need to talk now."

"Har, it's almost midnight."

"You're not sleeping."

"How do you know?"

"Because your voice is awake, and you usually sound like a zombie when you're tired."

I roll my eyes and sit on the edge of the bed. "Fine. What was the dream?"

"You were on a horse. Weird, right?"

"Mmm-hmm."

"Anyway, the horse was running fast along some beach. You looked so happy, Lil. And there was someone in the background, someone trying to catch up to you."

My heart sinks.

"You never slowed down," she goes on. "Then the horse bucked and threw you into the ocean. You looked like a lifeless ragdoll spinning through the air, and just as you came out of the water for a breath, a wave crashed down."

God, I'm in no mood to break down the meaning of her dream. Is it a warning? Does it have to do with Sam or the divination? "Did I drown?" I ask.

"I woke up before I could find out. My heart was racing,

and I could feel all these intense emotions coming from your direction. That's why I'm calling. Are you all right?"

"I'm fine."

"Lil, I need more than that."

I go over to the window, where the full moon sits low in the sky. I stare out at the flower fields, knowing Harlow won't let this go. I have to give her a crumb. But what? Should I tell her about my grief over Sarah or my agony over Sam?

Something painful and also lovely.

I reach into my jeans' pocket and remove the flower that carries Sam's memory. His touch vibrates through me and before I can even consider the words, they tumble from my mouth. "I fell in love."

"What!" Her voice is a decibel shy of a shriek. "When? How? With who?"

"Har?"

"Don't you dare tell me you can't talk about it."

"I'm so tired, and I do promise to tell you everything soon, but right now, I'm just trying to figure things out. I just need a little space." *And my nervous system is on overdrive because of what I'm about to do, which could be the reason you're sensing any of this, and no way can I tell you that. And I'm scared. Scared of how much this is going to hurt.*

I suddenly wish she were here. Harlow is the most powerful of us all with her ability to enhance magic, bending it to her will. Maybe with her help, I wouldn't have to burn to see and change Sam's future.

All divinations require flames, and once I set the enchanted bouquet ablaze, I'll have to hold on to it until I see the future and insert the memory.

Only then can I let go.

"Lil, you know I'm here for you, just like you were there for me when I was struggling with Ben. Remember?"

"How could I forget?" I laugh lightly. My sister was willing to dissolve all her memories of him just to make the pain of loving him go away.

"Just tell me this," she says, "does this have to do with the creepy corpse dream? Was this guy the secret?"

"It's complicated, but yeah, he was definitely a part of all that."

Harlow goes silent before she says, "Are you sure you're okay?"

"I am. And..." My voice cracks unintentionally. "I know you're there for me."

"Good. Okay, then I'm going to take myself and the kraken back to bed, but only if you swear on your life that you'll take care of that heart of yours and that I'm going to get all the details very soon."

"I promise and sorry my emotions woke you."

"It's fine," she says with a sigh. "I'm just so bummed I won't be there for the celebration. I mean, she isn't even due for another three weeks. I could fly in tomorrow and be gone two days from now. It would be fine."

"Harlow, the nearest hospital is an hour away."

"What if Mayahuel goes quiet on me?" Harlow nearly whispers. "What if she doesn't give the baby a name at all?"

"That's not going to happen."

"What if it does?"

"Then, we'll name her Kraken."

Harlow laughs quietly. "Perfect."

I've always loved the farm at night—the sharp shift in moods. Everything that's obvious and bright during the day turns mysterious and cryptic once darkness falls. Maybe it's because magic flourishes at night. Roots dig deeper, stems stretch higher, leaves and petals gleam brighter.

Sweet, earthy aromas fill the crisp air as Lana and I walk down a row of gladiolas, irises, hyacinth, and daffodils.

"So how is this going to work?" I ask, following behind her, clicking my flashlight on and off, off and on.

She glances over her shoulder. "We've been over this."

"I know, but I want to make sure I don't make any mistakes."

"I'm going to find the right flowers," she says, "or I should say willing flowers. Maybe pinkweed—they're usually very agreeable. Eucharis lily would be perfect for its powers of enchantment, but we aren't growing any right now."

"How do you know?"

"I asked the flowers."

I nod, thinking what a rare gift it is to commune with nature the way Lana can.

"So I made a list based on what's growing," she says, stopping midstride with her hands on her hips as she turns in a circle like she's looking for something. "We need blue rose," she says.

A flower for attaining the impossible.

I feel a bolt of panic that makes me want to run for the hills. But I won't give in. I can't keep running, thinking I can distance myself from grief or pain. I have to face this even if I'm struggling to find the courage I need.

"We also need a lavender rose for its enchanting properties," Lana says as she stoops near a small patch of clary sage. The purple flowering herb is known for its ability to clear the mind and lift the spirit. I watch as Lana leans closer to the plant, whispering and bending her ear toward its long stem. Then, with the care of a finely skilled surgeon, she clips the stem and hands it to me. "You'll need to breathe this in right before the divination—it'll help with clarity."

For the next few minutes, we walk silently, Lana repeating

the same gestures until we've collected a lavender rose bud, bloodroot for its powers of protection, Devil's Eye for pleasurable memories, and foxglove for divination.

I consider the countless variations of magic, the alchemical process of weaving together the right spell for the right purpose, as I stare across the moonlit fields. All these flowers carry the promise of hope, each growing their magic in the soil beneath our feet, soil blessed by the goddess herself.

When I was a little girl, I could feel the vibration of magic floating from the earth, fluttering around my legs like tiny butterfly wings. I could almost hear the flowers' whispers. Then, as I got older, I lost the ability to connect so easily.

It reminds me of a painful truth: *time is a monster with the power to erode all sense of magic and wonder.*

We make our way past the moon garden, a place guarded by the Hylocereus tree, a thirty-foot night-blooming cactus also known as the Night Queen. She's always been here, extending her angular arms up toward the sky like she's caught in the middle of an ancient dance. Her waxy honeyed blooms practically glow, but as beautiful as she is, her nightly flowers are only temporary. They will die in a matter of hours.

Still, she feels powerful. Unstoppable.

Once we arrive at a small clearing at the edge of the farm, Lana turns to me. Her eyes ask the question she won't say aloud. *Are you sure?*

No. Yes. Maybe.

With a hesitant nod, she says, "Did you bring it?"

I reach into my pocket for the boot lighter. The same one I bought in a Tijuana convenience store, which now feels a million miles away.

She repeats what I already know. Maybe it's her nerves or maybe she just wants to make sure I am hyper aware and clear on her instructions.

"Burn the bouquet while it's still in your hands," she says. "Hold it as long as possible, focusing on the request to see Sam's future."

My heart hammers in my chest, reminding me that if I let go too soon, I won't be able to insert Sam's memory into the divination. I won't be able to secure his future.

"The flames will be unbearable," she warns.

Perhaps a security measure to make divination so painful most will never attempt it.

But if I do this right, the fire won't leave scars; I'll only feel the pain. And I can do that. I can withstand the agony.

I bring the clary to my nose and take a deep breath, allowing its essence to wash over and through me.

"Lana?"

"Yeah?"

"Please don't interfere. No matter what."

Then, with the bouquet clutched in one hand and Sam's memory in the other, I open the lighter, steel my nerves, and set the flowers ablaze.

32

I stare into the flames, watching as they grow, burning the flowers.

A terrible heat consumes me as I speak the words of divination in my mind.

Show me Sam's future.

There is too much hope in these words, too much want and need.

For a breath, I want to take them back, but the world is already falling away in dreamlike fashion and a dark tunnel is materializing before me. A long and narrow space that feels both threatening and welcoming.

I hear Sam's laughter, his voice echoing back to me. There's no shape to his words. No shape to any of this and I suddenly feel small and weak, unfit for the task.

The air ripples and sways.

It would be easy to pretend I'm simply in a dream, but I'm not. I'm straddling two worlds, never too far from the knowledge that the flames are rising and expanding, drawing closer to my hand.

Closer to a pain point I'm not sure I can bear.

Fear washes over me like a wave of nausea, and I feel a terrible sense of urgency. For the magic to reveal what I want... what I *need* to know.

The fire finally reaches for me, twisting up my arms, burning across my skin. The pain is agonizing. Shocking.

Don't let go.

Don't let go.

I scream. A horrific, animalistic sound that terrifies me.

Then I see him. Sam. He's standing in the middle of the tunnel, backlit by a pale white light.

He turns and looks over his shoulder at me. A wan smile that tells me nothing.

"Sam!"

"Let go, Lily." His voice moves through me, a warning I don't understand.

I won't let go.

Show me his future!

I reach for him, thinking that if I can just touch him, I can prove myself worthy of the divination. But he's too far away.

And the tunnel is narrowing.

No!

I remember the memory flower still in the palm of my hand. I need to throw it into the tunnel. I hesitate. Is it too soon? Too late? I curl my fist closed around the peony petal, drawing my magic up to activate the memory.

For a single instant, all the pain ebbs. I'm back in Sam's bed, reliving this morning.

I feel his warmth. His tenderness. His love.

This is the world I want to live in. This is the one that should be his future.

The images begin to change quickly, spiraling forward with a velocity I can't grasp.

Stay with me. Don't go. Please.

As if begging has ever influenced magic.

The memory vanishes, and in its wake is the unforgettable pain. The flames burn through me with a new vengeance.

Another primal scream tears from my lungs. *I can't do this. I'm not strong enough.*

"Lily!" Lana's voice ricochets from far away.

I can't. Not yet. I need to drop the memory petal into the vision, but I can't move. I can't seem to find my footing. It's like I'm caught in quicksand, sinking and burning, burning and sinking.

And where is Sam's future? Why can't I see it?

Every cell in my body is screaming, raging against the anguish.

I can't breathe. Can't hold on. Can't let go.

Lana shouts, "Stop!"

I can't.

Like prying a charm from a deathly grip, I uncurl one finger at a time.

It's the fury that drives me, that gives me the strength to blow the memory petal into the vision like an unspoken wish.

Everything falls silent.

The pain goes dormant. And for the briefest of moments, I feel Sam's arms around me, holding me, keeping me safe.

His voice comes to me in a slow, painful whisper, "I'll always love you."

And then everything goes black.

33

I see Mayahuel.

She's there in the misty distance, near the moon garden. An ethereal figure with a translucent veil draped over her face.

The air smells of orange blossom and lilac.

The world is still and silent. There's no pain. No suffering. Only a vague recollection of what brought me here.

Sam. The divination.

The goddess sweeps back the veil. I meet her gaze. It takes a moment to absorb her beauty. Her flawless complexion. Her exquisite features. A goddess once hidden in the farthest recesses of the universe who managed to escape.

I take one breath. Two.

"Mayahuel?" My voice is hoarse, like I've inhaled too much smoke. I glance down at my hands and arms. There are no flames, no scars to tell the story of what I endured.

She walks toward me, a graceful creature in a gossamer gown whose feet don't seem to touch the ground.

Is she here to tell me Sam's future?

When she reaches me, her astonishingly dark eyes rest on

my face. Her gaze is both soft and penetrating, a goddess to be loved and feared. "Lily."

She says my name with near reverence, a name she gave me so long ago.

My heart fills with panic, dread, hope. "Yes?"

"You chose wrong."

I wake up on the ground.

I'm trembling uncontrollably. Sweat trickles down my neck and spine as a sickly panic floods my body. I roll over and vomit into a pile of ashes. The divination bouquet. Gone, burned to nothing.

"Lily!" Lana is kneeling next to me, holding my hair back as I retch a second time. She's cursing, saying words that make no sense because I'm still a million miles under the earth with Mayahuel.

You chose wrong.

Tears rolls down my face, cold and bitter.

Lana's rubbing my back in slow circles. "It's okay," she says more than once. It's not. I can feel it.

Sluggishly, I sit up. I drop my head into my hands, squeezing my eyes closed, but I can still see. The tunnel. Sam. Mayahuel.

"Lily…"

Dread gives way to anger. I didn't see Sam's future. I merely threw away a memory I can no longer remember.

I open my eyes, meeting my cousin's gaze reluctantly. I don't want to hear how I failed. I don't want to know what I've lost. I don't want to face the consequences.

Her eyes are wide, her mouth is quivering. "Let's go home."

"What happened?"

She shakes her head, takes hold of my arm to help me stand. I take a wide step back. "Tell me!"

"I tried to stop you," she begins. "Why didn't you just let the goddamn bouquet go?"

"Lana, please." A sob works its way up my throat. "What happened?"

"The flowers..." Her voice comes out painstakingly slow, sharp edged like a rusted blade. "Their magic. It's all gone."

I go cold all over, refusing to accept what she's telling me. Still, I know it's true. I *knew* this was the risk. And I went ahead with it anyway.

I stumble-rush down the hill toward the night garden, needing to see the destruction with my own eyes. Lana is right behind me.

Maybe it's not that bad. Maybe...

I come to a grinding halt.

The Hylocereus's once-powerful arms are shrunken and shriveled. Her shimmering white blooms are now sickly gray and wilted. She's nothing more than a wasted version of a used-to-be queen.

I scan the rest of the garden, hoping the devastation didn't reach beyond, but the moonflowers, the jasmine, and primrose— they're all ash-colored. Nothing more than rotted memories.

I can't breathe, can't think. I'm suffocating with guilt, dread, and a fear that feels too big to ever contain.

Lana stares at me wordlessly.

"It's not your fault," I manage, although the words hit a false note.

Her expression is rigid, cut from stone. "We have to wake—"

"Lana, please," I plead. "Maybe it's only the moon garden." And we can fix it. We can bring the flowers back. I can bring Sarah back.

The desperation is familiar, half crazed and so reminiscent

of the night Sarah died. The utter helplessness, the remorse, and just like then, all I can think is *I did this. I did this.*

"Did you at least see his future?" Lana asks, her voice threaded with what feels like the last traces of hope, but she doesn't have the knowledge of the last few minutes, when the world caved and my life shattered. She doesn't yet know all of it and for a moment I envy that.

I shake my head numbly.

"So this was all for fucking nothing?" she cries.

I don't blame her for being pissed. For needing to spend that anger on the one person who fucked it all up. "Maybe, maybe only the moon garden died," I say, realizing how pitiful those words sound. "Maybe the divination didn't deplete the rest of…"

She presses her fingers into her eyes, takes a long breath. "It didn't deplete the flowers. It killed them, Lily. Killed!"

I freeze. I'm not sure if I should scream or laugh like a woman descending into total madness. She's exaggerating, painting a woeful picture. "We should go look," I say. "Make sure… I mean we can't see the whole farm from here and maybe—"

"Lily," she says, cutting me off. "I'm already sure."

"How?"

"Because I heard them dying."

34

Everything happens in slow succession, like winding a jack-in-the-box, waiting for it to spring.

With each turn, I fall further into despair. This is no longer about Sam. This is about my family, our magic, our vow to protect love and beauty. A vow that I broke.

Lana and I walk in painful silence back to the hacienda.

You chose wrong.

Evidenced by the dreary fields, the lifeless roses, the withered sunflowers, the sagging hydrangeas. What was once a thriving sea of magic is now reduced to a field of corpses.

Once Mom and Rosa are awake, once I assure them that everyone is okay, at least, to some degree, we go into the upstairs study, a small space that boasts prized collections like first edition books, antique globes, old stone busts, and other miscellaneous artifacts from another time.

"What's so important you had to wake us at one in the morning?" Mom asks as she lowers herself onto a floral-patterned settee and adjusts her robe over her legs.

Rosa stays on her feet, scowling, arms crossed over her chest. A defiant pose that tells me she's ready to strike if need be.

I avoid Lana's gaze, afraid I'll shatter into a million pieces if I look at her. I made her an accomplice, and now I worry that she might never forgive me.

My family stares at me expectantly as I force the words out of my mouth as quickly as possible. "I tried to do a divination," I say. "I failed. And now the flowers are...dead."

There.

The worst has been spoken, laid at my mother's and aunt's feet.

For a beat, there is silence, the calm before the storm, and then the room erupts into a flurry of emotion and questions and agonizing truths that I'd rather not tell. I have no choice but to own up to it, because I did this, and if there is any way to salvage the farm, my family needs to know everything.

Except I can't bear to tell them about Mayahuel's words: *you chose wrong.*

What good would such an obvious message do now?

I expect my mom and aunt to launch into a how-to-fix-it plan, but they don't. They do something worse. They look at me resigned. Empty. Betrayed.

Mom's on her feet, pacing, her gaze locked on the stone floor. I'm surprised when she doesn't ask about Sam, about how someone could be worth all of this, but her attention is on the immediate destruction. I have no doubt those questions about him, about my breaking heart, will come later. "Why didn't you come to us first?" she asks.

"You wouldn't have helped me." My voice is small like a child's. In the dimness of the study, my reasoning for the divination feels so clearly wrong. If it had worked, if I had secured Sam's future, would I still feel this way? Would the cost have been worth it?

Rosa glares at Lana. "I can't believe you did this. With no regard for anyone, for…" She closes her eyes and takes a deep breath.

Lana holds her head high, a gesture that aims for confidence. She looks anything but. "I thought we could handle it."

"Well, you thought wrong, didn't you?" Rosa chides.

"And now the celebration," Mom says evenly. "All those flowers, those hopes and desires…gone. Our vow to the goddess…" Her voice trails off. I know what she meant to say, *broken*.

She's right.

Our celebration is a sacred tradition, when we form a union and ask Mayahuel for her blessing. It's a quiet and tender moment that has always felt like a renewal. And now that's gone along with the dreams that my mom and aunt have been tending all year.

I destroyed it all with one decision.

Rosa walks to the door.

"Where are you going?" Lana asks.

"I need to see the damage."

A minute later, we're outside. A death march down row after row of lifeless flowers. Mom stoops every few steps, cradling the stems, the destruction of it all. It hurts to see her in such pain, to know that I'm the cause of it.

Rosa turns in a circle, tears holding at the edge of her eyes. "I can't hear them. I can't hear—" her voice falters and the tears fall "—anything."

"So how do we fix this?" Lana asks. Her tone treads cautiously.

"Some things can't be fixed," Rosa growls.

Mom shoots her sister a sympathetic glance. "Camilla and Dahlia will be here in a few hours." She pauses, rubs her forehead, "We will try to use our collective powers, but there's no precedent for this."

I stare at her confused. "I'm not the first to try divination. I mean, the flowers have been depleted before." It's how we learned about the risks in the first place.

"These crops aren't depleted," Rosa says angrily. "They're dead."

If only I had listened to Lana when she begged me to let the bouquet go. Those few precious seconds might have made a difference.

"I know I screwed up," I say. "I thought I could do it, that I could change Sam's future, and..."

"If you had come to me," Mom says, "I would have told you it was impossible. To manipulate a future takes more power, more magic than you and Lana have."

Her words sting, yet I can see the curiosity in her eyes—the details she wants to understand about Sam, about our love. But that's not the most pressing concern right now.

"I'm so sorry," I cry. "I'll do anything to make this right."

"We might not be able to make it right at all," Rosa says. "Do you understand?" Before I can answer, she kneels, closes her eyes, and presses her hands into the soil. "Lana, help me. Do you feel any bit of magic?"

I watch as my cousin and aunt search for a pulse, for any sign of life at all. There isn't any—even I can feel the barrenness, the desolation. As if the thread that binds us all has been cut.

I don't know how long we stand in the darkness, searching for a hope that's been extinguished. Eventually we make our way back to the house.

When we get to the courtyard garden, Mom pulls me aside while Lana and Rosa head inside.

The dim garden lights cast shadows across her face. "I didn't want to believe it," she says.

"What do you mean?"

"I dreamed of a huge fire," she says, hesitating for an unbearable moment before she adds, "one that burned the farm to the ground. And you were there, you were the one lighting the blaze."

Her last words are a whisper, one that fills me with both shame and revulsion.

"Please forgive me," I say.

Mom looks away. "Let's hope Mayahuel can forgive."

"If anyone should understand, it's her," I say. "Even she sacrificed everything for love."

Mom's gaze meets mine, cold and unpleasant. "No, Lily. She sacrificed *herself*. Nothing more."

35

I spend the next couple of hours wandering the farm, replaying my mom's comment in my mind. She's right.

The goddess sacrificed *herself*. Nothing more.

Mayahuel was willing to break, to die in order to protect beauty and love. And so, when all hope was lost, she transformed into a beautiful agave plant.

A choice that gave her eternal life.

I place one foot in front of the other halfheartedly, feeling sick, broken, overwhelmed by what I've done. I've betrayed my family, my magic, the goddess herself. And Sam.

I've betrayed him too.

For a moment, I pretend that he never left me, that he never got sick, that we've been together for the last decade doing all the normal things couples do—brushing our teeth side by side, fighting over who forgot the milk, curling up under a quilt to watch our favorite show.

No lies. No sins.

No helpless hunger or echoing grief.

I think about the memory I gave away, the one I'll never

remember. Was it warm and lovely? A stolen moment between lovers? Or was it a violent collision of wants and needs?

Before I know it, I find myself in the tunnel of jacaranda trees. The once-vibrant purple blooms are now ashen, hanging limply like cobwebs from the gnarled, twisted vines.

My grandmother Azalea's words come to me, *Time stands still here, amor. And if you visit under the light of a full moon, you can change a single moment in time.*

Show me, I asked her.

Only your magic can do that.

Simply a fairy tale to delight a child, I now realize as I pass beneath the skeletal branches.

Besides, there is no full moon—only a few garden lights that illuminate my path of destruction.

A cool breeze rustles through the trees, curling around me in a soft whisper.

When all has been destroyed, the goddess shall rise.

I'm not imagining it. The words are distant, fragile things that vibrate through me.

I hold my breath, waiting for more. For guidance, for a hope that will never come, but my fear drives me forward, carrying me to Mayahuel's agave.

A plant that is very much alive.

I freeze. Afraid to move, to disrupt the moment.

The agave's leaves are succulent, fleshy, bearing healthy spines.

A symbol of transformation. A ghost with a story that tells of the exact place where my ancestor made her choice to accept the magic, and to always protect beauty and love.

A sound escapes my throat—a child's whimper, a gasp. I can't even be sure because I'm on my knees, crying with relief.

My memory magic emerges. It dips and swirls like a bird winging across the sky.

I see a vague image, a woman at a crossroads met by the goddess. I feel worry, doubt—these are my great-grandmother's emotions wedged deep within her heart.

The memory is a sharp, cold ache. It's then that I hear Mayahuel's voice: *you no longer need to hide your wounds.*

Words meant for my great-grandmother, and yet here they are, served up to me on a silver platter I don't deserve.

My wounds: Sam. Sarah. And now the flowers.

I realize my teeth are clenched. My jaw is painfully rigid as I reach out and touch the underside of the agave with the lightness of a feather. A ripple of energy glides through me, one that tells me all can't be lost.

"I chose wrong," I whisper. "I know that. Please let me make it right."

The world tilts, neither welcoming my plea nor ignoring it. I couldn't save Sarah. And maybe I can't save Sam, but perhaps...

A shiver works its way up my spine. I count to five slowly. I fist and unfist my hands. *Please be enough. Please be enough.*

"Take my magic," I say. "Let it be my sacrifice to you."

The logical part of my brain considers saying more, something like, *in exchange for the flowers' lives, in exchange for Sam's,* but my magic is more powerful than logic—it lives on intuition. And it's telling me to let the goddess decide what my sacrifice is worth.

I don't know how long I stay like this, pleading silently, hoping daringly. Soon the sky begins to lighten, a rosy expanse punctuated with dark clouds that looks like mottled bruises.

Gradually, I stand. The goddess's silence is loud and clear.

My sacrifice is worth nothing.

36

I float between consciousness and sleep, that dreamy state when everything is possible and pure. When I can pretend everything is as it should be.

It's close to 11:00 a.m. when I finally pull myself out of it, roll over, and dazedly check my phone.

There are a few texts from Sam. A photo of Spirit in the pasture with her mom, which brings a small smile to my face, and another message that reads: How does steak sound?

And then another: Or ribs?

Bullet votes ribs.

But no pressure.

My heart sinks.

I stare up at the timbered ceiling blankly. How in the hell am I going to explain any of this to Sam?

There was a fraction of a moment when I thought I could just avoid telling him. Then I remembered how secrets have destroyed so much already. The idea conjures images of Roberto, of that day in his café when he told me, *Secrets are like devils waiting to burn you.*

There's been enough burning for a lifetime.

I have to tell Sam the truth.

For now, I text back: Can't make it today. So sorry. Getting ready for the celebration.

The half-truth tastes bitter, but it's for his own good. He's got enough on his plate; he doesn't need to worry about the woman he loves destroying generations of magic.

Chewing my bottom lip, I send another: Miss you and Bullet already.

And that, at least, is not a lie. I do miss the ranch, the ease of Sam's arms around me. I miss the moments before I knew the truth of his illness, when we had nothing but open road before us.

I won't let myself think dark thoughts. I won't wander into what if territory.

The house is unusually quiet. I guess that everyone else has gone to the airport to pick up Camilla and Dahlia.

The idea brings a sense of relief.

I need some time alone, to unpack all of this. To find a solution.

And I know the first place to look.

The "Libro de las Flores," the hand-written book my ancestors compiled over generations, is still in my nightstand drawer. I drag it out and begin to leaf through the pages, pass floral sketches, symbolic meanings, spells, and more.

I land on the entry I dog-eared just days ago.

I left my heart in the dark
And there it rusted, a decomposed box of memories lost in

the cold. Until spring came. Until it emerged from a cocoon of dreams.

Rereading these words sparks a longing in me, a longing for spring, for renewal. Maybe Rosa's wrong. Maybe the flowers aren't dead, but simply hibernating like the heart that was left in the dark.

I examine each page, looking for any entry related to divination. The only thing I find is short and cryptic, written in a choppy hand that's hard to read.

The future isn't to be seen. It's to be experienced.
Not to be waited on, but to be hoped for.

"Not helpful!" I slam the book closed in frustration.

I won't take no for an answer. I won't give up until the flowers are restored.

After a quick shower, I dress in jeans and a light sweater and head downstairs into the kitchen. The faint aroma of eggs and bacon drift through the air. A few mugs are tossed into the sink haphazardly; whoever tossed them was likely in a hurry.

"Hello?" I call out, thankful when there's no answer.

I pour myself a much-needed cup of coffee and head out to the courtyard garden, where the sun is brazenly cheerful and the bright pink geraniums and purple zinnia grow in bunches.

One garden I didn't destroy.

Great.

These blooms aren't growing in magical soil, so their lives were spared.

Which only makes my guilt swell painfully. I killed the flowers. I suffocated the magic.

The painful thought marinates for a moment, maybe two.

Until I realize that dwelling on the dreadfulness won't bring the flowers or the magic back. It won't set things right. And so what that I've struck out twice—first the goddess ignored my sacrifice, second the libro held nothing of significance.

I still have another swing.

There must be a way.

I'm shaken from my reverie by a distant noise, like a shovel turning the earth. I make my way through the archway, following the sound around a bend of hedges.

That's when I see Lana standing in a row of dead flowers, jamming a shovel into the barren earth.

"Lana?"

She looks up, peering at me through wavy red hair. "Hey."

"What are you doing?"

"Digging."

"I can see that. Why?"

She sighs and shakes her head. "This is all so fucked-up."

"Listen," I say tremulously, "I'm an ass and I'm so sorry I ever dragged you into this. I—"

"No one twisted my arm."

"I should have let go," I argue. "I should have listened to you."

She meets my gaze now. The corner of her mouth turns up, not into a smile, more like a mischievous sneer. "I hate 'should haves,' you know that?"

I nod. I hate them too—they're filled with shame and regret and are useless at changing anything for the better. "So no 'I told you so'?" I'd rather just get them all over with if that's what's on her agenda for today.

Lana stares at me defiantly. "I might hate those more than 'should haves,'" she says, jamming the shovel into the ground again.

"So, what's up with the digging?"

With the back of her arm, she wipes the sweat from her forehead. "I thought I heard something."

"What do you mean?"

"The flowers—I thought I heard a whisper or..." Her eyebrows knit together. "Or something."

My heart tilts. "You mean...you think they're alive?"

She exhales sharply, staring at the small hollow she's already dug. "I'm digging a hole to see if I can get closer. Get a better listen."

"Oh my God!" I cry, snatching the shovel from her. "If they're alive, then..." My pulse races as I begin to dig where Lana left off. "Then, we can bring them back, right?"

"Maybe."

Maybe has never sounded so promising, so hopeful, so perfect.

I turn the earth feverishly, never taking my eyes from the work, never letting them wander to the death that surrounds us.

Several minutes go by. The soil yields to my efforts and just when I think I've dug enough, Lana gasps. "What the holy hell!"

I stop, look up. Half expecting her to tell me she's heard a whisper. Her gaze is frozen, locked on a figure that's rushing toward us.

It's a mirage. It can't be.

It's Harlow.

37

"Harlow!"

My heart is a rapid-fire drum as I race over and embrace my very pregnant sister. "What the hell are you doing here?"

"Aren't you ready to pop?" Lana asks as she goes in for a hug.

Harlow angles her head to the side and takes a deep breath as she stares wistfully at the destruction before her. "It's worse than I thought."

"Har," I say, suddenly breathless. "Explain!"

She grimaces, cradling her stomach. "Can we sit first?"

A minute later, we're in the courtyard. Lana's gone inside for some drinks while Harlow sits and tilts her face toward the sun. Her dark hair spills over the chair effortlessly. Her skin really is aglow, and even with the shadows under her eyes, I'd say she's never looked more stunning.

"Well, it's official," she says, blowing out an exaggerated breath. "Kraken hates planes. She plunged her bony little feet into me the entire time."

"Harlow," I say, staying on track. "Why are you here?"

"I sensed it," she says softly. "Yesterday, I felt sick, and not pregnant-sick. I was so dizzy I had to sit down, and that's when I had the vision."

The cold returns, settling low in my belly. "Vision of what?"

"I saw the farm," she says. "The flowers were withering, there was all this rot and decay." Her gaze circles back to me. "Lil, what happened?"

Lana arrives, carrying a tray with three glasses and a pitcher of lemonade. I quickly fill her in on the vision, more than glad to avoid Harlow's direct question.

What happened?

How can I begin to answer that succinctly, honestly? Without feeling like a wretched failure?

Lana ties her hair up into a bun and begins to fan herself with a hand. "Har, how did you have a vision? I thought your pregnancy blocked all that?"

"Yeah, well magic and growing babies are mysterious things," Harlow says before looking back to me expectantly.

I reach over and touch her stomach. The kraken rolls, then kicks forcefully.

"She's got super-powered legs," Harlow groans. "She likes to jam her heel under my ribs. I'm sure she does it on purpose just to let me know who's really the boss."

Lana's face twists. "I'm never having kids. They're like little aliens possessing your body."

Harlow looks down at her belly. "Monsters, you mean."

A small round of amusement and then Harlow narrows her gaze again, sits straighter, and says, "Quit stalling, Lil."

I study her for a long moment, wondering if there might be a way to save her the painful reality, but there's not. There never is.

Lana clears her throat and says to me, "Start with Sam."

So I do, never deviating from the truth, never sugarcoating, and for once, painting only the most detailed brushstrokes. I need Harlow to understand. Or maybe I need her to validate my decision, the risk I took.

Harlow listens attentively as she sips her lemonade. She never once gasps or rolls her eyes or interrupts with questions, and when I've come to the end, her expression softens. I can't tell if it's pity or just the discomfort of being nine months pregnant.

"Okay" is all she says, but I can see the wheels turning in that mind of hers.

"That's it?" Lana balks. "You came all this way to tell us, *okay?*"

Harlow frowns. "I'm still processing. That might sound easy, but it's really hard when you're growing a monster and your brain feels like it's shrunk to half its size."

"Ben actually let you travel alone?" I ask.

Harlow screws up her face and averts her gaze.

"Oh my God," I blurt. "You didn't tell him!"

"What!" Lana shouts.

"Calma," Harlow says with a guilty wince. "I told him once I was on the plane. I knew he'd try and stop me, and I had to come. I felt like it was the most important thing in the world to be here. Like some thread was tugging me home."

As reckless as the move was, I've never been happier to see my sister. Just her presence has a reassuring effect.

"Samuel James, huh?" she says to me with a twisted grin. I nod.

She sighs and squints against the morning sun. "I would have done the same thing, Lil."

"Well, let's not get carried away," Lana says.

Harlow chuckles. "You would have too, Lana."

"Unlikely."

"Lana," Harlow says, "you already did when you chose to help her. And here I thought you were ruled by logic alone.

But mira," she teases, "you actually have a romantic bone in there somewhere."

Lana rolls her eyes. "She was a mess, okay? I had to help her. And you would have, too, if you'd been here."

"Of course I would have," Harlow says. "I'd bury a dead body for any of you."

"It's better not to bury the whole thing," Lana argues. "I mean, if you want to get away with murder."

I stifle my laugh.

There's comfort in the loyalty that runs through this family, the unbreakable bonds of sisterhood that I can count on no matter what. And for the briefest of moments, I don't feel any dark clouds hanging overhead.

"Listen," I begin before telling my sister and cousin about my visit to Mayahuel.

"You offered up your magic?" Lana nearly shrieks.

"I'm the one who fucked this all up and I'll do anything to make things right again."

"Mayahuel doesn't want your magic," Harlow says.

I meet her gaze. "How do you know?"

"Because no one gives a gift expecting it back," Lana asserts.

"Exactly," Harlow says as she stretches her legs and rubs her enormous belly. "So, you sacrificed a memory to change his future?" she asks me.

"Yeah, why?"

"Just piecing things together."

"Well, how about you piece them together out loud," Lana suggests.

"That's not how it works," she tells Lana, then asks me, "Where's Mom?"

"She and Rosa went to the airport to pick up Cam and Dahlia," I say, feeling an odd sense of fragility but also relief. Maybe Harlow is right. Maybe the goddess didn't shun my sacrifice because it wasn't good enough but because she'd already given it away.

I wonder if Mom will tell Cam and Dahlia about all of this on the trip back, if they'll be just as furious that they came all this way for a Celebration of Flowers that isn't going to happen. If they'll ever forgive me.

Lana takes a swig of lemonade, capturing an ice cube. "You must have passed them on the road."

"Good," Harlow says.

"Good that you passed them," Lana says in between ice-chews, "or good that they aren't here?"

Harlow offers a barely there smile. "Good that they're coming."

"Why?" I ask, thinking the exact opposite.

My sister reaches over and takes my hand, giving it a squeeze. "I have an idea."

"That sounds like trouble," Lana grunts.

"What kind of an idea?" I ask.

Harlow studies me for a long moment, like she's weighing how to say whatever is on her mind. "Well, you're definitely not going to like it."

38

The moment I see Dahlia and Cam waltz into the hacienda, I know.

My mom has shared my story. All of it. Sam. Sarah. The divination.

I thought that I would feel relief that I didn't have to relive it again, but I feel only a strange disappointment that I wasn't the one who did the telling.

There's a ripple effect to stories, to how they're told, to the stops and starts. The bits and pieces that are included or left out.

In the foyer, my cousin Dahlia falls into my arms like a limp cloth doll. Her black hair is slicked back into a perfect bun and her nose is dusted with the same freckles that I used to count when I was a kid.

A wedge of sunlight slants through the half-open door. From here, I can see that Mom and Rosa are still at the car, likely falling back to give us this moment alone. A sentiment shared by Harlow and Lana, who are waiting in the living room.

When Dahlia breaks free, she studies me with her hazel-brown, deep-set eyes. Her expression is soft with a sympathy I'm not sure I deserve. "It's going to be okay," she whispers. "It's going to be okay."

I cling to her promise, but Camilla, my oldest sister, is in the doorway now, eyeing me with a mistrust that breaks my heart. After a compulsory hug, her voice comes low and bitter. "Mom told us everything and I..." She shakes her head slowly, tucking an unruly brown hair behind her ear, which is studded with three diamonds. "I don't understand, Lil. How could you?"

Camilla, the classic beauty whose road has been paved with granted wishes and a love most could only dream of. Years ago, she married Amir, a man who, I swear, she conjured from a love spell.

For the first time, I don't melt, I don't feel stricken. I own the decision. "Cam, I love him, and if there was even a chance..."

"Except that you chose for all of us!" she argues. And while her voice is severe, her expression is one of compassion. Tears prick her eyes. The moment they fall, I begin to cry too.

"We need to focus on a solution," Dahlia says, switching into therapist mode. "Shaming does no one any good."

"I'm not shaming," Cam says, wiping an eye where crow's feet are just beginning to form. "I love you, Lil. I just..." Her voice trails off and I understand that there aren't words to convey that kind of sorrow or regret. Or disappointment.

The three of us embrace, like magnets drawn to each other. I can feel their magic intensifying—Cam's spirit magic and Dahlia's healing magic, a power that is only reserved for broken souls or hearts; otherwise, I would have enlisted her help to heal Sam.

Spirit. Healing. Memory.

Powerful magic we were born with, but it's never felt so empty. Or so far away.

Just then Mom and Rosa come inside, and we all go into the living room where chaos erupts at the sight of Harlow.

"Why would you take this risk?"

"You have to get back on the first flight home!"

"Oh my God, that baby is going to be huge."

Harlow sits on the sofa and plants her swollen feet on the table with an annoyed huff. "I'm not due for three weeks!" she insists. "And I promise to go home tomorrow. After the ceremony."

It's then that Harlow shares the idea she teased earlier, refusing to tell me and Lana until everyone was here.

"The Celebration of Flowers is going to look different this year," she says. "We're going to use our collective powers, like always, but—"

"That won't bring the flowers back," Rosa interjects.

"It's worth a try," Dahlia says.

Harlow turns her gaze to meet mine. "Lily is the key."

"Me?"

"You need to collect your most cherished memories," she says, "and offer them to the land."

The room goes silent. Everyone's eyes are on me, and I suddenly feel hot and dizzy.

"That's the sacrifice," Harlow says gently.

"How do I know which memories?" I ask, fighting the tremble working through me.

She hesitates, glancing around the room as if they're all a few steps ahead of me and are deciding who should be the one to share.

"You did this for Sam," Harlow says, "and so the memories need to be of him."

I'm aware of the immediate resistance I feel. Of my memory magic swirling furiously as if to deny the request. "I already gave a memory away when—"

"This is different," Harlow says. "You were trying to change the future. We need to change the present."

"How's it going to work?" Cam asks, looking unconvinced.

"I'll enhance the memories during the ceremony," Harlow says almost cavalierly.

"It might be enough," Mom puts in.

My magic expands, spreading like mist. No. No. No!

Cam says, "But won't that affect her feelings for him?"

"There has to be another way," Dahlia says. "Our memories inform identity and…" Her voice trails off gloomily.

"So how many memories are we talking?" I ask.

Harlow gets to her feet clumsily and comes over to stand in front of me. "Lil, I need to keep feeding the memories into the land until it's revived. And I need your permission to do that."

I feel like I can't breathe. Like all the oxygen in the room has evaporated. "But…" I shake out my hands. "What if it takes all of my memories of Sam?"

I'm met with blank, uncertain stares.

"What if it doesn't work and I've given my memories away for nothing?" I ask. "What if the land takes every memory that matters?"

"That's the risk, just like the risk you already took," Rosa says and not unkindly. It's simply fact.

Dahlia comes over and rests her hand on my shoulder. I feel a ribbon of healing magic pulsing from her fingertips, and all I want to do is lean into it, allow it to wash over me, through me. "You get to decide," she says, "and no one will judge you if you don't want to do it."

I look into the faces of my family. Women with magic in their veins. Women who have been the grounding force in my life for as long as I can remember.

"Yes," I whisper. "I'll do it."

39

That night, before the ceremony, I call Sam.

More than anything, I wanted to go see him, but the risk is too great. I know I'll waver; I'll melt into his arms and refuse to give even a fragment of him, of us, away.

"Hey!" he answers. His voice is jubilant, not the tone of a man who might be handed a life-changing sentence next week. A sentence I couldn't change, not even with magic.

"Hey."

"What's wrong?"

"Nothing," I lie, gripping the phone as I stare out across the dead crops. In the moonlight, they've taken on an even ashier appearance, more skeletal, and for a moment, the land looks like it's buried under piles of bones. "I just wanted to hear your voice."

"Bullet!" he shouts away from the phone. Then, to me, "Hang on." I hear rustling, a chuckle, and finally, "*This is your bone, girl. Not the ribs.*"

"Is she eating my dinner?" I ask with a dry laugh.

"I saved some ribs for her, too, but she's impatient and

doesn't understand the word *marinating*," Sam says with an upbeat tone that breaks my heart. "You'll get them tomorrow, Bullet. Okay?"

Bullet yelps as if to say "why?"

What I wouldn't give to be at the ranch with them, snuggled under a quilt on the porch, staring at the stars.

"Well, I better get to the celebration," I say, not meaning it, not wanting to hang up or cut the line that connects me to Sam. To the version of myself that loves him, that carries a thousand memories of *us*.

"Okay," he says. "I'll see you tomorrow?"

I nod, fighting the tears that are determined to come. I can't cry now. He'll hear; he'll know something is wrong. And something is. I feel it like cold fingers scraping over my scalp.

My hand tightens around the phone as I take a moment to collect myself, to catch my breath. "Sam?"

"Yeah?"

"I love you." I imagine his arms around me, his breath on my skin, his lips on mine. A lovely fantasy. Maybe one I was never meant to have beyond the last few days.

"I love you too." There's no reticence or fear in his voice, only a man who trusts me. Is that what love is? Giving your heart away to someone who can destroy you and trusting they never use that power?

After we hang up, I consider hiding a memory, one to remind myself of the thread that binds us. Ultimately, I decide it's too risky. What if that's the last one needed? What if it's the final breath to give life to the farm again?

I find a pad of paper and a pen, choosing instead to write a letter. Not to Sam, to myself.

But everything I write feels unworthy of what I want to say. How can anyone encapsulate love with mere words?

My memory magic awakens, growing like misty vines, coiling tighter and tighter.

Life will never be the same.

I close my eyes, surrendering myself to the magic, to the cold spreading through me. I don't need to run anymore, to deny the existence of pain or regret or fear.

I left my heart in the dark

And there it rusted, a decomposed box of memories lost in the cold. Until spring came. Until it emerged from a cocoon of dreams.

Gripping the pen, my hand quivers. I stare at the page through a blur of tears, wondering how it is that I'm possibly saying goodbye to Sam all over again.

If all goes to hell, if every memory of Sam is given away, I'll need a reminder, a catalyst to open my heart and force me to remember.

Finally, I press the pen to paper and write the seven truest words I know.

Your heart belongs to Samuel James forever.

The night air is chilled. My family and I stand in the circle of dead flowers, the same flowers I planted just two days ago.

There is a stillness, a quiet I wasn't expecting. As if the entire farm is holding its breath in anticipation.

No one needs to be told what to do next. We've been doing this ritual since I was a child. Pressing our hands into the soil, feeding the earth with our magic. Waiting for the vibration to rise out of the land, connecting to our power, to our promise.

But tonight, things are different.

Tonight, I will be giving more than my magic.

Votive candles glimmer around the circle as we all stand at the inner edge.

Shadows flicker across my family's faces, quick pulses of darkness while dead blossoms sag at my feet.

I wonder how deep the death goes.

When I was a little girl, I used to imagine the flowers' roots reaching beneath the ground—a complicated matrix of long, entwined, powerful beings, creating worlds none of us could see.

Harlow leads me to the center of the circle. "While they focus on feeding their magic into the earth," she says, "you need to draw up memories of Sam."

"How do I possibly remember them all?" I ask.

Her expression twists into something like regret or maybe pity. "Your magic will bring them to the surface, but you have to allow it." She takes a shuddering breath. "Then you just need to let them flow out and—"

"Let them go."

She swallows and places a gentle hand on my arm. "I'm sorry, Lil."

My entire body feels heavy with a pain I've never experienced; it's like I've been put through a meat grinder and handed all the pieces to put back together again.

I did this. I'm the one who killed the flowers. It doesn't matter if it was unintentional, the fact remains. Just like Sarah's death. Maybe it's a blessing that I get to make at least one thing right, even if it means surrendering my heart.

We all drop to our knees, except for Harlow. In my periphery, I see my family, five or six feet away, laying their hands on the dirt, focusing their energy and their magic.

The earth is cool to the touch as I call on my own magic. It stirs, moving like a long slow tide, asking me, *What do you want to do?*

I take a deep breath, close my eyes, and think of Sam.

Hazy images form, worn with time. My magic brings them closer, into focus. As the world recedes around me, I see Sam as a boy, his mop of dark hair, his long skinny arms, his reckless spirit.

At first the earth is unyielding, then gradually...

I'm walking in the woods. It's a warm summer day. Sam's boyish voice is calling out to me, and I follow it until I reach the fort we built. Its walls are made of cardboard and discarded bits of wood. Sam's inside making paper birds, hanging them from the lopsided roof.

We each write our names on a bird, suspend them among the rest of the flock.

Sam says, "Race you back."

And then I'm running. I can feel the pliant ground beneath my feet. The rush of warm air. His laughter echoes all around me as the sun slants through the thick trees.

And then, like the paper birds, I'm hovering above, watching the scene evaporate.

It's slipping through my fingers like sand.

I let the memory go.

My magic conjures more images, more memories.

With each, I try to linger, to trace the details, but inevitably, I release them. I feel each draining out of me. One by one by one.

Then, out of the blue, I see Sarah's face. I feel the pain of her death, of my failure. I long to release the images of that night forever, and yet I know if I do, I'll always be a coward.

I hold onto Sarah. She deserves to be remembered.

I'm vaguely aware of Harlow's hand on my shoulder, of her magic enhancing my own as it flows between and through us.

The land's ravenous energy wants more.

Tears stream down my face.

God, I don't want to do this. I don't want…

How much more do you need?

I've already given away so many memories, enough that I struggle to find Sam in all the usual places: my mind, my heart, my soul.

It's Mayahuel's voice that breaks into my consciousness: *Will you give it all?*

No. No. Please.

But in the end, I know. I know I will give away every memory of Sam to restore the flowers.

Worn and defeated, I respond to the goddess with the only answer I have. *Yes.*

There's a jolt of energy, hot and painful, expanding inside of me.

And then everything goes still, quiet.

I'm no longer standing on the rotting soil of my family's farm. I'm sitting beneath a wide, shady tree. I look up. A purple balloon floats stringless into the sky. I feel the warmth of Sam's hands as he ties the stolen string around my finger, and whispers, "It's a promise."

The memory, like all the others, vanishes, carving into my heart, hollowing me out.

A moment later, I feel a vibration in the earth as if the roots are awakening, as if they're emerging from a cocoon of dreams.

Mine and Sam's.

That's when it happens.

A distant memory emerges from the earth.

It glides into my hand, courses through my veins.

I'm in his bed. The sheets are cool, soft. His touch is tender, his body so warm against my own.

We collide in pleasure just as he calls out my name. "Lily."

And then, cruelly, I'm ripped away, out of his arms.

Out of a memory I didn't know I possessed.

"Oh my God!" Harlow cries.

There's a rush of energy, an eruption of panic as I return to the present.

As I open my eyes, the flowers are still dead.

And Harlow's water has broken.

40

Harlow looks stricken as her gaze locks on mine. Searching, pleading. Asking me silently, *Will my baby be okay?*

There's a rush of voices, panic surges. A vortex of hysteria spinning round and round.

The thread between my sister and me closes out the chaos.

"We need to get to the house," I tell her, forcing the shock of what I just experienced as far away as possible.

"We need the hospital!" Cam cries.

Rosa throws up her hands. "That's more than an hour away!"

"Everyone needs to calm down," Mom commands.

In the commotion, Harlow never takes her eyes from mine. "I don't think I can make it."

"I'll check to make sure," I tell her.

Within minutes, she's in the guest room, lying on clean sheets.

Besides our mom, I've thrown everyone else out of the room so I can concentrate. I need to check to see how dilated she is and assess best next steps.

When I discover that she's already six centimeters dilated, I realize two things simultaneously: there is no way we can make it to the hospital, and Harlow's been keeping some secrets.

"Have you been having contractions?" I ask her, even though I know the answer. No first pregnancy progresses to a six without discomfort. I want to wallop my sister for not telling me.

Harlow screws up her face. "Some cramping here and there. I—I didn't think it was anything."

"Okay, listen," I say, holding my exasperation at bay. "You're six centimeters dilated, and that means this baby is coming now. We can try to get to the hospital, but we probably won't make it."

"No!" Harlow insists, grimacing, groaning through a contraction. A minute later, she takes a deep breath and says, "I want you to deliver the kraken, Lil."

"I don't have the tools, Harlow." I've never completed a home birth. I need my instruments and monitors. I need a damn hospital!

"You'll do a better job than anyone!" she cries.

Except that this is my sister. My niece.

Coolly, I tell my mom to bring me sterile towels, scissors, and gloves.

She takes my orders and runs with them, flying out of the room and returning minutes later with the items. She's clearly been crying, but she pulls herself together now for Harlow's sake. Maybe even for mine.

In the minutes that follow, we stand by, trying to comfort Harlow through more agonizing contractions. With each, she goes from grinding out expletives to groaning softly into her pillow.

I feel helpless, powerless.

It's made worse by the aftereffects of emptying my memories of Sam into the earth. But not all of them. I remember a moment from our childhood, something about a waterfall, and I remember driving to his ranch, fighting with him. There was a storm. He told me he had been sick. That's why he left me all those years ago. Right?

Fragmented images drift through my mind: holding him, kissing him, laughing with him. Memories lost to the shadows.

Still, the extraction of so many memories wasn't enough to erase my love for him. This feels like a small triumph. Well, until I remember that it didn't work. The flowers are still dead.

And Sam, he could be sick again.

His words still haunt me: *a shadow on my liver.*

Of course, the goddess would leave me that painful moment like some kind of cruel souvenir.

Will you give it all?

And then I remember. The land fed me a memory too. But why?

Clearing my head, I check Harlow again. She's fully dilated.

"Listen, Har," I say, removing a pair of latex gloves from their package. "It's time."

"Can I change my mind?" she asks, pushing a matted lock of hair back, looking like a small child who's just woken from a nightmare.

If she only knew how many women have asked me this question.

"On the next contraction," I say, "I need three pushes, ten seconds each."

Her eyes bulge. "Three?!"

Before we can argue about it, another contraction arrives. Harlow bears down, and excruciating cries escape her mouth. She fists the sheets, writhing in pain.

"I hate Ben!" she screams as the contraction subsides.

Ben. I look over my shoulder at my mom, her stance a show

of false stoicism, but beneath that veneer, I know she's just as scared as I am. "Did someone call him?" I ask.

"We tried. No answer."

"This is his fault!" Harlow shouts. "HIS!"

Redirecting Harlow's energy and focus, I say, "You're a really good pusher, Har. You're almost there. Okay?"

She glares at me like I'm her worst enemy. "Get her out of me!"

Mom's stroking Harlow's forehead, pushing her drenched hair away from her face, but it does nothing to comfort my sister.

After several more contractions, I nearly double over in relief. "I see her head!"

Mom gasps, looking on. Now her tears flow freely.

"Only a couple more pushes," I say, fighting my own urge to cry. Pleading silently. *Please be okay. Please let everything be okay.*

The seconds, moments between my prayers and Harlow's pain feel like hours stretched too thin.

When the time comes, when Harlow bears down again and again, when the baby's shoulders pop out one at a time, and her body glides from Harlow's into my hands, a beautiful cry pierces the air and then...

Time stills.

A wedge of sunlight streams into the room.

My breath stops.

I stare in awe at my niece, her wispy black hair, her pinched face, her clenched hands.

Each pulse, breath, movement unfolds in a strange slow-motion fashion, and in the microseconds before the perfect O of her mouth releases another wail, a thread of magic hums between us.

It's then that I hear a whisper.

"Laurel."

For abundance and strength.

For divine protection.

I wrap Laurel in a clean towel and hand her to Harlow before tying a knot in the umbilical cord and cutting it.

Relief floods my senses once the placenta is delivered smoothly. In the moments that follow, there is a sort of sacred hush as Harlow embraces her daughter, gazing at her in awe.

But why did Mayahuel whisper the baby's name to me?

Harlow tells me, "You did it."

I force out something between a grunt and a laugh. "It was all you."

"She's beautiful," Mom says softly. "What's her name?"

"Laurel," Harlow whispers.

I stiffen as her eyes meet mine and she says, "You heard it too."

"How...how did you know?" I ask.

"Because Mayahuel whispered something else with it," Harlow says. "She told me something I don't understand."

"What?" I ask.

"She said, *cocoon of dreams.* Does that mean anything to you?"

I feel a sharp pain in my chest, remembering the passage.

I left my heart in the dark

And there it rusted, a decomposed box of memories lost in the cold. Until spring came. Until it emerged from a cocoon of dreams.

After I tell my mom and sister about the libro's entry, Mom whispers, "It's a promise."

"Promise?"

"Spring is coming," she says.

I swallow. "What does that mean?"

Her expression is both hopeful and cautious. "Renewal? Growth?" I don't like the inflection after each word—she doesn't know definitively. There is no precedence here, all of this is just one big guess.

I bolt to the window, to look out across the farm, hoping that maybe...

But no. Everything is as lifeless as it was before.

Nevertheless, here in this room there is new life, and for now, that's enough.

Laurel stirs, throwing a fist into the air. That's when I see a tiny half-moon birthmark on her left wrist.

"So, do you know her brand of magic?" I ask.

Harlow looks up at me and smiles. "Abundance and prophetic dreams."

41

Right after midnight, while Harlow sleeps and the house is still, I sit, cradling Laurel by the bedroom's expansive window.

Beyond, even in the dimness of the garden lights and half-moon, the flowers are as limp and lifeless as they were before.

Laurel stirs gently. A warm bundle of so much hope and love.

I close my eyes, thanking the goddess and anyone who will listen for delivering her into this world safely. The entire experience reminded me of why I chose obstetrics to begin with. And yet something is gnawing at me, something that feels off-kilter. Something that tells me everything's changed.

I can't help but wonder if it's because of the lost memories. Which only makes me think of the one the land gave back to me. But why return to me what I had already given away?

I consider my mom's words: *Spring is coming. Renewal. Hope.*

And then I recall what Harlow said about the cocoon of dreams, the words the goddess spoke to her, which makes me feel cautiously optimistic.

With Laurel tucked safely in my arms, I lean my head back, close my eyes, and drift off.

I dream of a long white shore, shrouded in fog. I'm planting daisies in the sand, pressing my hands around the delicate stems as the waves break across the beach rhythmically.

Dimly, I recall that the daisy symbolizes love and strength, but its power eludes me.

"Can I help?"

I look up and see a girl, maybe eight or nine. She's willowy with dark wavy hair, large curious eyes, and a strong chin that juts out just enough to tell me she's confident or defiant or maybe both.

"Yes," I say, handing her a plastic shovel.

She drops to the sand and begins to dig. It's then that I notice the half-moon birthmark on her wrist.

"Laurel?"

She looks up at me and smiles. In that split second, she looks so much like her mom.

"These won't grow in the sand," Laurel says with a huff that is neither sorry nor attached.

I know this. Still, I tell her, "This is just a dream. We can grow whatever we want."

She nods, keeping her attention on the flowers.

"How are you so big already?" I ask.

"Like you said, this is just a dream."

And then I remember Laurel's magic: abundance and prophetic dreams.

I remember that in the waking world, I'm cradling her newborn body in my arms.

"Is this your dream or mine?" I ask.

Laurel doesn't answer. She's too busy gazing at the daisy

she's just planted. Her eyes expand in fascination as it grows taller and taller, reaching a good twelve inches.

"Did your magic do that?" I ask.

She gives only a small nod. "Did you know that the daisy's power is awareness?"

"Yes," I say. "And there's something else."

"Prediction." She tugs the flower from the sand and begins to pluck the petals. "He loves me. He loves me not. He loves me. He loves me not."

Halfway around the bud, she hands it to me. "Want to finish?"

I laugh. "I already know he loves me."

"You can ask a different question."

I stare into her dark eyes. Then back to the flower. I'm torn between asking about Sam or the farm. Maybe I'm not meant to know about either, maybe some things shouldn't be predicted. Maybe...

I glance up at my niece. "Is this real?"

"This is your dream," she says. "You get to decide."

I take a shaky breath. "Sam's healthy." Pluck. "The farm's going to be okay." Pluck. I can't bring myself to speak the alternatives, even though I know that's how this game works.

In the same moment, the petals I've just removed grow back. I pluck another and another, only to have them sprout again. "Hey!"

Laurel giggles.

A wave rolls in, its frothy edges swallowing the planted daisies and carrying them out to sea. A terrible sense of loss grips me, and yet I know—this is how it's supposed to be. Nothing lasts forever. Not love. Not life. Not even magic.

Sam's voice echoes across the beach: *life is a long string of surrenders and learning to let go.*

The words he said to me only days ago. Words that felt so

burdensome then, and now? I feel myself embracing them, accepting them.

The fog thickens, wrapping around us so tightly I can barely see Laurel. Her hand darts out and takes hold of mine before she says, "He's coming for you."

And then I wake up.

42

The day after Laurel's birth, the house is a peculiar blend of celebration and serenity. There is laughter, warmth, comfort. Even the hacienda seems to fold in around us, to witness each moment, like a collector of memories.

But more than anything, I feel a fragile mood of forgiveness. Or maybe forgetting.

Either way, it's a reprieve from all the worry and doubt and dread and fear. As if Laurel's magic has filled the hacienda with the abundance and light it was built upon.

I can't stop thinking about the dream, about Laurel's words: *he's coming for you.*

Sam.

I haven't even told him about the birth yet. Everything happened so fast with Harlow and then the dream, and then Ben arrived early this morning.

He parked himself next to Harlow's bed, never once questioning her decision. The fact that he looked so worn-out was nearly masked by the utter gratitude I saw in his eyes. And as I watched him cradle Laurel, whispering into her ear as he walked her through the house, I felt a sense of unexpected peace.

It occurred to me that doing nothing is a decision. *Trusting* is a decision. I've never been good at either, always demanding control. Always choosing action, creating a life that allowed me the freedom to cut and run anytime I wanted to.

I see now that all that movement was about protecting myself. If I moved fast enough, nothing could catch up to me, and yet there Sam was, always in the rearview mirror drawing closer and closer.

And now as I consider the farm, and Sam's potential diagnosis, I know I can choose differently. I can plant my feet firmly on the ground and face whatever is meant to come tomorrow and the next day and the day after that.

I've barely stepped out of the shower when I hear the bedroom floors creak under the weight of footsteps. I bind my hair with a towel, throw on a robe and step out of the bathroom, only to find Lana standing there.

"I wanted you to be the first to know," she whispers.

I stare at her attentively as the steam trails into the bedroom. "First to know what?"

"I heard the flowers."

The towel on my head drops to the floor with an unexpected *thwomp*. "What?"

Lana paces to the window and I follow, looking out. "They're still dead," I say.

"Maybe on the surface," she says with a tilted smile. "But their roots are strong. Underneath all that, they're alive!"

Blood rushes my ears. "How…? Why…? Are you sure?"

With a huff, Lana says, "Seriously? You're going to question my magnificent powers?"

I'm already shaking my head, trying to process the fact that all isn't lost, that the enchantment in our soil is still there, that I didn't kill the magic!

I open the window. The faint scent of honeysuckle drifts up into my room, a message, a welcome confirmation.

Lana throws her arms around me, and we simultaneously laugh and cry. When we break apart, I ask, "Did the flowers tell you how it happened?"

"No, but maybe it was the memories you gave away? Maybe our collective magic?"

"Maybe Laurel," I say, pondering her magic of abundance.

"Or maybe all of the above."

A surge of emotion, one that I can't name, overcomes me. It's all rolled up into joy and relief and thankfulness. It feels like I've been walking around in a stranglehold that's finally released its grip on me. For the first time in so long, I can take a breath.

"During the ceremony," I say, "something weird happened."

"Weirder than Harlow going into labor?"

"A memory rose up. The one I gave away during the divination. Why would the flowers give that back to me?"

Lana considers the question, then twists her mouth and says, "Maybe it was their way of telling you they didn't need it. That all is forgiven?"

I fiddle with my robe's tie, wondering if I'll ever really know the truth. Then I realize that, in the end, it doesn't really matter. Some questions aren't meant to be answered.

"Why did you tell me first?" I ask.

She blinks at me, then says, "They asked me to."

It's late morning when I head out to the farm.

A soothing honeyed scent hovers just out of reach. Nothing has changed, only a weary ghost garden that was once beautiful.

As I draw closer, as I wander down a row, I see bits of beautiful green poking through the earth. Tiny, determined stems.

My memory magic swirls gently. In my mind's eye, I can see the farm awash in color, vibrating with magic once again.

Spring.

I continue to walk, to greet every new sprout, but no matter how far I get from the hacienda, I can still hear laughter, Laurel's cries, music, life.

And just as I'm about to turn back, I feel Sam's presence before he speaks. "Hey," I hear.

I spin to find him walking toward me. His strides are long and purposeful and so quick he reaches me in two heartbeats.

"What are you doing here?" I ask as he draws me into him.

"I couldn't wait until tonight." He leans back, tucking a hair behind my ear. There is a certain restraint in his pose that's making me nervous.

"I have so much to tell you," I say, glancing over his shoulder. I don't even know where to begin: the divination gone wrong, the surrender of so many memories.

"Like what?" he asks.

"You might not like it, but we said no more secrets and…" My voice is a rush of emotion, bordering on blabber. "I bet you're wondering about what happened to all the flowers and then Harlow showed up, and you won't believe this, but she had her baby."

"I heard."

"How?" Yes, news travels fast in La Ventana, but not that fast.

"I saw Cam leaving as I was coming through the main gates. She told me you delivered the baby."

His expression is one of pride. The richness of it is like a wedge of sunlight that I want to bask in, and I let myself do so as I unfold every little detail of the birth. Sam listens attentively, and as I watch him there among the rot and ruin, I feel a strange hollowness. I *feel* the memories that have been lost. Distant, frayed things I can't grab hold of. And yet I don't love him any less.

"Lil?"

I meet his eyes expectantly.

"I have something to tell you too."

His phone rings. He quickly silences it and looks back at me. "I got my tests back this morning." He doesn't punctuate the sentence with a period. He goes on quickly, putting me out of my misery. "The shadow was nothing. I'm clear. I'm all clear."

Clear.

The word sinks into me as easy as a stone in still water.

I leap into Sam's arms, knocking him back. A burst of laughter escapes his lungs.

"Sam! Oh my God! Sam!"

We're kissing and clinging and beaming like two people who've never tasted luck. And yet here it is. By any other name: blessing, fortune, destiny. It doesn't matter how or why it's landed here at our feet, because it's ours.

For this sliver of time, it's all ours.

I sock him in the chest. "Why didn't you lead with that?"

"I dunno. I sort of got caught up in your story."

Sam's gaze is open, warm, an endless horizon I could search forever. With his thumb, he brushes a tear from my cheek. "So…"

"So."

His arms are still wrapped around me. For the first time, his eyes seem to notice the withered crops. Before he can ask, I say, "It's a long story."

"Good thing we have time," he says, grinning goofily. "Let's go meet this niece of yours."

I lean into him, into his strength and love. I'd forgotten

what it felt like to have someone to break my fall, to hold me up. "Okay."

"And then..." He tilts my face up and kisses me softly. "Let's go home."

43

It's nearly sunset by the time Sam and I get to the ranch.

We spent a good part of the day with my family, lounging in the main courtyard while feasting on enchiladas, arroz, freshly made tortillas, and salsa with a killer bite.

There was a simplicity to it, an ease that filled me up that made me think that this—this is what I want.

Now we're sitting on the sofa in front of a low-burning fire. Sam's reading a book on World War II and I'm perusing his Moleskines, studying his sketches—his plans and dreams for the ranch.

Bullet is wedged between us, sleeping and obviously dreaming, based on the way she's bouncing her legs and whining every few breaths.

"I definitely think you should knock down that wall in the back part of the house," I say, pointing to Sam's notes that say otherwise.

He lowers his book and looks over at me. "Oh yeah?"

"It'll make the room brighter."

"That's a load-bearing wall though," he says, getting to his feet and walking over so as not to disturb Bullet's dreaming. Sam sits down in the sofa's corner next to me, staring at the sketch he's drawn.

"How about this wall?" I ask, pointing. "Then you could expand the room. I mean you have enough land."

Sam's eyebrows come together in concentration and then he looks up at me and smiles. "I like it."

I lean over and kiss him. "Good."

He lowers the journal that's in my hands. I meet his gaze, and before he speaks, I know what he's going to say. The words that are going to break the spell of all this perfect normalcy. "When do you have to leave?"

I fall back against the sofa and sigh. "Two days."

Sam's expression tightens. "That soon?"

I nod. "I wish you could come with me."

"Me too."

"Look," I say, taking his hand. "It's only five more months and then…"

Neither one of us has addressed the fact that we live in two different places with careers and responsibilities, and they aren't exactly interchangeable. Sam can't just give up the ranch and move to LA and I can't just give up my career.

"We'll make it work," he says.

Make it work.

I roll the words around in my head. What does that mean? And how? Reducing our relationship to phone calls and weekends? I've spent so long without Sam that the thought of going back to a life without him sounds miserable. Still, I made a commitment and I worked hard to be a chief in my last year of residency. It's then that I think about the memory ceremony, about how I chose to remember Sarah. It would have been so easy to let her fade from my consciousness, but I would have cheated myself out of the forgiveness and the healing. It's this realization that actually reenergizes my love of medicine, and for the first time since, I feel ready to face the hospital again.

And every time I imagine him in LA, I chuckle. Sam's too much a part of this place to ever be happy in an overly populated traffic hell like Los Angeles.

"Lily?"

"Yeah?"

"Stop worrying."

"I'm not."

"You are. You always frown like that when you can't figure something out." He runs his hand over my hair gently. "I have an idea."

"I'm all-in."

"You haven't even heard it yet," he says, grinning.

I roll my eyes and sit up. "Okay, fine. Let's hear it."

He pulls me to my feet. "Come on."

Fifteen minutes later, we're walking in the woods.

The sun is blazing, casting a burnt-orange color over the land, creating an enchanting kind of glow.

"Where are we going?" I ask.

"Nowhere."

"Sam."

"I'm serious." He stops, turns to face me. "I just thought you needed to get outside, clear that chaotic mind of yours."

"It's not chaotic."

A husky laugh bubbles out of him. "Whatever you say."

We walk side by side until we find a clearing where wildflowers sprout in patches. They remind me of the farm, of all I still haven't told Sam.

I don't want to lie anymore. I don't want any secrets between us.

"I have something I want to tell you," I say.

Sam frowns.

"Don't look so worried," I say, feeling suddenly tense. "It's not that bad. I mean, I hope you don't think it is."

Sam plops down onto the ground. "Okay, lay it on me."

And so, I sit next to him and tell him about the divination, the aftermath, and all the memories of him that I gave away.

Sam's eyes circle my face, and I can't tell if he's confused or upset or stunned. "You risked a divination for me?" he asks.

I nod, plucking a yellow flower from the earth.

"Is that why my tests...?"

"I don't think so," I say, twirling the long stem. "I mean, magic is so weird and mysterious, we may never know."

"But your memories, how much do you remember about us?"

"Enough to know that I still love you," I say. "I'm sad that I won't remember so many times we shared and..."

"Hey," he says, pulling me into him and resting his chin on my head. "I'll remember for both of us. Got it?"

I glance up and meet his gaze. There's a flash of a memory, of him as a boy. Chocolate ice cream is smeared across his mouth and he's laughing.

My memory magic hums to life. Maybe the memories, like the flowers, will come back in time, but even if they don't, I have everything I could ever want. I have Sam. I have his love.

I press my mouth to his, soft at first, like an exploration, but soon the kiss intensifies. Our bodies come together naturally, the want, the desire, the insatiable need to be closer.

Sam slides his hand under my shirt, stroking my skin. His rough, calloused hands are perfect, more than perfect. Soon we're naked, making love on the soft earth.

As we find our rhythm, as we open ourselves to each other, the remembrance of another time, the first time, burns brighter and brighter in my memory. The way Sam kissed me, touched me so tenderly. The way we both trembled afterward as if the world was about to explode.

Clinging to him now, I take in the sky above us. It's on fire, a brilliant shade of red that is fraying at the edges. Soon, everything will be dark. That's the immutable nature of time, always moving forward.

It's why we were given memories.

I pull Sam closer, and for the first time, I want for nothing more than what I have right now.

EPILOGUE

One week later

I've just pulled a twenty-four-hour shift consisting of five vaginal deliveries, two C-sections, twelve gyn consults, one dull encounter with a lower-level resident, and zero carbs, which is why I feel like I'm running on fumes as I make my way into the parking garage.

My head is so fuzzy I can't remember where I parked.

It was the second level, right? Or maybe it was the third. Jesus, I'm drawing a blank. To be fair, it was just as dark as it is now when I came in. I glance at the black sky beyond the garage.

Did the sun even shine today?

The thought of it reminds me of that unbelievable sunset last week when I was with Sam in that flower field. When everything felt right.

My phone vibrates.

It's a text from Harlow. A photo of Laurel sleeping.

Angel, I reply.

Three blinking dots and then, more flowers grew in today.

My heart swells and before I can respond, she sends another text. It's going to be a rainbow out there within a week!

I send her three heart emojis just as a message from Sam lights up my screen. Hi.

Hi.

What are you doing?

Just got off work. You?

I'm staring down at my phone, walking aimlessly, wearing a ridiculous smile because this is always the best part of my day: when I can talk to Sam.

As I wait for him to reply, I hear *click click click*.

I look up. A gray dog comes tearing around the corner, running straight for me.

I'm about to bolt when I realize that this dog looks just like Bullet, but that can't be. As my brain's trying to compute what's happening, the dog leaps up to greet me.

"Bullet?" I rub her face, laughing, glancing around for...

Sam appears from behind a parked car. He's walking toward me, wearing an old flannel shirt, worn jeans, and a pair of scuffed boots. He's got something behind his back, but I'm too shocked to register what it is.

"Sam!"

I'm in his arms in two seconds flat. "Oh my God. What are you doing here?"

He doesn't answer because he's kissing me hungrily as Bullet dances around our feet.

Finally, he pulls back. He hands me a bouquet of daisies. Just like the ones from my dream.

He's coming for you.

"For the ones I never gave you," he says.

I throw my arms around him for the second time, breathing him in, clinging to him like a lifeline. "I'm so happy you're here. How long do we have?"

"As long as you'll have me."

I must look incredibly confused, because he adds, "I can't do this, Lily. I can't do this long-distance thing."

"What about the ranch? Your new clients?"

"Alonzo is holding down the fort, and I can go back and forth. It's only five months, right?"

I'm going to lift off any second. Can this be real?

"And then what?" I ask as Bullet sits at our feet, wagging her tail wildly.

"And then we can do anything we want."

I feel my memory magic quicken faster than my already-racing pulse. "I know what I want," I say.

"Oh yeah?"

"When Harlow went into labor, it made me think about all the women who have to travel over an hour into the city. What if they could get their care right there in La Ventana?"

"Are you saying you want to practice—"

I'm nodding vigorously, hoping he'll see my logic.

"Are you sure that's what you want?" he asks. "I just want you to be happy."

"And I want that damn porch and those open skies. I want you."

Sam's mouth curls into a half smile. "That's three things."

I sock him in the chest. "Smart-ass."

Bullet barks her agreement.

I laugh, then glance back at Sam. "I should tell you now that my apartment is not the ranch."

"So no horses?"

"Not a single one, but there's this amazing dog."

Sam looks down at Bullet. "Did you hear that, girl? She thinks you're amazing."

Bullet's tail whips back and forth.

"Hungry?" I ask Sam as we turn to leave.

"Definitely."

"How about pasta?" I ask. "I know a great place."

"Maybe barbecue?" he says. "Or steak?"

"Or tacos?"

He throws his arm over my shoulders and pulls me closer. "Maybe."

I used to hate maybes—their cryptic uncertain nature. Now I see them for what they are. Possibilities.

And for me and Sam, the possibilities are endless.

For the first time, I don't need to see the end of the road, I don't need to control the future.

For the first time, all those possibilities sound like paradise.

★ ★ ★ ★ ★

ACKNOWLEDGMENTS

When I was writing *The Enchanted Hacienda*, I quickly realized that the next book would follow Lily Estrada, self-professed nonromantic with the ability to manipulate memory. I knew she was harboring a secret, one that shaped her hard-edged demeanor, one that had broken her heart. Like most writers, the joy is in the discovery, the gems we excavate and collect along the journey of telling stories. I'm grateful to have had a team who went on this book's journey with me.

A big thanks to my editor, Gabriella Mongelli, for her keen eye and exceptional feedback, which made the story so much richer. And to the entire Park Row team. I'm grateful for all of you and the unique energy you each brought to this book.

Many thanks to: Nicole Luongo; Sophie James in publicity; Rachel Haller, senior manager of marketing; Randy Chan, director of channel marketing; Lindsey Reeder, senior manager of digital marketing; Brianna Wodabek, assistant manager of digital marketing; Riffat Ali, digital marketing coordinator; Ciara Loader, social media coordinator; Katie-Lynn Golakovich, managing editor; Alexandra Niit, cover designer; and last but not least, fellow gardener Jerri Gallagher, copy editor.

Thirteen books in and I'm still finding new ways to thank my incredible agent, Holly Root. We've been on this story-telling expedition many years and I couldn't imagine the road without her and the entire team at Root Literary.

A heartfelt thank-you to my amazing publicist, Brittani Hilles, who is the epitome of sunshine. Your creativity, dedication, and warmth are more appreciated than you know. And to my assistant, Sarah, I know without a doubt that I can always count on you, your inventiveness, and your lioness nature.

I'm so grateful to my early readers, friends, and family members, who are my pillars. Your care, brilliance, and support mean more to me than you could ever know, and I love you all.

Finally, I want to thank my readers. You keep the magic alive every time you turn the page. Abrazos!